THE *S*ECRET *B*LISS OF *C*ALLIOPE *I*PSWICH

MARCIA LYNN McCLURE

Published by Distractions Ink
1290 Mirador Loop N.E.
Rio Rancho, NM 87144

Published by Distractions Ink
©Copyright 2014 by M. Meyers A.K.A. Marcia Lynn McClure
Cover Photography by ©Larry Mateyer/Dreamstime.com and
Cover Design and Interior Graphics by Sandy Ann Allred/Timeless Allure

First Printed Edition: May 2014

McClure, Marcia Lynn, 1965—
The Secret Bliss of Calliope Ipswich: a novel/by Marcia Lynn McClure.

ISBN: 978-0-9913878-5-4

Library of Congress Control Number: 2014943232

Printed in the United States of America

To my beautiful, inspirational mother—
You fill my heart with love and tender memories,
My mind with images of simpler, more romantic times,
And my soul with faith, hope, and strength!
I love you so much, Mom!
~Marcia

The following is a short but lovely memory reminisced upon and quickly written down by my mother, Patsy Christine States Reed, in 1991. Her sweet, handwritten memories will forever continue to inspire me!

Sometime when I was four years old, we moved to the Walker Ranch at the foot of the Sangre de Cristo Mountains. This was a beautiful setting! The house was a rustic brown and sat back at least a half-mile from the main road. It had an upstairs in which the ceilings were pointed because they went up to the pitched roof of the house. The bedroom I loved had a small window that swung open like a door, and the bubbling sounds of the creek could be heard. There was another window in that room on the outside sill of which a robin built her nest one spring, and Mom and I lay on the bed sometime each day watching her first build her nest, then sitting on her eggs, then the eggs hatching, then feeding her babies. I will always remember those blue speckled eggs, the speckled breasts of the young birds, and their feeding them. What a wonderful experience!

In the spring, summer, and fall, I would go out to the wood pile and, from the round, short pieces of quakies which had been cut for the winter wood, find some pieces that were flat enough on both ends to stand up and be used for furniture. I sat these up in little make-believe rooms. Mom cut out paper doilies for the tops of them, and I would play house. I had some little pans. I took little petals from the dandelions for corn, the little fuchsia petals from another very tiny little plant for beets, small green leaves for greens, and just had an imaginative good time.

CHAPTER ONE

"Oh! *Do* link arms with me, Calliope," Blanche whispered, her brown eyes widening with apprehension. She took Calliope's arm, tightly linking it with her own. "The old Mulholland house still gives me the willies every time I walk past it. I hate to think on what might have gone on inside. It's truly terrifyin'!"

"Oh, don't be silly, Blanche," Calliope said, feigning calm. "Poor Prudence's lunacy…it's sad. And besides, her fiendish acts were not committed inside the house. There's nothing wrong with it. It's just…it's just a sad, empty building." Calliope Ipswich felt the hypocrite, however, as an uncomfortable shiver of residual dread and unease shuddered down her spine.

More than six months had passed since the All Hallow's Eve when the dangerous state of Prudence Mulholland's fracturing mind had been revealed to the townsfolk of Meadowlark Lake. And now, each time Calliope thought of poor Prudence and her family, her heart ached for their family's unhappy lot, and a chill of lingering horror rippled through her being.

In truth, at times Calliope wondered if it had all been simply a bad dream—a nightmare. But it hadn't. It really had happened—all of it. Jealous of Calliope's older sister Amoretta at having won the heart of the handsome Brake McClendon, Prudence Mulholland had endeavored to scare Amoretta—at first. Yet when Brake and Amoretta's love proved unalterable, Prudence's fracturing mind had prompted her to attempt to eliminate Calliope's sister altogether.

Thankfully, Brake McClendon was a strong, heroic man and had stopped Prudence from taking any human lives, especially that of his beloved Amoretta. Yet Amoretta and Brake would both forever bear the physical scars of Prudence's attempt to separate them, all the same.

As Calliope studied the now empty house where the Mulholland family had once lived, that fateful Halloween night somehow seemed so long ago. But it was still far too fresh in the minds of those who dwelt in Meadowlark Lake, especially Calliope's. The terror had ended six months past, and Prudence Mulholland was now tucked away in an asylum, while Brake and Amoretta McClendon were happily married and living in the nearby town of Langtree. Her sister and brother-in-law were safe, as was everyone else in town. Hence, Calliope wondered why she still trembled whenever she passed by the old Mulholland house.

"Well, empty, sad buildin' or not, no one will ever buy it and move in again," Blanche noted. "Not after what happened to Prudence. That new family in town—the Chesterfields?—even they did not consider the old Mulholland house once they'd been told what had happened with Prudence."

Calliope sighed, feeling rather compassionately heartbroken. "Poor Pru," she said. "Even now I can't believe it most of the time. All of us were such dear friends with Prudence! We sat in sewing circles with her, got into mischief in spying on the men at the mill with her. And all the time...all the time none of us even suspected she was suffering as she was, hearing strange voices in her head...killing animals, people's pets."

"I know," Blanche sighed, glancing over her shoulder once more to the abandoned house. "Poor Prudence...and poor Samuel."

Suddenly remembering that Blanche had been very sweet on Prudence's brother, Samuel Mulholland—realizing that Blanche's melancholy was far deeper than perhaps even her own—Calliope reached up, tucking a flaxen strand of breeze-blown hair behind one ear, and said, "Well, we have a lovely path before us today, anyway.

All springy and sunshine, with bright blue skies and the delightful conversation that awaits us at Winnie's house."

Blanche rolled her eyes and giggled. "I do not understand why it is you enjoy the sewin' circle so much, Calliope." Blanche's eyes narrowed with suspicion. "I'd say that it was for the sake you might catch a glimpse of the handsome Fox Montrose. Yet somethin' inside me thinks maybe you aren't as sweet on Winnie's older brother as he is on you, Calliope Ipswich."

Calliope giggled, her sky-blue eyes twinkling with amusement. "Oh, every girl in town is sweet on Fox Montrose, Blanche. You know that. To some degree or another, all the young ladies in Meadowlark Lake like to catch a glimpse of him."

"He *is* very handsome," Blanche confirmed. "You're so lucky that his interest has settled on you, Calliope." She giggled. "Perhaps I should have your stepmother brew me up a batch of some sort of love potion. Then I might be blessed with his smile when he looks at me the way you are when he looks at you."

"Kizzy is a gypsy, Blanche, not a witch," Calliope teased. "And besides, since she married Daddy, she doesn't really sell her gypsy wares anymore."

Blanche laughed, and her coiffed brown hair bounced in rhythm with her vocally expressed amusement. "Oh, I so adore that your father, the important county judge, fell in love with the gypsy from the wood. It's so romantic!"

"It is romantic," Calliope sighed contentedly. "And Daddy loves little Shay as if she were his very own child, which she is now, I suppose, being that the adoption has been final for some time. The way Daddy dotes on Shay, one would never guess she'd been Kizzy's alone before Daddy and Kizzy met."

Blanche's smile broadened. "Your whole family dotes on Shay! You Ipswich girls are gonna spoil your little stepsister rotten if you're not careful," she teased.

Calliope giggled and nodded. "We do adore her so much. But I don't believe you can spoil children by loving them. Perhaps sparing discipline and teaching or giving them too many material things might spoil them. But there is no such thing as too much love."

"That's true," Blanche agreed. She exhaled a heavy sigh. "Oh, Calliope, what I wouldn't give to be in your shoes—a successful judge for a father, a beautiful young gypsy woman for a stepmother, two older sisters who love and adore you, and a little sister who thinks the sun and moon rise and set by you. And let's not forget Fox Montrose being sweet on you too! Why, you've got everything a girl could ever wish for!"

Calliope smiled and admitted, "I'll not deny the fact that God has blessed me and my family with love and comfort, for he has. I would be selfish to wish for anything other than what I already have."

Blanche quirked one eyebrow and studied Calliope for a moment. "And yet?" she ventured. "That's what you're thinkin' right now, isn't it?"

Calliope shrugged. "Sometimes I do wish I could one day have the kind of love my sister Amoretta has with Brake...what Daddy and Kizzy have."

Blanche's pretty forehead puckered with a slight frown. "You don't like Fox as much as he likes you, do you, Calliope? You're not in love with him."

Calliope silently scolded herself for having let her countenance and words reveal her secret to Blanche. The truth was that she was not as sweet on Fox Montrose as he was on her. Yet there were secrets in her heart that could never be revealed to anyone—not even to Blanche, not even to Calliope's own sisters.

Therefore, she chose a counter maneuver with which to distract Blanche and said, "Oh, I adore Fox! I just think these things may take time, you know, for me to...to..."

"To really fall in love with him, you mean," Blanche finished.

"Yes. Perhaps that is what I mean," Calliope responded.

"But you seem to forget that you're out west now, Calliope. This isn't Boston," Blanche reminded. "Many people out here marry for practical reasons—simply to survive hardship and to work together."

"Well, in Boston, one lives in fear of being saddled with an arranged marriage," Calliope countered.

"Still? Truly?" Blanche gasped.

"Sometimes," Calliope answered.

Blanche inhaled a deep breath of determination, however, straightened her posture, and said, "Don't you worry, Calliope Ipswich. You'll fall in love with Fox Montrose eventually." She giggled, lowered her voice, and whispered, "And if you don't, I'll do it for you and gladly take him off your hands, all right?"

Calliope giggled as well, agreeing, "All right."

Yet as they neared the Montrose house—as Calliope returned a friendly wave that Sallie Ackerman tossed to her as she entered Fox and Winnie's home—trepidation welled up in Calliope's bosom, for she knew that if she hadn't fallen in love with Fox Montrose by now, she never would. Furthermore, she didn't want to.

A secret bliss was nestled deep inside Calliope Ipswich. It had been nestled there from nearly the moment the Ipswich family had arrived in Meadowlark Lake all those months past. And though it was a bliss she owned in knowing something about herself that even her own sisters did not know, it likewise brought her pain at times—for it was the very reason she knew she would never fall in love with Fox Montrose. Calliope's love was already spoken for—and no one in all the wide world, save Calliope Ipswich herself, would ever know it.

"And I swear that little darlin' Shay of your father and Kizzy's just gets cuter every day!" Ellen Ackerman chirped.

"Oh, I think so too," her daughter, Sallie, agreed. "She looks so much like her mother, and Kizzy is just the most beautiful woman I've ever seen!"

"Shay is an angel," Calliope agreed, smiling at the thought of her sweet little sister, Shay. Calliope giggled. "And she gets into more mischief even than I do!"

"Is she the pretty little dark-haired girl with the long, long rag curls? I saw her walking a marmalade cat on a leash in town yesterday," Callie Chesterfield said, smiling.

Calliope laughed. "That would indeed be my little sister, Shay."

Callie's sister, Pauline, exclaimed, "I have never seen a cat that would take a leash, not in my whole life!"

Calliope nodded to the two newcomers to Meadowlark Lake and the sewing circle. "Molly is a very patient cat. She lets Shay dress her up in doll dresses, lead her around town on a leash, and all kinds of things most cats would never endure. You should see her when Shay is serving make-believe tea! Molly just sits right in her place at Shay's little table and waits. Then when Shay fills Molly's teacup with water, Molly just laps it up like she thinks she's as human as Shay is." She paused for a moment as the ladies of Mrs. Montrose's sewing circle smiled and laughed with amusement. Then, sighing with satisfaction, Calliope added, "I can't imagine life without her now…or Kizzy."

"Yes. Your father and Kizzy are a such a lovely couple," Sallie Ackerman said.

Dora Montrose looked to Callie and Pauline then. "And I see you girls have some younger siblin's as well."

Calliope smiled. Mrs. Montrose, Winnie and Fox's mother, was the most wonderful hostess. She always made sure everyone felt included in everything they attended, whether or not they were newcomers to Meadowlark Lake. Her heart warmed at remembering the first time she and her older sisters, Evangeline and Amoretta, attended Mrs. Montrose's sewing circle. Amoretta had met Brake that very day! It was divine intervention at the very least.

"Yes," Callie answered.

Callie was nineteen, one year older than Pauline, so it made sense she answered.

"We have one older brother, Tate. He's twenty-one. Then our sisters Eva and Lena are thirteen and eight, and our two little brothers, Willis and Albert, are seven and six."

Looking to where Mrs. Chesterfield sat across the room, Dora Montrose exclaimed, "My goodness, Josephine! With all that you must have pressin' in havin' so many children still at home, I'm quite flattered—rather honored—to have you takin' time to come to my sewin' circle today."

In truth, Calliope thought that Josephine Chesterfield didn't look like much fun. Her dark eyebrows wore what looked to be a permanent pucker of worry and concern. Yet her blue eyes owned a softness—a kindness that was calming. Her raven hair had a sheen to it that was rare for a woman of her age, and coupled with the natural pink that still graced her cheeks, it gave her the look of health and vitality. Still, there was no countenance of great happiness or joy about her. But Calliope mused that with seven children—most of whom were still young—Mrs. Chesterfield was most likely perpetually tuckered out.

"Oh, it's me who is grateful to you, Mrs. Montrose, for the invitation to attend," Mrs. Chesterfield said.

"Oh, do call me Dora, please," Mrs. Montrose said, smiling.

Mrs. Chesterfield smiled at last then, and it brightened her face all the more, though Calliope noted it did little to ease the worried pucker of her brow.

Exhaling a heavy sigh, Calliope decided that Mrs. Chesterfield deserved to have something kind done for her. She determined to mull the idea over and find some way to make the woman's brow relax—at least, someday.

"So you say you have an older brother, Callie, is that right?" Winnie Montrose inquired.

Calliope grinned with mild amusement and exchanged understanding glances with Blanche and Sallie. Winnie Montrose was always in search of a handsome young man to flirt with. Not that Calliope, Blanche, and Sallie didn't enjoy a bit of flirting with the eligible men of Meadowlark Lake, but Winnie wasn't a bit clandestine about it. Whereas Calliope and her friends went about their flirting in a more proper manner, Winnie just said whatever came into her mind when she was talking to a young man. Therefore, Calliope and her friends knew it would not be long before Tate Chesterfield knew exactly who Winnie Montrose was.

"Yes, Tate," Callie answered.

"And, yes, our brother Tate is a very eligible bachelor," Pauline added.

"Pauline!" Mrs. Chesterfield scolded.

"I only told her what she wanted to know, didn't I, Mother?" Pauline defended herself. Looking to Winnie, she asked, "Didn't I?"

It was Mrs. Ackerman who laughed and said, "Yes, Pauline, you only told us the answer to what we all were curious over."

Everyone laughed, and though Pauline blushed, Calliope nodded to her with reassurance when their glances met. Calliope fancied that Pauline and Callie both resembled their mother. She thought that it was easy to know what Josephine Chesterfield had looked like when she was near the ages her daughters were now, for they both boasted the same lovely raven hair, as well as their mother's dark eyes.

"Oh, I'm so sorry to be late!" Evangeline Ipswich sighed as she hurried into Mrs. Montrose's parlor. "But I just had to stop and check the post. I've been waiting for a letter, and I was hoping it would arrive today."

"And did it?" Calliope inquired of her oldest sister.

"It did!" Evangeline exclaimed.

"A letter from whom, Evangeline?" Mrs. Montrose asked. "For you do seem quite delighted."

"And I am!" Evangeline confirmed with enthusiasm. "My dear friend Jennie and I have been corresponding more often of late, ever since she and her husband moved out west several months ago. Jennie has had some anxieties over the move, which is to be understood, our lovely west being so vastly different from Boston, and I have been trying to be very prompt in answering each of her letters. And so I do try to check in with Mr. Perry at the general store very often when I'm expecting a letter from Jennie."

"Wouldn't it be nice if all of us had as good and loyal a friend as you, Evangeline?" Mrs. Ackerman noted sincerely.

Calliope smiled as her older sister blushed, for she knew how truly uncomfortable Evangeline became whenever praise was offered to her.

"What did I miss?" Evangeline said, taking a seat next to Calliope on Mrs. Montrose's sofa.

"Only that Callie and Pauline have a very handsome and eligible bachelor for an elder brother," Winnie offered.

"Do tell," Evangeline giggled.

"How do you know our brother is handsome?" Pauline teased Winnie.

"I can answer that," Calliope interjected, "for you and Callie are the image of your mother. And being that you are all so lovely, it only stands to reason that your brother is attractive as well. Isn't that what you're thinking, Winnie?"

All the ladies in the room smiled, and Winnie's smile was broadest. "Exactly!" Winnie confessed without pause. "You know me too well, Calliope Ipswich."

"Well, our brother is a handsome young man," Pauline confirmed. "Yet Callie and I have decided that your own brother is quite the good-looking fellow himself."

Everyone looked to Calliope—she knew they did—though she kept her attention on the stitching she was working on in her lap. Still, the heat of her own blush caused her to feel as if her head might explode at any moment when she heard Winnie say, "Oh, Fox has almost always been the most handsome man in town. But he's sweet as sugar on Calliope, and I know there won't be any turnin' his head."

There was an uncomfortable silence for a few moments, but Calliope thanked the heavens for her elder sister when Evangeline said, "My good friend Jennie told me in her letter I received today that...well, that she is expecting a baby. I'm quite overwhelmed with excitement for her!"

"As well you should be," Mrs. Chesterfield exclaimed.

Thankful that Evangeline had guided the attention of the ladies in the room from the subject of Fox Montrose and his being sweet on Calliope, she was likewise surprised that it was Mrs. Chesterfield who had been the first to respond to Evangeline's announcement about her friend. Therefore, she glanced up and was somewhat astonished to see that Mrs. Chesterfield's worried brow was relaxed—that she was smiling, her eyes atwinkle, as if she'd never before heard the wonderful news of a baby to be born.

"Any baby is such a blessing, such a joy," Josephine said, smiling. "I cannot wait until my own children are married and begin having families of their own. I miss babies so very much."

"I do too," Mrs. Ackerman announced.

"As do I," Mrs. Montrose added. She looked up to Calliope and winked. "I hope I won't have to wait too very much longer to see Fox and Winnie with spouses and babies."

Again Calliope blushed, looking to Evangeline for saving.

"Yes," Evangeline said, staring at her sister with understanding. "It's one reason we're all so glad to have Shay with us now. Though she's not a baby, she is so wonderful—so young and fresh and, more often than not, wildly entertaining."

"Winnie did mention that she saw Shay walking her cat, of all things, through town just yesterday," Blanche added.

Evangeline laughed, her ebony hair flouncing in its coif, her dark green eyes sparkling with remembered amusement. "Why, just this morning at breakfast, Shay said...Shay said..." But giggles had overtaken the usually composed eldest Ipswich daughter.

Calliope began to giggle as well at the memory but managed to finish for her sister. "Yes, just this morning at breakfast, Evangeline had agreed to read a book to Shay, and Shay picked a Christmas book. And Evangeline..." She paused to giggle to herself a moment and then continued, "And Evangeline read, 'And they found the baby, lying in a manger.' And Shay jumped up from her chair, looked more closely at the illustration in the book, and said, 'But I don't see a baby lion in the manger!'"

As Calliope erupted into laughter at the memory of confusion on Shay's pretty little face, each and every other woman, young or older, did too. There were several long minutes of ladies' laughter echoing through the room before at long last tears of mirth had been dabbed from every eye and moist handkerchiefs returned to apron pockets.

"Oh, you Ipswich girls are so good for my heart!" Mrs. Ackerman sighed as one last giggle escaped her before she returned to her stitching.

"Mine too," Winnie Montrose agreed. "Shay was certainly cut from the same cloth as Calliope, wasn't she, Evangeline?"

Evangeline smiled lovingly at Calliope and confirmed, "That's what Daddy has been saying for months now too."

Calliope smiled. After all, it was a gift to be able to bring mirth and joy to people the way she and Shay seemed to do—albeit accidentally more often than not. Calliope knew she had misunderstood a thing or two herself of recent and caused just as many chuckles at her own home. But long ago Calliope had discovered that she liked to make people smile and feel happy, and she'd accepted that it was worth a few dents in her pride.

And so she smiled as she sat stitching on the special little dress she was making for Shay, glad that the ladies' hearts had been lightened—that Mrs. Chesterfield's brows had not been puckered for quite a few minutes now. Smiling was so preferable to scowling, after all. At least in Calliope's opinion.

"I thought spring would never come, Calliope," Evangeline admitted as she and Calliope meandered home from Mrs. Montrose's house late that afternoon. "And yet here it is, in all its hopeful glory! I don't even mind the rain, for Kizzy says the lilacs will bloom soon, and you know how I adore lilacs."

"I do too, Evie," Calliope agreed. "Though I do miss the daffodils and hyacinths. The earliest flowers of spring are some of my very favorites, you know."

"Mine too," Evangeline sighed. "But, oh, doesn't the warmth of the sun on your face feel divine?"

Calliope stopped walking when her sister did. Glancing to see Evangeline's eyes closed, her face tipped upward toward the warm sun of late afternoon and early evening, Calliope followed suit. Closing her eyes, she lifted her face to the sky and imagined that her cheeks were soaking up the yellow warmth of spring's sunshine. In those moments, she was aware of other things—sensations other than the warmth of spring's sky. In those moments there was the sweet scent of new, wild grasses, of burning applewood in someone's cookstove. There was also the feel of the gentle breeze playing with her hair and caressing her cheeks and the lovely arias of returning birds who whistled sweet and lulling melodies.

"It's true, Evie," Calliope admitted. "I feel as if I've just woken from a slumber that lasted weeks on end—weeks of wind and snow and cloudy skies. And now I'm—"

"Good evenin', ladies."

Calliope and Evangeline both gasped as the sound of a male voice nearby interrupted their tranquility.

"Oh, hello, gentlemen," Evangeline greeted, having recovered her senses more quickly than Calliope.

It seemed the men from the gristmill had finished earlier than usual and were finding their way home. Calliope smiled as she saw Fox Montrose, Dex Longfellow, Rowdy Gates, and a young man she had never seen before standing before her and her sister.

"Have you ladies met Tate Chesterfield?" Dex Longfellow inquired, his attention darting from Calliope to Evangeline and back.

"Why no, Dex. We haven't yet had the pleasure," Evangeline answered.

Calliope smiled at Fox Montrose when he grinned and winked at her. Dex nodded to her in greeting, though she knew Fox had warned Dex long ago not to be too hopeful where she was concerned—being that Fox had had eyes for her the moment he'd met her last fall. Rowdy Gates reached up, giving the brim of his hat a quick bend in greeting, and Calliope smiled at the group of hard-laboring men, for they all looked quite done in.

"Well, let us introduce you to him then," Dex offered then. "These here lovely ladies are the Ipswich girls, Tate. Well, two of the Ipswich girls, at least."

"My pleasure," Tate Chesterfield greeted with a proper nod and a slight bow.

Calliope smiled, for he was a handsome young man, and he did resemble his sisters and mother. Tate Chesterfield was tall and broad-shouldered, with raven hair and deep blue eyes. Calliope thought that perhaps all the young ladies in Meadowlark Lake might be well tempted to swap their infatuations with the handsome Fox Montrose in favor of new fascinations with the handsome Tate Chesterfield. She felt sorry for Fox a moment, for she knew how much attention he was used to.

"I'm Evangeline Ipswich, Mr. Chesterfield," Evangeline said, offering her hand to Tate.

Tate Chesterfield accepted her handshake and then turned expectantly to Calliope.

"And I'm Calliope Ipswich," Calliope said, taking Tate's hand as he offered it to her. "Welcome to Meadowlark Lake."

"Again, it's my pleasure to meet you both," Tate said as his smile broadened. "I've heard a lot about you young ladies."

"Tate here is gonna start workin' at the mill with us tomorrow," Fox interjected. "It took some doin', but Dex and me talked ol' Rowdy here into givin' Tate a chance. We've been shorthanded since losin' Brake and Sam last fall."

"Well, that's wonderful, Mr. Chesterfield," Calliope congratulated. "The mill is settled in such a perfect venue. The trees and shrubs and wildflowers that grow around it are magnificent, especially when they're greening up as they are now. A body couldn't ask for a more lovely scene to work amidst."

"Yes...a lovely scene," Fox playfully teased. "And I'm sure that's what Tate was thinkin' when he asked about hirin' on at the mill."

Calliope good-humoredly sneered at Fox. She smiled just after, however, and said, "Well, you gentlemen have a nice evening. Evangeline and I are off to help Kizzy with supper." She looked to the handsome Tate Chesterfield and said, "It was very nice to make your acquaintance, Mr. Chesterfield."

"Oh, do call me Tate, Miss Calliope," Tate said. "And you too, Miss Evangeline."

"Of course," Evangeline said. "Good evening then, gentlemen."

"Good evenin'," the men chimed in unison.

Calliope and Evangeline nodded to each man in turn as they walked on toward their home. And once they were out of earshot of the men, Calliope exhaled the nervous breath she'd been holding.

"Oh, Evie! I thought I might faint dead away when he looked at me!" Calliope confided before she thought better of it.

"He's not *that* handsome, Calliope," Evangeline giggled.

"Who?" Calliope asked.

"Tate Chesterfield," Evangeline answered, her beautiful dark brows puckering with curiosity. "That's who you're referring to, aren't you?"

"Oh, I…I…" Calliope stammered.

"Oh, you mean *Fox* took your breath away?" Evangeline asked, somewhat perplexed. "Hmmm. That's funny…being that I didn't think you were as sweet on him as he is you."

"Oh, it's no matter. They all looked quite handsome returning from their day's labors," Calliope tried to redirect. "Father's right. Men who work hard and are willing to work hard…I do find them more attractive than most of those tight-collared sorts we knew in the city."

"I do too," Evangeline admitted, "though I do fear that you've got every eligible bachelor in this town so tightly wrapped around your finger that I'm bound to be an old spinster."

"Oh, nonsense!" Calliope argued. "You're just the kind of beauty that intimidates men, Evie. When the right man comes for you, you'll know it, because he won't be afraid to pursue you."

Evangeline laughed for a moment. "Oh, poppycock, Calliope! You are so full of flattery it's ridiculous sometimes." She laughed a moment more and then looked to Calliope as her smile faded. "And what about Fox, Calliope? What will you do if he comes to Daddy, asking for permission to formally court you? Do you want him to? Do you like him enough?"

Calliope's smile faded. She inhaled a long breath and exhaled a heavy sigh. "I don't like him the way Amoretta *likes* Brake or the way Kizzy *likes* Daddy, if that's what you're asking."

Evangeline sighed then as well. "In truth, I don't know if any woman *likes* any man the way Amoretta *likes* Brake and Kizzy *likes* Daddy. Maybe you and I will never find that kind of love. Maybe you and I will just have to settle for...for rather lackluster love."

"Well, that's the most depressing thing I've ever heard you say, Evangeline Ipswich!" Calliope scolded. "No. No. You and I are meant to have great lovers, to love and be loved just like Amoretta and Kizzy love and are loved. I won't believe we are meant for anything less. After all, we are Ipswiches, are we not?"

Evangeline's countenance brightened. She smiled and strongly affirmed, "Yes! We are Ipswiches."

Calliope and Evangeline linked arms then, straightened their postures, and walked more quickly toward home.

A thought struck Calliope then, and she began to giggle.

"What is it? What's so amusing to you?" Evangeline inquired.

Still giggling, Calliope answered, "A baby lion in a manger! Ha ha ha ha!"

Evangeline burst into laughter then as well, and they were still laughing when their little sister, Shay, scurried down the front porch steps to meet them both with such loving hugs and kisses that their laughter continued—long after they had reached their destination of home.

CHAPTER TWO

When Calliope awoke the next morning, she didn't feel quite as rested and refreshed as she usually did, even for the gentle coos of the mourning doves outside her bedroom window and the cool morning breeze wafting in through it. She'd slept fitfully all through the night, for the sake of something Evangeline had mentioned the evening before. What if Fox Montrose actually *did* approach Calliope's father and ask permission to officially court her?

The truth was that any of the eligible young women in town would simply swoon with euphoria at the mere prospect of the handsome, charming Fox Montrose calling upon her father to ask permission to court her. Fox was, after all, a wonderful young man—polite, kind, hard working, and ambitious. His family was certainly wonderful, as well. His sister, Winnie, was one of Calliope's dear friends. His mother, Dora Montrose, was pleasant company, always kind and making certain that everyone felt important. And his father, Dennison Montrose, was sheriff of Meadowlark Lake, very often working with Calliope's own father, Judge Lawson Ipswich, in matters of the law.

Hence, there really wasn't any commonsensical reason why Calliope herself shouldn't have been elated at the fact that Fox seemed, for all outward appearances, to have settled his interest and affections on her. And it was well accepted through town that of all the lovely young ladies of Meadowlark Lake, Fox Montrose obviously favored Calliope Ipswich—well accepted by everyone save

Calliope herself. Lucky as all her friends thought her to be, Calliope was greatly unsettled. Oh, she liked Fox well enough—enjoyed his company, but only in moderation—and Evangeline's question of what Calliope would feel if Fox did decide to ask their father for permission to officially court her had caused a great anxiety to begin stirring in her.

Therefore, as she sat at the kitchen table with her family enjoying a comforting breakfast of warm biscuits and soft butter, bacon, and poached eggs, she decided to broach the subject of Fox Montrose's possible intentions with her father before her fretfulness swelled any further.

"Daddy," Calliope began.

"Mm hmm," Lawson Ipswich mumbled as he broke open a steaming biscuit and slathered butter on it.

"You know Fox Montrose?" Calliope ventured.

Immediately Lawson looked up from his biscuit, glancing to Calliope and then to his beautiful young wife, Kizzy. "Mm hmmm," he answered.

"Well, I was just wondering…I was wondering that if…well, if Fox ever came round asking to court me—you know, officially, and of course this is only if he ever came round asking to court me, which he probably never will—but if he ever did…" Calliope stammered awkwardly.

"Mmm hmmm," Lawson urged, grinning with amusement at his daughter's discomfort.

"Well, would you please *refuse* your permission for him to court me, Daddy?" Calliope blurted.

Lawson's eyes widened with astonishment, though Kizzy smiled with a woman's understanding.

"What?" Lawson asked. "You…you're telling me you don't want Fox to come courting you?"

Calliope sighed. "No, Daddy. I don't."

"Calliope don't like Fox Montrose in that romantical way, Daddy," Shay interjected.

"Calliope *doesn't* like Fox Montrose that way, Shay darling," Kizzy corrected her little girl.

Shay frowned. "That's what I said, Mama. Calliope don't like Fox Montrose enough for him to come courtin' her."

Evangeline and Lawson giggled as Kizzy sighed with amused exasperation.

"I mean to say that Fox Montrose is handsome and all, Daddy," Shay continued as she took a bite of soft breakfast bacon. "All the girls in town think so, but Calliope just...well, she just doesn't want him courtin' her, that's all. Do you understand, Daddy?" Shay reached over, tenderly patting the back of her father's hand in a soothing gesture.

Calliope smiled at her little sister. Never was there a more loyal soul than little Shay. Calliope glanced up to Kizzy a moment, noting how much Shay looked like her beautiful young mother, both dark-haired beauties. Calliope quietly offered a prayer of thanks to God in his heaven for bringing Kizzy and Shay into her father's life to love—into all of their lives.

"I think I do understand, honey," Lawson answered Shay.

"And since you *do* understand, Daddy," Shay continued, "and since you always, always, always tell us Ipswich girls—Evangeline, Calliope, and me, you know, the three daughters you still have here at home with you—since you always tell us that you'll always, always, always protect us and do everything to make us happy, please don't let Fox Montrose come courtin' on Calliope. All right?"

Lawson exchanged amused glances with Evangeline and Calliope, an unspoken recognition passing between them that Shay ever needed assurance that she was as much Lawson's daughter as Evangeline, Amoretta, and Calliope were.

"All right," Lawson agreed. "If Fox Montrose ever does come to me to request permission to court Calliope, I'll kindly let him know that...well, that I don't think the time is right or some such similar reason."

"That sounds perfect, Daddy," Shay approved. She looked to Calliope and smiled, whispering, "See, Calliope? You can always count on me to help you out."

"Oh, I know it!" Calliope giggled.

"But, Shay, darling," Kizzy began then, "what if Fox Montrose comes around to ask Daddy's permission to court Calliope, and Daddy refuses, but he wants to court Evangeline instead?"

Shay's pretty little brows puckered in puzzlement. "Well, I don't know about that," the child said. She looked to Evangeline and asked, "What about that, Evangeline? Would you want Fox Montrose courtin' you?"

Evangeline laughed, shaking her head. "Heavens no! Even if I did have some infatuation with him, I want a man who wants *me* and *just* me, not one who wanted someone else as his first choice."

Shay smiled. "That's what I thought you would say, Evie." Shay sighed and shook her head as she picked up the biscuit her father had just buttered for her. "Poor Fox Montrose. I don't know what will become of him if he can't have one of us Ipswich girls for a wife."

Evangeline and Calliope exchanged mirth-filled glances with their father and Kizzy. Shay was so tenderhearted, sincerely concerned for Fox Montrose's future happiness.

"You're an angel, my Shay Shay," Calliope said, leaning over and placing an affectionate kiss on Shay's forehead. "How did we ever get by before you came along?"

Shay shrugged and bit into her biscuit.

"Now remember, Shay," Kizzy began gently. "This discussion, about Fox Montrose and what Daddy will tell him if he ever does come callin'—"

Shay interrupted with an exasperated sigh, rolling her dark eyes with impatience. "It's a matter of family loyalty," she quoted the instruction her mother and father had given her time and again about such matters. "Don't tell nobody else about it because somebody's feelin's might get hurt or somethin' like that. I know, Mama." Popping the rest of her warm, buttery biscuit into her mouth, she daintily wiped her mouth with her napkin and exclaimed, "It's time for Molly's mornin' walk. Would anyone like to come along with us today?"

"I'd love to come, Shay," Calliope chirped. "And maybe today will be the day we see some lilac blossoms, hmm?"

"Ooo, maybe so," Shay giggled. "I can't wait for the lilacs! Mama, will you help me gather bunches and bunches for our new house the way we used to for our old house in the wood when they're bloomin' well?"

"Of course, my sweet pea!" Kizzy assured her daughter. "As long as there are lilacs in spring, we'll fill as many vases as we can for the house, all right?"

Shay clapped her hands with excitement. "Oh, I can't wait for the lilac bunches! I think they smell so…so…well, I think heaven smells like lilacs!"

"I'm sure it does," Lawson chuckled. "Meanwhile, I'll help your mama with the breakfast dishes so you and Calliope can be on your way with Molly. All right?"

"Thanks, Daddy," Shay said, leaping up from her chair and throwing her arms around her father's neck as she kissed him quickly on one cheek. "You know how impatient Molly gets if we don't get her mornin' walk in early."

"Ah yes," Evangeline said, smiling. "*Molly* gets very impatient to get out and about." Evangeline winked at Calliope knowingly.

Calliope sighed with resplendence born of contentment. Oh, she missed her sister Amoretta—missed her something awful. But she adored the new family environment that Kizzy and Shay brought to the Ipswich home. It was new, fresh, and filled with hope and endless possibilities of happiness. She enjoyed being the big sister for a change too, instead of the little sister as she'd always been to Evangeline and Amoretta. And Shay was the most adorable baby sister anyone could ever have wished for. And besides, Amoretta and Brake visited often, especially since winter had slipped away to welcome spring. Langtree wasn't so far away after all, only half a day's ride in the wagon. Amoretta and Brake would visit again soon, and meanwhile Calliope was joyous in the company of her family—

of her sisters Evangeline and Shay, her father, and her stepmother and friend, Kizzy.

And there was something more as well—her secret bliss. The warm embers of felicity that smoldered deep in her heart, ignited months before in a moment of unanticipated epiphany, elevated Calliope's delight in life to such a soaring height that she was certain no one in all the world could fathom it—even if someone did know of her bliss and its cause, which no one did.

Oh, she knew that her secret wouldn't always gift her the euphoria it did in that moment—not forever. But she'd determined some time ago to linger in her bliss for as long as her secret would keep safely cached in her own heart and mind. Thus, as she watched Shay put the collar of the leash around poor Molly's neck, as she saw Molly visibly sigh with buoying up her patience with her little friend, Calliope sighed as well. Winter was gone. Spring had arrived. And some secrets were well worth handing poor Fox Montrose over to some other young woman to adore—some other young woman who was not an Ipswich girl.

"Isn't it a little cool out here, honey?" Lawson asked as he joined his daughter on the front porch that evening. "Are you sure you're warm enough?"

"Oh yes, Daddy," Calliope answered with a sigh. "Resplendently so!"

As her father sat down next to her on north-facing porch swing, he laughed, repeating, "Resplendently so, is it?" Stretching one strong arm along the length of the swing at Calliope's back, he said, "That's quite a theatrical response in the positive from a young woman who just this morning informed her father that she does not wish to be courted by the handsomest young bachelor in town."

"Maybe I don't think Fox *is* the handsomest young bachelor in town," Calliope teased. "Have you *met* Tate Chesterfield, Daddy? My guess is poor dear Fox might lose his throne of handsomest to the charming Mr. Chesterfield."

Smiling, Lawson asked, "Oh! So it's this new young man that has you spurning Fox, is it?"

Calliope's smile faded. "I'm not spurning Fox, Daddy...am I? I mean, I've never cared for him as any more than a friend, a chum. I have tried my best to be kind to him, yet simultaneously attempting *not* to encourage him to liking me as anything other than a friend. But I can see it in his eyes sometimes, his determination to...to..."

Lawson's understanding laughter comforted her, for she did not wish to hurt Fox Montrose in any manner. "Well, my angel," her father began, "sometimes a young man can't keep from pursuing a beautiful young woman once that infamous old male determination kicks in." He winked at her, adding, "And you are a beautiful young woman, my Calliope." He paused a moment, thoughtful. "But if it isn't Fox Montrose that makes your heart beat a little faster, then who is it?" he asked. "I've known you long enough—all your life, in fact," he teased. Calliope smiled at him. "Long enough to know that there's someone who strikes your fancy. You're too loving-hearted, with your mother's romantic nature simply radiating from you. Why, I can't remember a time when you weren't always going on about love and romance and weddings and things. So who is it? It can't be this new Chesterfield fellow...not that quickly. Can it?"

Calliope smiled with mischief. "Well, wouldn't you like to know, Daddy?" she teased. "Maybe I'm between infatuations just now."

"Oh, I doubt that," Lawson said, pushing one foot against the porch floorboards and starting the swing to swaying a bit.

Calliope frowned. "You...you don't think I'm a bad person for not caring for Fox as much or in the same way that he might care for me, do you, Daddy?" she ventured. "I mean, Daddy, I've even *tried* to grow fonder of him. But I can't make myself."

"And you shouldn't try, sweetheart," Lawson assured her. "You can't force love, Calliope, and I wouldn't want you to."

Calliope sighed as a bit of discouragement entered her mind. "Blanche says that out here, out west, people often marry for convenience more than love. That just because of the need to survive, to have a helpmate and someone to be with, people out west often marry for practical reasons instead of love. But I can't even begin to fathom marrying someone without loving him."

Lawson looked down at Calliope, and when she met his gaze, it was to see him frowning at her with concern. "I would never want that for you, Calliope. Your spirit thrives on emotion, my girl. What Blanche says, well, there is some truth to that…a lot of truth. But don't resign yourself to that, Calliope. Don't you ever let me allow a young man to come courting you unless you truly want him to, all right? I want love for you—impassioned, thoroughgoing love the like Kizzy and I have…and Amoretta and Brake. I would never want to see one of my daughters marry for mere practicality or desperation or because they feel sorry for a young man who has inadvertently given his heart to her. Do you understand?"

Calliope sighed, smiled, and threw her arms around her beloved father's neck in appreciation. "Yes, Daddy, I do. And thank you! I was beginning to doubt myself and—"

"Never doubt yourself, Calliope, especially where your heart is concerned," Lawson whispered into her ear.

"Ooo, what a beautiful evenin'!" Kizzy exclaimed, as she and Shay stepped out onto the front porch from the house.

Evangeline followed closely, asking, "Are the crickets chirping yet, Calliope?"

Calliope released her father and smiled as she watched her two sisters and Kizzy take seats on the south-facing porch swing across from her and her father.

"Not yet," she sighed. "But I keep hoping they'll begin any night. I so love to go to sleep listening to them."

"And then in summer when the frogs are croaking in the grass behind the house and down by the creek—heavenly!" Evangeline added.

Lawson chuckled. "I guess you girls aren't missing the busy streets of Boston tonight then?"

"Not a whit," Evangeline answered.

The Ipswich family sat quietly in the cool tranquility of the evening for a time, the soft squeak of the porch swings swaying to and fro and the gentle breeze the only sounds.

"This is sublime!" Kizzy whispered, exhaling a heavy sigh as she closed her eyes, savoring the feel in the air.

"Here comes the lamplighter," Shay exclaimed, although quietly. "I love to watch Mr. Gates light the street lamps," she added. "Up that little ladder he carries to light a lamp, then down again and onto the next one. I wonder if he ever gets tired of lightin' the lamps, Daddy. Do you think he does?"

"I don't know, Shay," Lawson answered. "But I would guess that he wouldn't continue to do it if he didn't enjoy it to some extent."

Shay looked up to her mother. "Would it be wrong if I asked Mr. Gates if he ever gets tired of lightin' the lamps, Mama?"

Kizzy smiled. "I don't think it would be wrong, honey. Just make certain you ask in a very polite manner, all right?"

Smiling with excitement, Shay jumped up from her seat on the porch swing, racing down the steps to the street and the lamp in front of the Ipswich home.

"I notice that Mr. Gates's limp isn't nearly as severe as when we first met him last summer, Daddy," Evangeline noted. "I suppose that whatever his ailment was, it's improving."

"It would seem so," Lawson agreed.

Calliope smiled. Oh, how she loved the simple conversations of evening. Easy conversation was so consoling somehow, especially while enjoying out of doors and midst a sweet spring breeze.

Calliope joined the rest of her family as they watched Shay scurry up to Rowdy Gates. Her little voice carried on the evening air, and it seemed its melodic lilt brightened the spirits of the man lighting the lamps of Meadowlark Lake, for he smiled as Shay babbled on to him.

Rowdy Gates propped the small ladder he carried with him when lighting lamps against the lamppost just in front of the Ipswich home. He stepped up several rungs of the ladder, lit the gas lamp with the small torch he carried for that purpose, and then descended the ladder again.

Calliope smiled when she heard Shay ask the man if he ever got tired of lighting the lamps.

"Sometimes I sure do," the man answered. His voice was deep, with a resonance of strength that yet somehow conveyed calm.

"Then why don't ya quit doin' it?" Shay asked.

Rowdy Gates chuckled. "Well, somebody has to light the streets, right?" he asked. "And besides, I hurt my leg a couple years back, and it started stiffenin' up on me. But I found the more I made my knee bend, even when it pained me some, the better and better my leg got. Goin' up and down this little ladder every night and mornin' keeps my leg limber, you see?"

Shay smiled. "Why, Mr. Gates, that's the best reason I could ever imagine for lightin' the lamps of town," she exclaimed. "And I'm so glad it makes your leg better to do it."

Rowdy Gates chuckled, tweaked Shay's chin, and looked up to where the rest of the Ipswich family sat on the front porch swings.

"Good evening, Rowdy," Lawson greeted. "Why don't you come on up and visit a moment with us?"

Calliope watched as Mr. Gates paused, obviously uncertain as to whether he wanted to linger in visiting.

But Shay Ipswich was not one to be put off easily, and taking his hand, she said, "Oh, come on and linger awhile, Mr. Gates. You're almost finished with the lamp lightin' anyway."

Calliope was certain that there wasn't a person who walked the earth that would be able to refuse the sweet urgings of little Shay. Therefore, Calliope was not surprised when Rowdy Gates did indeed follow Shay's lead to the porch.

"Mr. Gates explained to me that *someone* has to light the lamps, Mama," Shay explained as she reined in Rowdy to standing on the top porch step. "But it's even better that all that goin' up and down the ladder helps keep his bad leg limber. I guess he hurt it awhile back somehow, but it's gettin' better now, and I think that's a good reason for lightin' the lamps, don't you?"

"I certainly do. Good evenin', Mr. Gates," Kizzy greeted.

Rowdy touched the brim of his hat and nodded, responding, "Good evenin', Mrs. Ipswich." He looked to Evangeline, adding, "Miss Evangeline."

Lawson stood from his seat next to Calliope and offered Rowdy his hand. "Rowdy," he said as the two men struck hands.

Rowdy Gates looked to Calliope then, touched the brim of his hat, and said, "Miss Calliope."

Calliope smiled and nodded in return. She was glad Shay had *convinced* the man to join them on the porch. As a general rule, Rowdy Gates wasn't the most social man in Meadowlark Lake—even for the fact that he was so very handsome and personable.

Rowdy Gates wore his facial hair heavier than most men in town and was tall, broad-shouldered, and brawny—in truth, a somewhat intimidating presence. Calliope knew this was why most people in town didn't seek out his company. Oh, he was an unusually attractive man—there was no denying that—even if his striking features were somewhat concealed by the length of his dark hair and heavy beard. But anyone who took a moment to look beyond the conscious or subconscious attempt to conceal his face, almost as if he were hiding from the world, would've known at once that hidden beneath the rough exterior was a man of profound good looks.

"I hope you don't mind that we allowed Shay to pose her curiosities to you directly, Rowdy," Lawson said.

"Oh, of course not," Rowdy assured him. "I'm always happy to answer the questions of a pretty little filly like this one here." He looked to Shay and winked.

Calliope almost giggled out loud when Shay blushed cherry red with delight.

"So lightin' the lamps helps the stiffness in your leg?" Kizzy inquired.

"Yes, ma'am," Rowdy assured her. "I'll admit it was a might awkward and painful at first. But it seems like that little ladder done the trick. And the pain isn't nothin' like it was before either. I guess I just had to work the cricks out of it."

"Oh! So you just have a stiff leg, Mr. Gates," Shay said then as sudden realization hit her. "You're not missin' half a foot like Warren Ackerman says!"

"For pity's sake, Shay Ipswich!" Kizzy scolded.

But Rowdy Gates just laughed. "Is that what Warren Ackerman thinks was causin' my limp?"

"Yes, sir," Shay ventured, glancing at her mother apologetically.

"Well, I'll tell you what. You just let Warren think that I was missin' half a foot," Rowdy began. "Then maybe when my limp is gone for good, he'll get to thinkin' I grew the missin' half back. What do you say?"

Shay giggled and nodded, still looking to her mother for reassurance. Kizzy smiled and winked, and Shay was relieved.

"I hear you hired the new Chesterfield boy out at the mill," Lawson ventured.

Rowdy nodded. "Yep. Today was his first day," he explained. "I think it's a little more laborious a job than he's used to, but once he builds up a bit more muscle, he'll do just fine." He paused a moment and then continued, "Between you and me and the fence post, I'm glad a new family has moved into town. Maybe now the absence of the one that had to leave last fall won't hover over all of us so heavy anymore."

"You mean the Mulhollands," Calliope blurted. She blushed when Rowdy looked at her, knowing she'd entirely thwarted his graciousness at attempting to leave the actual Mulholland family name out of things.

"Mmm hmm," he confirmed, however.

"I did receive a telegram from Ben Mulholland just last week," Lawson mentioned. "Seems he's settled in all right up in Denver, and I guess you know that he was able to sell the mill to...well, to somebody. He said you'd agreed to stay on as the mill foreman for the new owner."

"Mr. Mulholland sold the mill? To somebody? Who?" Evangeline interjected.

But Lawson Ipswich shrugged. "He didn't mention to whom he'd sold it."

"And what do you mean you received a telegram from poor Ben Mulholland? You never said a word to me," Kizzy said. "Is he well? And what about Sam and poor Prudence?"

Lawson exchanged amused glances with Rowdy as Rowdy said, "Hmm. Looks like you've got some questions to answer yourself, Judge." Looking down to Shay once more, he tweaked her chin again and said, "I guess I better get back to lightin' the lamps, just in case your daddy has to run off down the road for the sake of too many questions to answer, hmmm?"

Shay blushed again under Rowdy's kind gaze and agreed, "I guess so, Mr. Gates."

"You all have a nice evenin' now," Rowdy said, touching the brim of his hat and looking to each family member in turn.

"Good night, Mr. Gates!" Shay called as Rowdy descended the steps and headed back out toward the street. "And I'll just keep lettin' Warren Ackerman think whatever he thinks about your foot."

Rowdy tossed a wave to Shay over his shoulder.

"Now you tell me right now about this telegram from poor Ben Mulholland, Lawson Ipswich," Kizzy flirtatiously demanded. "You know how worried we've all been about him after...well, after everything that went on."

But Lawson shrugged. "There isn't much more to tell. He's settled in comfortably in Denver. Seems he has a sister and brother-in-law that took him in. Prudence is in the asylum—a very necessary, albeit sad, circumstance. Sam has found work, actually at the asylum as well. Still, considering everything, Ben sounded fairly hopeful...in good spirits."

"It's all so sad," Evangeline sighed. "Still, I can't believe Prudence tried to...well, she tried to—"

"She tried to kill our sister Amoretta!" Shay exclaimed with anger. "I don't feel sorry at all that she's in the asylum, whatever that is. As long as she can't try to hurt anybody else, especially Amoretta and Uncle Brake."

Evangeline smiled and gathered Shay into a loving embrace of comfort and security. "Well, let's go back to talking about how beautiful the evening is, shall we? I like that much better. And look at you, Shay Ipswich! You found out something that nobody else in town has ever known, and that's why Rowdy Gates limps...or used to limp anyway. That's something very interesting, isn't it?"

"It is!" Shay said, brightening. "And silly old Warren Ackerman thought Mr. Gates was missin' part of a foot. Pfft! Silly ol' Warren."

Calliope smiled as she listened to Evangeline redirecting Shay's thoughts from the terror of Prudence Mulholland's insanity and back to the lovely night at hand. She watched Rowdy Gates stride from one lamp to the next, ascending the short ladder he carried to light a lamp and then descending and moving onto the next. His limp was nearly gone altogether. And she was glad to know he wasn't missing half a foot, though she simultaneously wondered how he had injured his leg in the first place.

Suddenly, an idea leapt into Calliope's head, filling her with such instant excitement that she hopped up from her seat in the swing and announced, "I have the most *wonderful* idea!"

Kizzy giggled. "Uh oh! I know that expression. Looks like your big sister is about to pull us all into some sort of adventure of some kind or the other."

"Oh, I love Calliope's adventures!" Shay cheered. "What is it, Calliope? Tell us! Oh, do hurry and tell us!"

Calliope's bosom was so filled with excitement she could hardly catch her breath. She couldn't believe she hadn't thought of actually attempting the idea before. But for some reason, the notion had only just struck her as conceivable.

"Well, Shay is old enough now, I think," Calliope began. "And I have been thinking of this for so long, but for some reason I couldn't just...well, I couldn't just pull it together in my mind. Not until this very moment, when Shay mentioned Warren Ackerman and... and..."

"And what?" Evangeline urged impatiently. "For pity's sake, Calliope! What has your eyes so lit up? I swear you look like you're going to take to flight any moment."

"Oh, Daddy!" Calliope exclaimed, looking to her father. "Can't you just envision it? Can't you?" Quickly she looked to Kizzy and said, "We've got enough young children in town now, I think, with the Chesterfields having moved in and such. Don't you think, Kizzy? And wouldn't Shay be perfect?" Squealing with delight, she raced to Evangeline, taking her hands and pulling her from her seat on the porch swing. "I know you can envision it with me, Evie! A white cake, adorned with yellow roses, perhaps. I'm sure Mrs. Montrose would allow us some roses from her rose garden when they bloom."

Evangeline's eyes lit up then as understanding washed over her. "Bow ties, little top hats, the most beautiful little dresses…with lace, of course!"

"And Shay adorned in the most beautiful dress," Calliope giggled. "Can't you just see it?"

"I can!" Evangeline chirped. "It will be beautiful, Calliope. Oh, and everyone will love it. The whole town is bound to turn out!"

"The whole town is bound to turn out for what?" Shay asked. She looked to her father for an answer, but Lawson Ipswich merely shrugged, as perplexed as his young daughter about what the other Ipswich women were going on about.

Jumping up from her own seat, Kizzy squealed with delight as well. "Oh, Calliope, it's a wonderful idea! I've always dreamt of seein' one."

"Of seeing one what?" Lawson asked.

"A Tom Thumb wedding!" all three adult women exclaimed with exuberance.

"A Tom Thumb wedding?" Lawson repeated. "In Meadowlark Lake?"

"Yes, Daddy," Calliope chirped. "Oh, it will be so wonderful— and with Shay as the bride! She'll make a beautiful bride."

"And we can have edibles afterward, and cake," Evangeline added.

"And we can all help with the bridesmaids' dresses," Kizzy suggested. "And we'll have official invitations, and everyone in town can be involved."

But Shay's pretty brow puckered. "Me? A bride? Like a weddin'? *My* weddin'? I can't get married! I'm not even six years old yet!"

Lawson smiled and gathered his youngest daughter into his arms. "Oh, sweetie, it's not a real wedding. You won't really be getting married. It's…it's like a play, like an acting play when people pretend, only all the actors are children. Do you see?"

Shay shrugged. She looked to Calliope, asking, "Will it be fun to do, Calliope?"

Calliope smiled, her heart continuing to swell with delirious anticipation. "Oh yes, darling, it will! You'll get to be dressed up in the most beautiful dress we can make for you, with a lovely headpiece and veil and a beautiful bouquet. Everyone will dress up and come to see the pretend wedding, and then we'll have food and cake and dancing. Oh, it will be a dream come true, Shay!"

Shay sighed with determination. "Well, if you say it will be fun, Calliope, then I'm sure it will be."

"So you'll be the bride in our Tom Thumb wedding?" Evangeline asked.

"Yes," Shay answered, smiling, "especially if I get cake when it's over."

Kizzy, Evangeline, and Calliope all squealed with simultaneous gladness.

Throwing her arms around her father and Shay, Calliope hugged them both tight and said, "I have always, always wanted to put on a Tom Thumb wedding. Oh, thank you, Shay!"

"This will be so much fun," Evangeline said, clapping her hands together with glee. "We'll need Amoretta to choose a date that she and Brake can attend as well. And she'll want to help, as much as she can from Langtree."

"There will be plenty of sewin' to be done," Kizzy offered. "And the invitations—Amoretta's script is so lovely!"

"Let's you and I amble down the road a bit, shall we, darling?" Calliope heard her father ask Shay.

"Yes, let's, Daddy," Shay agreed. "You know how they get when there's plannin' to do. I'd rather walk along and just watch the lamplights flicker, if you don't mind."

"Not at all," Lawson said. He winked at Calliope as he took Shay's hand and led her down the porch steps toward the main thoroughfare of Meadowlark Lake.

Calliope watched them leave, commenting, "Won't she be the perfect little bride?"

Kizzy and Evangeline followed her gaze. "Perfect!" Evangeline agreed. "Now, you mentioned yellow roses, Calliope," she continued. "Were you thinking yellow dresses for the bridesmaids as well?"

"Or lavender. Lavender would be beautiful! And it goes so well with yellow," Kizzy suggested.

But Calliope shrugged. "I don't know. I just thought that it seemed like a good time to finally, finally present a Tom Thumb wedding. I hadn't gotten much further than that."

"Let's get some paper and pencils," Evangeline suggested, "write a few things down while our minds are fresh on it."

"Oh, Calliope," Kizzy sighed, hugging her stepdaughter and friend affectionately, "you've no idea the joy you bring to the world, my sweet thing. This is a wonderful idea—and just the sort of innocent, happy distraction this town could use...especially after what happened last Halloween." As Kizzy gazed into Calliope's eyes, Calliope was awed by the beautiful emotion in the countenance of her father's young bride. "You bring enchantment into the soul of anyone who is blessed to know you. Thank you for that."

Calliope was moved, nearly to tears, by Kizzy's words, for she could feel the fabric of their sincerity. And though she deemed Kizzy's compliment as far too kind, she was overwhelmed with knowing the woman meant her words. What greater gift could a person give to the world than enchantment?

Rowdy Gates spun around to look behind him. The squeals he'd heard coming from the Ipswich home were that of unmeasured female delight. In fact, the sound was so foreign to him—so long absent in his life—that it had taken him a moment to recognize it. Yet when he'd looked back to see the three Ipswich women giggling with joy and hugging one another—seen Lawson Ipswich standing and smiling with amusement at their goings-on—he did remember how marvelous the sound of female laughter was.

Returning his attention to the last lamp to be lit in Meadowlark Lake for the evening, Rowdy thought on what a lucky and truly blessed man Judge Lawson Ipswich was. Obviously he'd known immense love in his life—still knew it. No doubt there had been great pain as well, for Rowdy knew that the judge had lost the mother of his three eldest daughters years before. Yet to be surrounded as he was now, with the tender, loving hearts of women—with their nurturing ways, kindness, exuberance, and happiness—it was something he doubted most men ever knew, especially to the extent that Lawson Ipswich did.

Yet Rowdy was not resentful. He didn't envy the judge in any malicious manner. Rather he was glad for him. Lawson was a good and honorable man. He deserved the kind of happiness God had showered down on him. But before he began to think too much on what Lawson had that he didn't, Rowdy turned his thoughts to his own blessing of miracles. After all, he'd survived what few men could have—lived through it. Maybe he didn't have a beautiful wife or babies to bounce on his knee, but there was still time. At least he hoped there was. Perhaps if he could heal completely—walk without any limp at all—then he might find the courage to flirt a bit with the lovely young ladies of Meadowlark Lake the way the other bachelors did.

His thoughts were getting away from him, wandering to venues he knew were mere fantasy. And so once Rowdy had lit the last lamplight of Meadowlark Lake's main street, he turned and sauntered toward home—toward a cool evening breeze, perhaps some cold biscuits and a hunk of ham for supper.

But as Rowdy neared the house just outside of town where he dwelt, he was once again struck by the lonesome sense of the absence of a spirit. The terrifying events of the previous fall had hit Rowdy Gates hard, though no one knew how hard. The madness of Prudence Mulholland had peaked its malice on Amoretta Ipswich and Brake McClendon that dark All Hallow's Eve. But the poor girl's violent insanity had begun with the murder and mutilation of Rowdy's dog, Dodger, and each and every night since, Rowdy Gates missed the old mutt—missed his companionship at night when the house was dark and lonesome.

Dodger had been far more than a good dog; Dodger had helped save Rowdy Gates's life, and the man's heart still twinged with missing his faithful old friend. In fact, as had become his habit, Rowdy paused beneath the old willow tree where he'd buried his cherished canine friend, after managing to recover his carcass before Sheriff Dennison had put fire to it months before.

Hunkering down, Rowdy placed a hand on the stone-covered mound that was Dodger's resting place. "How you doin' tonight, ol' boy?" he asked in a lowered voice. "I sure do miss your barkin'." He chuckled as happy memories of the dog washed over him. "I even miss them slobberin' kisses of yours, I guess. Though I can't figure out why." His smile faded as he continued, "Still, it was somethin'— you lightin' up when you saw me comin'. Just between you and me and the fence, I get mighty tired of no one bein' glad to see me, you know?" He thought a moment and then smiled again. "Though that little Ipswich girl, that Shay, she seemed a might glad to see me tonight. That lightened my heart a bit." His smile broadened, and he added, "Of course, just settin' eyes on her pretty sister lightened my heart a bit more." Rowdy drew a slow, deep breath, exhaling a sigh of returning loneliness. "Still, girls like her…it's the Fox Montroses of the world they're meant for, not raggedy, banged-up ol' fellers like us. Ain't that right?"

Sighing again, Rowdy put down his ladder and sat down on the ground next to Dodger's grave. "Look at them stars, Dodger, will ya?" he mumbled. "As bright and as beautiful as the sparkle in Calliope Ipswich's eyes." He frowned. "Damn that Fox Montrose."

CHAPTER THREE

"We've chosen yellow and lavender as the colors," Calliope explained. She looked to Mrs. Montrose, admitting, "We were hoping you would allow us a few of your beautiful yellow roses to embellish the cake with, Mrs. Montrose. But we will understand if you'd rather not."

"Oh, I'd be delighted, Calliope!" Dora Montrose exclaimed with delight. "You may have as many roses as you like. Take them all if you need them. Goodness knows they'll only end up in a vase on my kitchen table or witherin' away if you don't use them up. If you're plannin' on mid-June for the weddin', my roses will be at their best just about then. Oh, this all sounds so delightful!"

"Have you chosen a groom yet?" Blanche's mother, Judith Gardener, asked.

Evangeline and Calliope exchanged nervous glances.

"Well, in truth," Evangeline began. She looked to Ellen Ackerman, sitting next to her daughter, Sallie. "We...well, we were hoping you might be able to convince Warren to be the groom, Mrs. Ackerman."

Every woman in Dora Montrose's parlor burst into merriment and laughter.

"Oh, I'd pay good money to see little Warren Ackerman cleaned up and wearin' a swallowtail suit coat!" Dora squealed with delight.

"Are we to understand that it might be a bit difficult to convince your son, Warren, to play the groom, Ellen?" Josephine Chesterfield inquired.

Again everyone laughed as Ellen said, "Like shovin' a live rooster into a cannin' bottle, most likely."

"Really?" Calliope asked with sudden disappointment, for she knew that, although Shay always pretended not to like Warren Ackerman, in truth she was sweeter on him than ants were to sugar.

Recognizing Calliope's thoroughgoing disenchantment, Ellen answered, "Oh, don't you worry a whit, Calliope. Warren will be the groom. His daddy and I will make certain that he will be."

"We were also going to ask if we might hold the wedding in your barn, Mrs. Ackerman," Evangeline ventured. "It's the perfect venue, and everyone in town is used to gatherings there."

"Of course you can hold it in our barn," Ellen assured her. "Oh, this will be somethin' to behold, won't it?"

"Is there anythin' we can help with?" Pauline Chesterfield inquired. "I know we're too old to actually be *in* the play, but Callie and me can help with sewin' or decoratin' or anything else you need."

"Oh, thank you, Pauline! There is so much to be done in preparing everything, we would be so grateful for your help," Evangeline graciously thanked Pauline.

"And I think your brothers, Willis and Albert, would be perfect ushers," Calliope said. "And Lena, did you say she's eight years old? She'd be a wonderful bridesmaid."

"My Eva plays the violin," Mrs. Chesterfield offered unexpectedly. She blushed when everyone in the room looked to her. "I-I mean, if you're needin' a musician of any kind. She's very good, and I'm sure it would be easier to have a violin for music than tryin' to get a piano out to Ellen's barn. Wouldn't it?"

Calliope leapt to her feet with sudden inspiration. "Oh yes, yes! Violin music would be perfect. Can't you just see it, Evie? Little Shay coming down the aisle with violin music playing the bridal chorus. But wait! Previous to Shay's entrance, someone should sing 'Oh, Promise Me' once the ushers have seated the guests."

"My Natalie could do that! She has a lovely voice," Ellen Ackerman exclaimed.

"Oh, she does," Sallie added. "And she's only nine—young enough to be in the play, right, Calliope?"

"Perfectly young enough," Calliope giggled with delight.

"We should be writing this down," Evangeline noted. She reached into her sewing basket, retrieved a paper and pencil, and began scribbling.

"Well then," Calliope said as she began to pace back and forth across Dora Montrose's parlor, "Evie and I worked out colors, fabrics, flowers, cakes, and refreshments. We cast Shay as the bride, of course. And, Mrs. Ackerman, you're certain you can coax Warren into being the groom?"

"He'll be the groom, Calliope. I promise," Ellen answered with a smile and twinkling eyes.

"Wonderful!" Calliope exclaimed, clasping her hands together with one loud clap. "Then we've got Natalie singing, Eva and her violin for music, Willis and Albert as ushers, Lena as a bridesmaid." She frowned a moment and then said, "We need a maid of honor, perhaps one more bridesmaid, a groomsman, a boy of about twelve to be the clergyman." She turned to look at Blanche and her mother. "Do you think Nigel would be willing to be the clergyman, Mrs. Gardener?"

Judith Gardener smiled, nodded, and said, "Yes. I think once Ellen has convinced Warren to be the groom, Nigel will want to be front and center to witness it!"

Everyone giggled, amused by the notion of the boys in Meadowlark Lake being put through the pomp and circumstance of a Tom Thumb wedding.

"What about flower girls?" Dora asked. "We simply must have flower girls."

"Maybe Mr. Longfellow will allow Mamie and Effie to be flower girls," Evangeline suggested. "They've just turned three years old, and wouldn't they be perfect? Little twins as they are?"

Everyone was quiet for a moment, exchanging worried glances.

Calliope doubted for a moment, as well—doubted that Mr. Longfellow would let Mamie and Effie out of his sight long enough to be prepared to be flower girls. She sighed, thinking how sad it all was. Floyd Longfellow, Dex Longfellow's father, had lost Dex's mother when Dex was just a toddler. Years and years later, when Dex was already in adolescence, Mr. Longfellow had found love again with a beautiful young woman from the next county. They'd married, and for a time Mr. Longfellow's heart was healed. But his young bride died in childbirth, leaving him alone once more, this time with twin daughters to care for.

As an understandable result, Floyd Longfellow kept watch over his twin girls, Mamie and Effie, like no one Calliope had ever seen. Oh, the girls played and attended church and things, but only when Floyd or Dex was present. Naturally, the girls were very young—far too young to be on their own. But the entire citizenship of Meadowlark Lake knew Floyd's fear for his daughters' well-being was so obsessive it was perhaps unhealthy for the girls at times.

"I know what everyone's thinking," Evangeline said, proceeding carefully. "But I'm sure Calliope and I can convince Mr. Longfellow into allowing the girls to participate. We can assure him that he or Dex can come with them to rehearsals. And of course, we'll make their dresses. He won't have to worry about that at all."

Dora was the first to speak up in support of the idea. "I think we should at least try. It would be so lovely, two little twin girls as flower girls. And perhaps it would help Floyd as well—to see that his friends in Meadowlark care for his children and want to include them in all the town events."

Judith Gardener said, "I agree. Perhaps if we feed the idea to him slowly, with lots of reassurance…well, I'm certain we can convince him to allow it, especially if he or Dex is with them."

Winnie giggled. "I'm not so sure Fox will like the idea of Dex being at every rehearsal—if Calliope's there, as well."

Calliope blushed, but not with delight. Why on earth did everyone assume that she and Fox Montrose someday being a couple was already a forgone conclusion?

Once again, Calliope was thankful for her older sister's uncanny ability to redirect the cumulative attention of the sewing group from one thing to another, as Evie said, "And there we have it! Our Tom Thumb wedding is nearly cast. Naturally, it's a small affair, being that we are a small community, but in truth, I think it will be far preferable to that large cast Tom Thumb wedding we saw in Boston when we were little. Remember, Calliope? Weren't there something like forty to fifty children in that one?"

"Oh, at least!" Calliope agreed. "And it wasn't at all very intimate, the way ours will be." Calliope sighed with pure joy in anticipation of the affair. "Ours will be so quaint and lovely—yellow and lavender everywhere, music, singing, flowers!"

"Indeed," Josephine Chesterfield agreed. "In fact, I've quite forgotten my sewin' for today." Calliope smiled as she watched Mrs. Chesterfield discard her sewing into the basket at her feet, lean forward, and with pure resplendence of delight ask, "What else can I do to help?"

"Me too," Dora Montrose said, abandoning her stitching as well.

Calliope laughed as soon every woman in Dora's parlor had put away her stitching in favor of discussing the details of the wedding.

She looked to Evangeline, who smiled at her with understanding. *Yes!* Calliope thought. A Tom Thumb wedding was just what Meadowlark Lake needed to begin looking forward to happiness, instead of lingering on a dark past.

As Blanche asked, "What is the refreshment menu? Other than cake, of course?" Calliope thought of Rowdy Gates—wondered whether he would find entertainment in attending the Tom Thumb wedding. Everyone else had family with whom to attend, but he didn't. She wondered if he'd be willing to join the Ipswich family at the wedding, just so that he wouldn't have to arrive alone.

Calliope quickly began to compile a mental list of the citizens of Meadowlark Lake. She wanted to make certain she wasn't forgetting *anyone.* She also wanted to reassure herself that Rowdy Gates was the only person in town without family nearby. Everyone needed to feel comfortable in being included in the guest list.

"We've got to get the guest list together right away," she said, speaking her thoughts aloud. "I'm sure Amoretta will agree to write out the invitations. We've written and asked her already, and I want to be sure we don't forget anyone."

"Excellent point, Calliope dear," Dora said, nodding. "Everyone must be included, and hopefully in attendance. We must make certain the invitations are given out in plenty of time for folks to include the weddin' in their plans."

"Definitely," Judith Gardener confirmed.

"Oh, I'm near tremblin' with excitement!" Josephine Chesterfield exclaimed. "I've never seen anything like a Tom Thumb weddin', not in all my life. And to actually have a hand in it...I'm so delighted!"

Calliope exchanged satisfied smiles with Evangeline, for the Tom Thumb wedding was already turning out to be exactly what she'd hoped for—a gift that everyone could look forward to with happy anticipation. She sighed with contentment in knowing that already the ladies of Meadowlark Lake seemed cheerier—and the wedding hadn't even happened yet!

❧

"But Warren Ackerman?" Shay whined. "How could you girls do this to me? My own sisters even!" Shay's dark curls bounced as she shook her head, feigning irritation.

Calliope giggled when Evangeline looked at her and winked with understanding. Oh, Shay was certainly putting on an act of being horrified that Warren Ackerman was going to be her groom at the Tom Thumb wedding. But both Calliope and Evangeline could tell that their baby sister couldn't have been happier about the fact. If nothing else, it was obvious in the sudden sparkle that had leapt to Shay's eyes when they'd informed her that Warren would play the groom—not to mention the manner in which she'd begun twirling around like some merry fairy.

"I'm sorry, Shay Shay," Calliope began, "but it just worked out that way. And Warren will be such a handsome groom. Don't you think?"

Shay quirked half a smile, shrugging. "Well, he's not as ugly as some bugs I've squashed, I suppose," she answered. "Still, will you and Evie play with me now—you know, to ease my bein' upset about marrin' Warren and all?"

Evangeline laughed. "Of course we will, darling. But we'll play with you because we want to, not to bribe you into letting Warren kiss you as part of the ceremony, all right?"

"Kiss me?" Shay exclaimed. "You mean we have to kiss as part of it all?"

Calliope was amused by the blush of pure delight that rose to Shay's young cheeks. "Well, of course, angel," she answered. "It's all part of the wedding. The bride and groom always, always kiss."

Shay exhaled a heavy sigh, again feigning unwilling resignation. "Well, I guess if it *has* to be part of the play, I'll just have to go along with it."

"We appreciate your willingness to make such a grand sacrifice, Shay Shay," Calliope told her.

Evangeline let a giggle slip, and Shay scowled at her.

"But let's just have some fun together now," Calliope suggested. "I could use something to distract me from all the sewing I'm behind on, now that we spent the sewing circle time planning the Tom Thumb wedding."

"Me too," Evangeline agreed. "What do you want to play first, Shay?"

Shay smiled, her eyes twinkling with mischievous triumph. "Ponies," she answered flatly.

Again, Calliope exchanged glances of shared emotion with Evangeline. Though they each smiled, Calliope knew that deep inside, Evangeline felt like moaning as much as she did.

Shay loved to play "ponies," as she called it, and the little girl that was still part of Calliope did too. Yet it was a fairly difficult pretense for grown-up young ladies. Playing ponies with Shay required a lot of running around (sometimes on all fours), neighing, and oft-times imagining one was a beautiful white horse performing in a circus.

Therefore, young as Calliope and Evangeline still were, early on they'd discovered that playing ponies with Shay found them both collapsing into bed afterward, having fallen asleep nearly before their heads hit the pillow.

Still, it was a fun game, and Shay enjoyed it so thoroughly. Furthermore, Calliope knew she could never, ever verbalize even one mild complaint, for she had been the one to teach Shay the thing in the first place (having adored playing ponies herself as a child).

And so half an hour later, Calliope and Evangeline found themselves out in the meadow near the stream, long pieces of satin tucked in their skirt waistbands at their backs to mimic a horse's tail, prancing around in pretending to be equines.

As was almost always the case, the moment Calliope was parading around in the meadow with her sister fillies, she found she enjoyed the frolic more than she'd expected.

It was a beautiful spring day, bold with warm sunshine. Birds filled the trees and bushes that lined the meadow opposite the stream. They warbled and twittered with excitement as they gathered different materials hither and yon that nature provided for them to use in building new nests. Great puffy white clouds billowed overhead and in the distance—not the sort of clouds to threaten the coming of a storm but rather the kind that were perfect fodder for the imagination.

Why, on the way to the meadow, in fact, it was Evangeline who pointed to one large, globular cloud and exclaimed, "Shay! Doesn't that cloud look just like a big bullfrog with bulging eyes?"

Shay had giggled and squealed with delight, "It does, Evie! Oh, you're so good at finding shapes and things in clouds."

Yes! The air was fresh with springtime, the grass cool beneath their feet, and the sun warm on their pretty faces, as Calliope, Evangeline, and Shay Ipswich pranced about, whinnying with lengths of satin cascading over their dainty posteriors.

Rowdy smiled as he watched the goings-on in the meadow from the small hilltop near the stream. Worn out from work at the mill (and the company of the men he labored with), he'd decided to lunch near the meadow, in hopes that the soft, tranquil babbling of the brook might soothe and rejuvenate him a bit.

But in a million years he never would've expected to find the distraction he'd happened upon. As he'd settled himself on the hilltop near a large laurel bush and began to eat the baked potato he'd brought along for his midday meal, he was startled to hear laughter. Yet when he'd looked down to see Judge Ipswich's three daughters dash into the meadow, whinnying like horses, long strips of fabric tucked into their skirt waistbands at the back, he smiled with amusement—glad he'd decided to leave the mill for a midday break.

It was an enchanting, almost surreal event to witness—two beautiful young women and an adorable little girl frolicking about in the meadow pretending to be horses. Rowdy marveled at how different the two eldest Ipswich sisters looked from a distance. Evangeline's hair was raven black, and Rowdy knew that if most of the men in town could see her now—hair unpinned and blowing in the breeze, laughing and playing with her sisters—they might not be as intimidated by her as they all were. And they *were* intimidated by her beauty and graceful carriage. As he looked to Shay Ipswich, Rowdy fancied that it would be easy for a stranger to mistake Evangeline and Shay as full-blood sisters, both having dark hair as they did—easier to think they were blood sisters and Calliope the added-in one.

Rowdy inhaled a deep breath, exhaling a low, slow sigh of admiration as he watched Calliope then. Calliope Ipswich—with her sky-blue eyes that pierced a man's heart clean through to his soul. Calliope Ipswich—with hair the color of sunshine and a smile even brighter. Calliope Ipswich—with a laughter that was the music of heaven and with the countenance of an angel.

It was no secret that every eligible man in Meadowlark Lake—though mesmerized and intimidated by the dark, graceful beauty of Evangeline—was immeasurably drawn to the bright, spirited beauty of Calliope. And no one was more drawn to Calliope Ipswich and the radiance of her heart and soul than Rowdy Gates himself.

Rowdy had never known such a young woman as Calliope—not in all his life. From the day she and her family had first arrived in Meadowlark Lake, it felt to Rowdy as if Calliope had somehow reached into his chest and with her soft, dainty little hands clasped his heart and withdrawn it to keep as her own.

Naturally, this was something he would hardly ever allow himself to admit—even silently to himself, let alone imply during conversations among the other bachelors in town. Even when his fellow mill workers lingered in verbal admiration of the Ipswich girls—how dark and beautiful Evangeline was, how bright and beautiful Calliope was—Rowdy Gates kept his thoughts mostly to himself. And whenever he was asked an opinion about the Ipswich girls and chose to answer, he never let on which was his favorite.

He'd simply say something like, "Well, I wouldn't deny either one of them Ipswich girls, if she wanted herself a little sparkin' time with Rowdy Gates."

Most times the other men would nod and laugh—chuckle their agreements—and go back to discussing their own fancies about either Evangeline or Calliope—or both.

But the truth was that if Rowdy Gates could have one thing in all the world to call his own, it would be Calliope Ipswich. Still, he wasn't stupid. He knew Calliope deserved a whole lot better then his banged-up hide and secret past. He wasn't sure Fox Montrose deserved her either, but Rowdy sure didn't.

After all, what did he have to offer a young woman like Calliope? Any young woman for that matter? A stiff leg? A past that still caused him to wake up shouting in panic some nights?

He'd be a good provider—there was no questioning that. Even if he hadn't bought the mill from Sam Mulholland, Rowdy had plenty of money. But physical comfort wasn't everything. Calliope had such a lively, bright spirit, and Rowdy was afraid a man like him might unintentionally squelch it somehow—simply because of the burden of truth he carried around inside him, the knowledge of who he was and where he'd come from.

Furthermore, even if Rowdy proved to Calliope he was a good man, her father was a judge. A judge! No judge would ever agree to allow a man with a history like Rowdy's to come courting his daughter—especially with serious intention.

Exhaling another heavy sigh of disappointment and regret, Rowdy retrieved the small pad of paper and small piece of charcoal he carried in his back pocket and began to sketch. He learned a long time ago that making sketches of the things he could not have seemed to soothe him a little. He'd never be able to know Calliope Ipswich as anything more than a casual acquaintance, but that didn't mean he couldn't sketch her and keep her portrait to himself.

Rowdy sketched for a few moments and then looked up when he heard the Ipswich girls squeal with delight. Calliope and Evangeline were playing ring-around-the-rosy with Shay. Squealing with amusement, the girls twirled faster and faster, holding tight to one another's hands. Suddenly, however, one of them seemed to lose her grip, and all three girls were flung back by the force of their spinning, to land on their fannies, feet and legs flying up in the air for a moment.

Rowdy laughed but quickly quieted himself for fear of being found spying. Fortunately, the Ipswich girls were giggling so loudly as they lay on their backs in the meadow grass that they hadn't heard him.

He smiled as he continued to watch Calliope and her sisters. They continued to lie on their backs in the grass for quite some time, pointing up to clouds here and there, giggling and talking. As he watched them, he sketched, until he had a fairly good likeness of Calliope to keep with him.

At last Rowdy Gates shoved his sketchbook and charcoal back into his pocket and left. As he walked away, he heard the Ipswich girls' laughter again and smiled, glad he'd abandoned the mill in favor of the hilltop as a venue to have his midday meal—for heaven itself would have to agree that watching Calliope Ipswich prance around like a pony in the meadow was far favorable to sitting in the mill, listening while the other men discussed women, work, and worry.

"Calliope," Rowdy mumbled out loud to himself. Even just speaking her name made him feel stronger somehow—more lighthearted.

❦

"I thought Shay was trying to *kill* us out there in the meadow today," Calliope teased as the Ipswich family sat enjoying light conversation in the parlor after supper that evening. "Ponies, ring-around-the-rosy, and then more ponies," Calliope sighed. "I swear I'm worn out!"

"You are not, Calliope," Shay argued with a giggle. The lovely little dark-haired angel hopped up into Calliope's lap, threw her small arms around her big sister's neck, and hugged her. "You love playin' ponies as much as I do, and you know it."

Calliope smiled and admitted, "Oh, you know me too well," Calliope said, winking at the others as she continued to hug her little sister.

"Well, I for one will sleep soundly tonight," Evangeline said. She covered her mouth as a revealing yawn escaped her.

Lawson chuckled. "I guess you older girls don't have the fortitude you used to when it comes to playing ponies, hm?" he teased.

"Shay," Kizzy began, "you should be very grateful and flattered that Evie and Calliope have chosen you to play the part of the bride in the Tom Thumb wedding. I'm not sure it was necessary to wear them clean through today."

"Oh, I *am* excited about bein' the bride, Mama," Shay explained. "It's havin' to kiss Warren Ackerman, him bein' the groom and all. That's why Evie and Calliope were in my clutches today!" Shay poised her hands as if they were claws and, employing her best witch's cackle, added, "Wah ha ha ha ha ha!"

Everyone guffawed, entirely amused by Shay's dramatics.

When the laughter had settled, however, Lawson offered, "But, Shay Ipswich, I thought you'd be tickled about being kissed by Warren Ackerman."

Shay gasped, exclaiming, "Daddy! What a thing to say! Me? Be glad that I have to kiss Warren in the play?" Shay's face was as red as a radish, but Calliope bit her lip to keep from giggling. "Why, I can't believe you would say such a thing, Daddy! Warren Ackerman? For Pete's sake, Daddy!"

"Well, forgive me then, angel," Lawson said, trying his best not to grin with lingering amusement. "Come give me a hug so that I'll know I'm forgiven."

Shay hopped off Calliope's lap, folded her arms determinedly across her small chest, and asked, "Promise not to tease me about havin' to kiss Warren Ackerman when we get married, Daddy?"

"Of course, baby," Lawson agreed.

Shay smiled and threw herself into her father's waiting embrace. "I love you, Daddy," she whispered against his handsome, whiskery face.

"I love you too, my angel," Lawson whispered in return.

Everyone in the room smiled, and Calliope sighed with pleasure. They were such a happy family, so content in one another's company. It was still strange that Amoretta and Brake lived in a different town, that they weren't with them every day anymore. Yet Calliope knew how blissful Amoretta was in the arms of Brake McClendon, and it seemed at times that the Ipswich family could almost feel Amoretta and Brake's love lingering in the parlor with them, even if they weren't actually there.

"Here comes Rowdy Gates," Evangeline whispered.

Calliope looked to see Evangeline looking over her shoulder and out the parlor window behind the sofa on which they sat.

Evangeline shook her head. "I admire that man's tenacity," she sighed. "Every night he goes along lighting the lamps, and every morning he turns them out before heading to the mill. You'd think it would wear him thin, don't you? Never having an evening or morning to relax?"

"He's one of the most steadfast men I've ever known," Lawson commented.

Shay dashed back over to the sofa, hopped up between Calliope and Evangeline, and stared out the window.

"With all this nonsense about Warren Ackerman, I almost missed wavin' to Mr. Gates!" she exclaimed.

Calliope's pretty brows puckered. "What do you mean, honey?" she asked.

Shay shrugged and explained, "Ever since I asked him about his limpin' last week, I've been waitin' at the window here to wave to him every night when he lights the lamps in front of our house."

Calliope smiled, instantly delighted. "You have?" she asked in unison with everyone else.

"Yep!" Shay answered. "I figure it's the least I can do—you know, bein' that he lights our lamps every single night for all eternity and such. I figure he at least deserves a smile and a wave."

"Why yes, he does," Evangeline agreed.

"*Indeed* he does!" Calliope added. Turning around to kneel on the sofa and gaze out the window in mimicking Shay, she giggled. In truth, she'd watched for Rowdy Gates each evening as often as she could—ever since the family had arrived in Meadowlark Lake. She watched for him each morning as well. But she'd never told a soul. She'd always wished she'd had the nerve to wave to him once in a while, smile at him, and let him know she appreciated his efforts in tending to the gaslights of the town's main street. Thus, she was soothed to know that at least Shay had taken to giving him some well-deserved acknowledgement.

"He's coming closer!" Shay announced.

Evangeline turned to kneel on the sofa and stare out the window as well. And when Rowdy Gates had lit the lamp to the left of their home—when he glanced up a moment to the parlor window—Calliope and Evangeline joined Shay in tossing a grateful wave to him.

He looked a bit astonished at first, and Calliope knew it must be a strange sight indeed—to look up expecting to find a little girl waving and instead see three smiling faces staring out into the dusk and waving.

But in the next moment, Rowdy Gates grinned, tugged at the brim of his hat in thanks, and moved along to the next lamp.

"See?" Shay said proudly. "He always waves to me or tips his hat at me. I think he likes that I watch for him."

"I'm sure that he does," Kizzy agreed.

"How sweet you are, Shay Shay!" Calliope exclaimed, hugging her little sister then. "To think of Rowdy Gates every night that way— you really are our little angel." Calliope hugged Shay and then immediately gasped. "Evie," she said, "Shay should have flowers woven through her hair for the wedding! Don't you think? Oh, how lovely would that be?"

Evangeline smiled and enthusiastically agreed, "Yes, that would be perfect! Yellow roses, some lilac blossoms…maybe a bit of lavender."

Calliope giggled, took Shay's hand, and pulled her to stand with her. "Come on, Shay. Let's go play with putting your hair up a bit so Evie and I can imagine how the flowers will fit."

"Yes, let's," Shay giggled with delight. "Warren Ackerman won't mind kissin' me at all if I have flowers in my hair!"

"Exactly!" Calliope said.

The girls were gone then, leaving Lawson's head spinning. "Now how can those girls go from waving out the window at Rowdy one moment to planning more fluff where this Tom Thumb wedding is concerned the next?" he asked his beautiful young wife. "They wear me out sometimes."

Kizzy Ipswich smiled, studied her handsome husband a moment, and then asked, "You're teasin' me, right, Lawson?" she asked. "You…you *do* know why the subject went from Rowdy Gates to this weddin' so quickly, don't you?"

Lawson leaned back in his chair and shrugged. "Well, probably because the girls can't keep a single thought in their brains for more than a second or two at a time, I would guess."

Kizzy giggled and hopped up from her chair, planting herself in her husband's lap. "Oh, Lawson, you idiot. That's one thing I love so much about you!"

"What's that?" Lawson asked as his arms encircled her waist.

"That the most amazin', most obvious things can be goin' on right under your nose, and you aren't any the wiser," Kizzy answered, giggling.

Lawson chuckled. "Well, the only thing I see right under my nose at this moment is the most beautiful woman on the face of the earth."

Kizzy blushed, for she recognized the expression—the smolder of desire—deepening in her husband's eyes. "Is that so?" she asked.

"Yes, ma'am," Lawson mumbled.

As her strong, handsome, skilled lover pulled her into his embrace, ravaging her mouth with a loving and wanton kiss that caused goose pimples to erupt over the entire surface of her body, Kizzy decided she'd keep the knowledge of why Rowdy Gates's appearance had spurred Calliope to thinking of the Tom Thumb wedding to herself for a while. Lawson would catch on eventually, one way or the other. But for that moment, Kizzy just wanted to kiss him—to be kissed by him—exactly the way she knew Calliope dreamt of being kissed by Rowdy Gates.

CHAPTER FOUR

"I promised Evangeline I would stop by and check the post, Mrs. Perry," Calliope explained. "You know how impatient she is in waiting for correspondence from her friend Jennie."

"Oh my, yes!" Mrs. Perry exclaimed with a quick burst of laughter. "Why, you'd think the fate of the entire world depended on Evangeline gettin' her letter from Colorado, wouldn't you?"

Calliope giggled and nodded her agreement with the sweet proprietress of the Meadowlark Lake general store and post office, Sophia Perry. Mrs. Perry was a jolly little lady, with hair the color of salt and cinnamon stirred together and a little round face, perfectly deep-wrinkled from a lifetime of smiling. Calliope liked Mrs. Perry and her husband, Maurice Perry. They were always happy, it seemed, and never uttered an unkind word about anything or anyone. To Mr. and Mrs. Perry, life was simply something amusing.

"And glory be, here it is!" Mrs. Perry declared as she removed a letter from a wooden box she had been using to sort the post.

"What's all the ruckus back here?" Mr. Perry asked as he entered the small nook of the general store that served as the post office. "It sounds like a bunch of geese just flew in," he teased.

"Oh, Maurice, it does not," Mrs. Perry laughed as Mr. Perry kissed her on one cheek.

Mr. Perry was round and plump. He had snow-white hair and a cherry-red nose that always gave Calliope reason to wonder if the man indulged a little too often in drinking spirits or if he were simply

St. Nicholas hiding out in Meadowlark Lake until Christmas Eve arrived.

"Ahhh," Mr. Perry said as he saw Calliope. "It seems another one of them letters from up in Colorado has arrived for your sister, is that it, Miss Ipswich?"

Calliope smiled and nodded. "It would seem so," she answered. "Evangeline and her friend Jennie have recently renewed their friendship. I'm so glad, for they were very close when they were little girls."

"Yes, Evangeline has mentioned that she and Jennie were nearly inseparable before...before..." Mrs. Perry stammered.

Knowing the kindhearted woman was uncomfortable and feeling awkward, Calliope finished, "Before our mother and baby brother died, yes." Calliope sighed. "I was still very little, but I can remember how Evangeline and Jennie would find themselves so amused over the tiniest thing that they'd burst into giggles that seemed to me to last for hours." She smiled as Mrs. Perry handed the letter to her. "I'm glad they're corresponding now."

Snapping her fingers to indicate she'd just remembered something, Mrs. Perry added, "Oh, I nearly forgot. There's one addressed to both you and Evangeline too. It's stamped 'Langtree.' I'm thinkin' it might be from—"

"Amoretta!" Calliope squealed as Mrs. Perry drew another letter from her wooden box, offering it to Calliope. She knew at once that it was from Amoretta, for the script was so beautiful and swirly and perfect, and no one in the world had handwriting as beautiful as Amoretta's.

"Oh, thank you, Mrs. Perry," Calliope said gratefully. "We've got such plans, we Ipswich girls! Just you wait and see what fun plans we have!"

Mrs. Perry laughed and said, "Oh, I'm sure you're up to something, Calliope. You always are! Now you run along and enjoy your post, all righty?"

"Yes, ma'am," Calliope agreed. "And thank you so much, both of you," she said, tossing a wave to Mr. and Mrs. Perry as she hurried out of the general store.

She couldn't wait to read Amoretta's thoughts on the Tom Thumb wedding she and Evangeline were planning. She missed her older sister so much, even for the fact that she knew Amoretta was blissful in her love for Brake.

Calliope was so excited about reading Amoretta's letter, in fact, that instead of waiting until she arrived home, she hurriedly opened the envelope in her haste to read it while she was walking out of the general store.

"*My Darlings*," Calliope read under her breath as she walked, "*I was so very delighted to receive your letters concerning the Tom Thumb wedding! I—*"

Calliope gasped and looked up, astonished into nearly dropping the letters, as she found herself face to face with Tate Chesterfield. She'd bumped right into him.

"Oh! I-I beg your pardon, Mr. Chesterfield," she apologized at once. "I was so engrossed in this letter, I wasn't paying proper attention to where I was walking."

But the tall, dark-haired newcomer simply smiled a handsome and somewhat alluring smile and said, "Oh, never you mind, Miss Calliope. The fault lies squarely on my shoulders."

"Are you all right, Calliope?" Fox Montrose inquired, taking hold of her arm in attempted support—or to show some sort of possession to Tate. Calliope wasn't sure which.

Calliope smiled at him and said, "Oh, I'm just fine, Fox." Looking to Tate, she added, "And thank you, Mr. Chesterfield, for forgiving me my bad manners."

"Oh, I can't imagine you ever havin' bad manners, Miss Calliope," Tate said, taking hold of her other arm. "Are you sure I didn't hurt you? That you didn't twist your ankle or somethin'?"

"No, I'm fine," Calliope said. She was uncomfortable. Fox was glaring at Tate Chesterfield, but Tate wore an expression of pure daring—even premature triumph. For pity's sake! All she wanted to do was read Amoretta's letter.

"But thank you, gentlemen, all the same," she said, gently trying to tug her arm free of Tate's grasp. But he held tight, as did Fox when she tried to free herself from his hold.

All at once the elation Calliope had felt over receiving a letter from Amoretta evaporated. She was suddenly anxious and felt unhappy. She didn't like the attention from Tate or even Fox. And she certainly didn't like the fact that Rowdy Gates had just stepped out of the diner next to the general store and was watching the goings-on as he placed his hat on top of his head.

Mrs. Ackerman walked past, grinning knowingly, and said, "Good afternoon, Calliope." Looking to Fox and Tate, she added, "Boys."

"Mrs. Ackerman," Tate and Fox greeted in unison—though they didn't release Calliope.

Calliope felt her face heat up like a hot coal had been plopped in her head as Rowdy Gates frowned and began walking toward the place where she stood being pulled like taffy.

"Fox. Tate," Rowdy greeted.

"Rowdy," Fox returned—still holding tight to Calliope's arm.

"Boss," Tate greeted—also still holding tight to Calliope's arm.

"You boys best get back before the foreman blows the end of lunch whistle…lest you be counted tardy and get your pay docked," Rowdy Gates said.

"B-but you're the foreman, Rowdy," Fox needlessly reminded. "And you're still out for midday meal."

Rowdy grinned a little. "Yep, but I'm on my way back to the mill now. And when I blow that whistle, if you're not…"

Tate let go first, bowing a bit to Calliope and saying, "You have a good day now, Miss Calliope."

"Thank you, Mr. Chesterfield," Calliope told him as he turned on his boot heel and headed toward the mill.

"Yes, Calliope," Fox said, also releasing her. "You have a good afternoon. But watch where you're goin' next time, all right? Maybe you ought not to walk and read at the same time, hm?"

"Good afternoon, Fox," Calliope said—though she thought the slight snip in her voice probably revealed how irritated she was at being reprimanded by him.

Fox cleared his throat, turned, and headed toward the mill.

Calliope's blush deepened as Rowdy Gates looked to her then, an amused glimmer of understanding in his dark eyes.

"I thought them boys were gonna yank you clean apart," he said. "It looked like two youngsters fightin' over the turkey wishbone at Thanksgivin' dinner."

"Th-they were just concerned for my welfare, I suppose," Calliope stammered. "I rather bumped into Mr. Chesterfield on my way. I was reading a letter and walking home, and…I-I didn't see him there and…"

"Well, you have a good afternoon, Miss Calliope," Rowdy said, saving her from any further awkwardness in trying to explain the situation he'd happened upon.

"Thank you, Mr. Gates," she managed.

Rowdy Gates nodded at her, touched the brim of his hat, and turned toward the mill. Calliope watched him go, fanning herself with Amoretta's letter—for she felt very overheated all of a sudden.

Glancing up into the blue, sunshine-kissed sky, she mumbled, "Hmm. It must be hotter out than it looks."

"There you are, darlin'!"

Calliope turned when she heard Blanche's voice from behind her.

Hurrying to meet Calliope, Blanche took her arm, exclaiming, "I have it, Calliope! I have found the most delicious cake recipe on the face of the earth. It was my grandma's, but Mama and I had misplaced it somehow. But we found it today, and believe me, it will make the most scrumptious weddin' cake ever for the Tom Thumb weddin'!"

Instantly, Calliope was caught up in renewed excitement about the event she and Evangeline—and now many other ladies in town—were planning.

"Wonderful, Blanche!" she exclaimed. "What sort of cake is it?"

Blanche sighed with contentment. "It's a buttercream spice cake, and, Calliope, I promise, you've never had anything at all like it. Not in all your life, even in Boston! It's truly delectable."

"Oh, how divine, Blanche," Calliope giggled. "I'm so excited that you and your mother have agreed to do the cake. I can bake a good enough cake, but I'm all thumbs when it comes to icing and decorating one."

"Well, no worries about that, Miss Ipswich," Blanche assured her. "Mama and I will have it well in hand. And with roses from Mrs. Montrose's rose garden, it's bound to be the most beautiful *and* delicious cake anyone in Meadowlark Lake has ever eaten!" Blanche's gaze fell to the letters Calliope was holding, and she inquired, "What are those? Letters? Is one from Amoretta? Has she agreed to write out the invitations?"

Still smiling, Calliope sighed. "I don't know for certain," she answered. "I haven't had a chance to read it yet. But I'm sure she's agreed to do the invitations."

"Perfect!" Blanche pronounced. "Oh, it's all comin' together so marvelously, don't you think?"

"I do," Calliope agreed. "I really do."

"By the way," Blanche began, quirking one eyebrow, "what was goin' on with Fox and Tate before?" she inquired. "As I was walkin' up, I saw them both tuggin' on you like...like..."

"Like two youngsters fighting over the turkey wishbone at Thanksgiving dinner?" she finished, echoing Rowdy Gates's comparison.

Blanche laughed. "Exactly. You said it exactly!" She paused, her lovely dark brows puckering with curiosity. "But what was it all about?"

Calliope shook her head, however, wanting only to forget the incident. "Nothing. I-I stumbled coming out of the general store, and…and…it was nothing." She linked arms with her friend, smiled, and said, "Let's get back to my house and see what Amoretta has said in her letter. Evangeline will be very excited to see she's got another letter from her friend, as well."

Blanche grinned and nodded. "Yes. Let's." She exhaled a happy sigh. "Oh, Calliope, I'm so glad you thought of this Tom Thumb weddin'. I think we all need something as entertaining and untainted as it promises to be."

"I think so too," Calliope agreed. Glancing back over her shoulder, she could see Rowdy Gates had almost reached the turnoff leading to the mill. "I just hope everyone will enjoy it as much as I hope they will," she sighed.

❦

As expected, Amoretta had proven in her letter that she was more than willing to write out the invitations to the Tom Thumb wedding. Calliope had read the letter aloud to Evangeline, Blanche, Kizzy, and Shay once she and Blanche had arrived at the Ipswich house. After Amoretta's letter had been read, the five of them lingered in the parlor discussing details of what the invitations should say.

Yet an hour or so later, Blanche had decided she should probably get home and help her mother with the laundering, Evangeline was wanting to answer Jennie's letter, and Kizzy went about preparing a dessert for dinner that evening. Thus Calliope and Shay found themselves sitting in the parlor, still excited about the wedding plans but with no one about still willing to discuss them.

"I was plannin' on havin' tea with Molly out on the back porch if you'd like to join us, Calliope," Shay offered.

Calliope smiled, her heart swelling with love and compassion as she saw the pleading hope bright in Shay's eyes.

"I'd love to join you and Molly, Shay Shay," she said. "It is a lovely afternoon, just perfect for cucumber canapés and butter cookies."

Shay giggled. "And don't forget the raspberry tarts, Calliope!"

"I could never forget the raspberry tarts, my darling," Calliope assured her little sister. "Now, you gather the cucumber canapés and set up the tea on your table, and I'll gather the butter cookies and raspberries, all right?"

"Yes!" Shay exclaimed, hopping to her feet. "And we can use the doilies Evangeline made for me today."

"Oh yes, we must use those," Calliope agreed. "Now off with you! Collect what you need, and I'll meet you on the back porch as soon as I've gathered everything."

Shay nodded with emphatic agreement and delight and hurried off in search of the things she needed to gather.

Calliope sighed with a feeling of mingled discontent and contentment. She so enjoyed playing with Shay. Furthermore, she knew that one way or the other, the moments with Shay would lessen, or at least slowly grow into something else. Shay would, after all, eventually stop playing ponies in the meadow, just the way Calliope had. Her pretended tea parties with Molly would give way to real tea parties with friends, or even sewing circles with the ladies of the town. This thought caused discontent in Calliope—a sadness that things would change. After all, things had changed when Amoretta married Brake and moved to Langtree. Things had changed when Calliope's father had married Kizzy and brought Shay into their lives along with her. But those were good changes, whereas the idea of Shay grown up and no longer a little girl distressed Calliope.

Simultaneously, however, Rowdy Gates had championed her in town that day. Calliope knew that Rowdy probably had no intention of docking Fox's or Tate's pay if they were a bit tardy getting back to the mill. He'd just somehow sensed Calliope's distress, or the impropriety of Fox and Tate taking hold of her the way they each had, and he'd diminished the situation instantly and without incident—and Calliope was much more flattered by the fact Rowdy had intervened on her behalf than with Tate and Fox pulling at her like taffy. The knowledge offered her quite a measure of contentment.

Thus, Calliope headed out to the grassy expanse behind the Ipswich home in search of butter cookies and raspberries with conflicting emotions jostling around in her mind and heart. Yet she smiled when she saw that, indeed, the space behind the house was simply speckled with buttercups and red poppies.

"Butter cookies and raspberries," Calliope giggled to herself as she began to gather the colorful blooms to use as treats at Shay's pretended tea party. She smiled as she held a buttercup to her nose, dusting off the pollen afterward. Her own mother had taught her to use different flowers to represent different sorts of foodstuffs when playing tea party—when she was just a bit younger than Shay was now. It was one of the most vivid memories Calliope owned of her mother, and it always made her a little melancholy to think on it.

When Calliope arrived at the back porch, she was delighted when she saw that Shay had already set up her tea set on the little round table their father had made for Shay at Christmas. Using round, short pieces of wood from the woodpile that hadn't been split yet as seats, Shay had set three places at the little table. Molly the marmalade was already positioned on her wood seat. As usual, Molly looked dreary-eyed but patient.

"Here's a plate for the butter cookies," Shay said, pointing to a small plate in the center of the table. "And a little bowl for the raspberries," she added, placing a small bowl next to the plate.

"I see you've already made the cucumber canapés," Calliope noted as she studied the green lilac tree leaves Shay had collected and set on another small plate on the table.

"Yes," Shay confirmed. "They took almost all afternoon to put together!"

"Oh dear," Calliope sighed. "I hope it wasn't too much trouble to have me to tea today."

"Not at all, my dear," Shay said, pretending to be grown up.

Quickly, Calliope placed the buttercups on the small plate meant for butter cookies and then carefully removed the petals from several poppies and put them in the raspberry bowl.

"Oh, thank you for contributing to our eats today, Miss Ipswich," Shay said as she sat down on her wooden seat and began to pour water from her tiny teapot into the tiny teacup set at the seat meant for Calliope.

"Oh, thank *you* for allowing me to, Miss Ipswich," Calliope graciously returned, taking her own wood seat.

"Miss Molly?" Shay inquired. "Shall I pour for you now?"

Molly slowly blinked as she watched Shay pour water into the cup before her.

"There," Shay said, pouring water from her teapot into her own cup. "Now we're all ready." She picked up her tiny teacup, crooking her pinky just so, and then took a sip of water. "And isn't it just the loveliest day, ladies?"

"Oh, absolutely the loveliest!" Calliope agreed. And it was another lovely spring day in Meadowlark Lake. The warm sun shone overhead, and the gentle breeze whispered through the new grass behind the house.

"You know, Miss Ipswich," Shay began, "I was thinking."

"You were?" Calliope exclaimed, feigning astonishment.

"Why yes. I often do," Shay answered.

"And what were you thinking about, Miss Ipswich?" Calliope inquired.

"I was thinkin' that perhaps you should wave to Mr. Gates every evenin' the way I do," Shay responded, "as an offerin' of thanks for all his hard work in tendin' to the lamps and all."

Calliope grinned. "Well, I think Mr. Gates enjoys *your* waving to him so much that, if I joined you, it might not seem so special as it does now."

Shay's smile faded. She inhaled a deep breath, appearing as if she were struggling to remain calm.

"Miss Ipswich," Shay began again, "you do realize that I am a gypsy girl, my mother before me bein' a gypsy herself, don't you?"

Calliope smiled. Yet her brows puckered with puzzlement.

"Why yes, Miss Ipswich. I do know that you are a gypsy girl," she acknowledged.

"Then you also know that I can see things others can't...don't you, Miss Ipswich?" Shay inquired.

"Such as?" Calliope prodded.

"Such as the fact that you don't have eyes for Fox Montrose at all, Miss Ipswich," Shay proceeded. "But you do look at Rowdy Gates every time you get the chance…and when you do, your eyes start to sparkle."

Calliope forced an amused laugh. "Oh, Miss Ipswich!" she exclaimed. "Surely you can't mean to imply——"

She was interrupted, however, as Shay reached out and took her hand. Gazing directly into Calliope's eyes, Shay dropped her adult manner of speech and whispered, "Don't worry, Calliope. I promise that I won't tell a soul!"

"A-about what, Shay?" Calliope asked, nearly gasping in astonishment. Could it be that Calliope's secret bliss was not so secret as she thought?

Shay winked at Calliope then, released her hand, and reached for a butter cookie. As she pretended to eat the buttercup, she slipped back into her adult manner and answered, "I think you should wait at the parlor window with me this evenin', Miss Ipswich. And when the lamplighter comes to our street lamp, I think you should toss him a wave."

Calliope was still bewildered. Somehow Shay knew! How *could* she know? Calliope had kept her attraction to Rowdy Gates—her strong, strong, strong feelings toward him—entirely to herself. Always! She'd never mentioned it to anyone—not Evangeline, not Amoretta, certainly not her father or Kizzy! Not Blanche or any of her other friends. Therefore, how was it that a six-year-old girl had discerned it?

A sense of something akin to panic began to wash over Calliope, and she couldn't help but ask Shay, "Shay, how do you know that…how do you suspect that…"

"You mean how to I know that you're sweeter than molasses candy on Rowdy Gates, Miss Ipswich?" Shay asked in return.

Desperate for her secret to be kept, Calliope reached out, taking Shay's hands in her own. "Shay, you can't tell a soul! Not one soul! Do you understand?"

Shay smiled a sweet, loving smile. "Dearest sister," she began, "I'm a gypsy. And gypsies are the best secret-keepers in the whole wide world. I already told you I wouldn't tell."

Calliope breathed a little easier, but only a little. "I still don't understand why you think—"

"I don't *think* it, Miss Ipswich," Shay interrupted. "I *know* it. And I've known it for a long time now. Your eyes light up like stars whenever he's around, Miss Ipswich." Shay paused, picked up the bowl of poppy petals, and offered it to Calliope. "Now, let's just get back to our tea, all right? Raspberry, Miss Ipswich?"

Without another word, Calliope picked a poppy petal out of the raspberry bowl and pretended to eat it. She was stunned—entirely stunned. All the while she thought she'd been keeping her secret bliss to herself, thinking no one could possibly know she was in love with Rowdy Gates—a thing even she herself had trouble understanding. And yet her little sister—a child—knew her feelings.

"Thank you," Calliope managed to whisper.

Shay smiled and set the raspberry bowl back on the table. "You're welcome, Miss Ipswich. Now, do tell. This Tom Thumb weddin' you're plannin', you say the bride and groom have to kiss at the end of the ceremony?"

"Uh...yes," Calliope answered. And then she smiled, for she understood exactly how Shay had figured out everything concerning Calliope's feelings toward Rowdy. For at the very mention of the Tom Thumb wedding, as she asked about the bride and groom kissing, Shay's own eyes lit up like stars! It was very well that Calliope knew Shay was sweet on Warren Ackerman. It's why she and Evangeline had decided on trying to coax Warren into being the groom in the first place. And there it was, in all its obviousness. Shay's pinked-up cheeks and sparkling eyes told the entire story— revealed just how sweet Shay was on Warren. A body didn't have to be a gypsy to see it either.

"Yes," Calliope continued, taking another poppy leaf and pretending to eat it. "They do need to kiss at the end of the ceremony; otherwise it will ruin the entire event."

"Hmm," Shay hummed, feigning innocence. "I see your point."

Calliope relaxed a bit more. Shay would keep her secret; she knew she would. No one else would ever know how madly Calliope loved Rowdy Gates. And as she thought more on it, she realized that, if it were meant to be that someone else on earth knew of her secret bliss, it was best that it was little Shay, for she would never think to question why Calliope felt the way she did about a man she'd hardly ever spoken to. To Shay, there needn't be an explanation.

And so Calliope sipped her water from her tiny teacup and pretended to eat leaves that represented cucumber canapés and buttercups that proxied butter cookies. And when Shay had had her fill of playing tea party—when she'd looped her leash about poor Molly's neck and headed off for an afternoon stroll—Calliope did what she often did when everyone else was busy and careless of where she was or what she was doing. Once Molly and Shay were well on their way down the main street of Meadowlark Lake—once she was certain everyone else in the house was occupied with their own doings—Calliope hurried to the much less traveled trail leading through the trees and brush to the gristmill.

CHAPTER FIVE

Calliope sighed with awed admiration as she gazed into the gristmill through the opening provided by a loose board on its outer wall. There he was—Rowdy Gates—in all his handsome, alluring glory! She never got tired of looking at him, of staring at him. Her thoughts quickly flittered back to the very first moment she'd ever laid eyes on the attractive man.

It seemed so long ago, though it had only been the previous autumn—the day Winnie Montrose had led Calliope, her sister Amoretta, and several other girls from town out to the mill. Calliope and Amoretta had assumed that Winnie and the others had intended to share the scenic beauty of the mill's setting with them, for the old mill in its picturesque surroundings was indeed a sight to behold—a veritable haven of isolated, charming respite.

Yet Calliope and Amoretta both soon learned that it wasn't just the gentle and rhythmic whoosh-whoosh of the paddle wheel in the water, or the lovely brown cattails alive with shiny-winged dragonflies that surrounded the millpond, that made the mill so beautiful. Rather it was what was inside!

Four men had been working inside the mill that day, and while Amoretta and the other girls had been delighted, near to swooning, at the sight of the brawny and handsome Brake McClendon, Calliope's attention had instantly settled on the mysterious, intriguing, and guardedly handsome Rowdy Gates.

When Calliope had exclaimed, "He's magnificent!" that day, Amoretta, Winnie, Blanche, and the other young ladies had naturally assumed it was Brake Calliope was referring to. But it hadn't been Brake who had instantaneously captured Calliope's interest. It had been Rowdy.

Of course, Calliope quickly realized that every other young lady was fawning over Brake McClendon, and she'd happily allowed them to do so—and to think she found Brake to be the most attractive man working at the mill too. She was glad all the other girls were distracted by Brake, for it left Rowdy for her alone to admire.

And admire him she had! From that day forward, Calliope Ipswich had been smitten with none other than Rowdy Gates. Oh, certainly she was kind to the other young men in Meadowlark Lake, agreeing to their requests to dance with her at various town events and so on. But all the while, it was Rowdy Gates who made her heart leap in her bosom whenever he appeared—Rowdy Gates who lingered in her daydreams, as well as the dreams she owned at night.

Calliope watched Rowdy ever so closely, but in secret—very guardedly—for she didn't want him, or anyone else in Meadowlark Lake, to know that she was so blissfully taken with him. And there were many reasons Calliope had chosen not to openly flirt with Rowdy—had chosen not to be obvious in her affections for him (and in desperately wanting his in return). First of all, it was obvious that Rowdy was a very private man. He didn't talk very much, even at social gatherings (which he only sometimes attended). He was polite and gentlemanly, of course, but reserved and rather solitary. Calliope had often wondered if Rowdy's reclusive manner was due to whatever accident had caused the injury to his leg. Still, his limp that had been so pronounced when first the Ipswich family had moved to Meadowlark Lake was nearly indiscernible now, and still Rowdy seemed to prefer detachment to socializing.

Of course, Rowdy's tendency to withdrawal and manner of privacy actually appealed to Calliope. She'd decided long ago that, when she fell in love with the man she was meant to fall in love with, she would prefer to have him all to herself.

Rowdy wiped the sweat from his brow with the back of his hand. "It ain't even summer yet, and it's already hotter than hell in here," he said to Dex.

"Well, I imagine you are hot, Rowdy," Dex responded. "You're wearin' long sleeves when the rest of us stripped our shirts off long ago."

Rowdy frowned. "Well, the rest of you don't seem to be the favorite target of them dang pigeons to try and crap on," Rowdy pointed out.

Dex chuckled, and so did Fox.

"What do you mean?" Tate asked. He paused in his work to look at Rowdy with curiosity.

Fox smiled and explained, "There's a couple of pigeons up in the rafters that we ain't been able to chase out or shoot, and both of them seem hell-bent on crappin' on Rowdy every other day or so." He laughed. "I swear, it's like they wait up there 'til he ain't lookin' and then just let go."

Tate smiled. "You're kiddin' me."

"Nope," Dex affirmed, shaking his head. "They get him a couple of times a week."

"It's because he's so purty under that mess of a beard," Fox teased.

Rowdy sighed yet smiled with amusement. "It does seem that they've been bullyin' me around and leavin' everyone else alone, though I can't figure why. I sure ain't the shiniest new penny in here."

"How old are you, boss?" Tate asked.

Fox and Dex exchanged glances. "Yeah. How old are you, Rowdy? You've never said."

Rowdy shrugged broad shoulders and easily clarified, "I never said 'cause it never came up in conversation."

Rowdy knew he hadn't answered their question, and he waited to see who would press the issue further.

He wasn't at all surprised when it was Fox that prodded, "Oh, come on, Rowdy. You can't be more'n a few years older than us."

"Well, you're right. I ain't," Rowdy said.

Tate Chesterfield frowned. "You ain't what, Rowdy?"

"He ain't more than a few years older than us," Dex explained. "So somewhere in the range of twenty-five, maybe twenty-six?"

"Yep," was the only answer Rowdy would give. He grinned, knowing it drove the other men at the mill plum loco when he would avoid giving them direct and specific answers about himself when they asked questions. It was a bit impish of him to ring them around the way he did, but he couldn't help it. It offered him such a measure of amusement that he couldn't seem to keep himself from the mischief of it.

Tate Chesterfield shook his head. "You're a hard man to figure, boss," he said.

"I try to be," Rowdy admitted, feeling he needed to give the newcomer a little stretch of slack in the reins. "And you can call me Rowdy, Tate. As long as you remember who's boss, you don't need to be callin' me boss, all right?"

Tate nodded. A moment later, however, the young man gasped and then burst into laughter as a long white and black trail of bird mess fell directly onto Rowdy's left shoulder.

"Dammit to hell!" Rowdy exclaimed in a growl as he looked at the large glob of bird manure that had begun to dribble from its landing place on his shoulder, down over his chest.

Dex, Fox, and Tate, however, were roaring with laughter.

"Rowdy, them birds just do not like you!" Fox announced as he continued to whoop and howl with amusement.

Rowdy shook his head, reining in his temper. Angrily he pulled his suspenders from his shoulders, unbuttoning the front of his shirt before stripping it off. Seeing the moisture left on his shoulder from the watery bird manure having already soaked through his shirt, he turned his head and sniffed at his shoulder, swearing under his breath.

"It already soaked through," he grumbled. "I gotta go rinse this off in the pond. You boys get that twenty-two that's behind the desk over yonder and shoot them dang pigeons!"

"Sure thing, Rowdy," Dex agreed, still laughing.

Wadding up his shirt in one hand—for he figured he might as well rinse the bird mess out of his shirt before it dried stiff while he was at the pond—Rowdy stormed off toward the door. Yet he had a good enough sense of humor that, by the time he'd stepped outside, he was chuckling as well. After all, it was fairly amusing that the pigeons only ever seemed to hit him with their stinky bird-mess.

Calliope gasped as she saw Rowdy Gates stride across the inside of the mill toward the door, intent on heading to down to the millpond. What if he found her spying on him through the loosened board? What would she say if he simply saw her alone out by the mill?

Quickly she hopped up from the place she'd been kneeling in the grass. Glancing around, she knew that she couldn't go the way she'd come, for if she did, Rowdy would certainly see her as he made his way out the door of the mill. She realized there was nothing to do but make her way around to the slope that led down to the pond, even though it was the same route Rowdy would take. At least that way, when he saw her, she could say that she's simply been out on a leisurely stroll down to the pond herself—just to enjoy the lovely spring day.

Yet as she began to walk along the edge of the high bank surrounding the millpond on her way to the slope, she heard Rowdy call from behind her, "Good afternoon, Miss Calliope. What finds you out this way?"

Whirling around to face him, Calliope was astonished to see that Rowdy was almost directly behind her already. He must've been in a hurry to wash off his shoulder indeed, for she'd only just left the side of the mill where the loose board hung.

"Oh!" she exclaimed. "You startled me, Mr. Gates. I just thought...well, that I'd take a stroll out away from town this afternoon, and..."

71

"Be careful, Miss Calliope," Rowdy warned, frowning at her. "The spring rains have softened the edge of the—"

But Rowdy's warning came too late—for in that very moment, Calliope felt her heels begin to slip. Her back was turned toward the edge of the high bank above the millpond—the high bank that was in the very least thirty feet above the water.

As she screamed, flailing her arms in an ineffectual effort to regain her balance, she felt the moist soil of the edge of the bank beginning to slip away beneath her.

Without pause Rowdy tossed his wadded-up shirt aside and rushed forward. He knew that if Calliope Ipswich slipped down the side of the high bank, she would be torn to shreds by the sharp rocks jutting out of the bank on her way down. Therefore, his reflexes and instincts knew that, though it was a high distance to fall, it would be far better for her to hit the water and avoid the side of the bank altogether.

He heard the young woman scream as he grabbed her under her arms, pulled her against him, and pushed against the wet, slippery ground with every ounce of strength in his legs. With any luck, he'd pushed hard enough to throw them both clear of the jagged rocks protruding from the high bank. Twisting in the air as his arms locked around Calliope, Rowdy next felt the air be forced from his lungs as his back hit the water's surface, plunging he and Calliope into the millpond.

He felt something sharp strike the back of his head and right side of his face an instant before he pushed against the bottom of the millpond to send him and Calliope rising toward the water's surface.

As their heads simultaneously broke the millpond's surface, he heard Calliope gasp for breath. His own breath was more difficult to inhale. The punch of hitting the water so hard on his back had rendered his lungs empty and too stunned to take an easy breath. But in another moment, he inhaled and began swimming them toward the opposing bank of the millpond where the ground was level with the water.

As Rowdy Gates pulled her up onto the bank of the millpond, Calliope found she was dizzy. Everything had happened so fast! It was only moments ago—literally only moments ago—that she'd felt the soft soil of the high bank begin to give way beneath her feet. Instinctively, she'd gasped and held her breath when she realized that she and Rowdy were falling through the air on their way into the millpond, and she was thankful for the instinct. Otherwise she might have inhaled water after plunging into the pond, rather than already having her lungs filled with air.

"Are you all right?" she heard Rowdy cough.

She nodded as she wiped water from her eyes.

"Are you sure? You're not hurt at all?" he repeated. She heard him cough again and then spit.

"I'm all right," she panted as she struggled to push her wet hair out of her face.

All at once, however, she felt something else on her face—something warm. When she felt it next on her lip, she licked her lip and recognized the salty taste of blood. Calliope didn't feel any pain, other than a grueling soreness that was beginning to overtake her arms and legs. Therefore, she angrily pushed her wet hair from her eyes and looked up to where Rowdy Gates was hovering over her.

"You're bleeding!" she cried out then. And it was true! Blood was everywhere over Rowdy's face. And though she could see that some of it originated from a large wound on his right cheek, she knew there was far too much blood pouring over his forehead and dripping off the tip of his nose to be from that wound.

"I just bumped my head a little," he answered, however, wiping blood from his forehead with the back of his hand—as if it were no more than a little perspiration.

"Bumped your head?" Calliope squealed with horror. "You're bleeding to death! We have to get you to the doctor in town, Mr. Gates!"

Hurriedly, Calliope sat up, pulled up the hem of her sopping wet skirt, and tore a length of ruffled cotton from her petticoat.

As tears began to stream over her cheeks, she whimpered, "I almost killed you! Maybe I did! You still might bleed to death! I can't believe I—"

"I'm fine, Miss Calliope," Rowdy interrupted, however. "It's just a scratch. Head wounds bleed like hell. It ain't as bad as it looks. I promise."

"Hold this against it," Calliope wept, handing him the length of sopping petticoat ruffle. "It won't absorb the blood, but push hard on the wound, and it might slow down the bleeding until we can get you into town."

"What in tarnation?" Fox hollered as he and the other men from the mill hurried across the narrow bridge that spanned the millpond just behind the mill. "Calliope? Is that you?" he shouted.

"Mr. Gates has been terribly hurt, Fox!" Calliope called. "Someone run into town and bring Doctor Gregory! Hurry!"

"I'm fine," Rowdy hollered up, however. "But come down and help me get Miss Ipswich back to town."

It didn't take long for Fox, Dex, and Tate to reach the place where Calliope and Rowdy sat on the bank of the pond. Blood was still streaming from Rowdy's face and head when they arrived.

"What the hell happened?" Fox asked angrily as he helped Calliope to her feet.

"I-I was walking along the higher bank...and the ground started to give way," she stammered. "Mr. Gates saved my life! But now he's bleeding to death, and we have to get him to town."

"I ain't bleedin' to death," Rowdy grumbled.

Dex and Tate exchanged glances a moment, however, and then Dex said, "Well, from the looks of it, I beg to differ on that, Rowdy."

"Me too," Tate agreed. "We best get you into town to the doctor."

"Are *you* all right, Calliope?" Fox pressed Calliope, even so.

"I'm fine!" she nearly shouted. "Nothing hurts but my pride. Just get Mr. Gates to town, Fox...please!"

"I can walk it," Rowdy said, struggling to his feet. But as more blood gushed from the wound at the back of his head, he stumbled a bit.

Dex and Tate both reached out to help steady Rowdy.

"You're losin' blood mighty fast, Rowdy," Dex needlessly stated.

"You best let us get you back to the mill and mounted on your horse," Tate suggested.

"I'll run up ahead and bring Rowdy's horse down to meet us," Fox said. He dashed up the incline toward the mill.

Tate and Dex each draped one of Rowdy's large, muscular arms across their shoulders. "Let's get you back up to the hill here, Rowdy," Dex said.

The problem was that, since none of the men assisting Rowdy was wearing his shirt, blood from the wound at Rowdy's head was still streaming over his face and shoulders, causing his body to be very slick and difficult to move.

Lifting her skirt hem once more, Calliope tore a very long strip of fabric from it. "Just a minute," she called to Dex and Tate. They stopped, and Calliope used the wet strip of fabric to bind Rowdy's head wound. She wrapped the cotton around his head and forehead, and though the wound still seeped blood, she secured it tightly, with enough pressure to slow the bleeding.

"You sure you're all right, Miss Calliope?" Rowdy asked as Dex and Tate helped him stumble toward the mill.

"I'm fine," Calliope assured him as renewed tears streamed over her cheeks.

As she watched Fox coming down the hill with Rowdy's horse—watched Tate, Dex, and Fox struggle to get him mounted—Calliope began to sob, whispering to herself in utter despair, "I may have just killed the only man I'll ever truly love!"

CHAPTER SIX

"Head wounds bleed much worse than others," Doctor Gregory told Calliope as she sat in his office watching him stitch Rowdy's lacerations. "But he'll be fine, Miss Ipswich. I assure you of that." Doctor Gregory paused to offer a reassuring smile to Calliope. "I wouldn't want to see you come down with pneumonia or some such thing. You oughta run on home and get dried off yourself. "

"I will," she responded, "as soon as I see the bleeding is stopped." She shook her head and wiped a tear from one corner of her eye. "This is all my fault you see, Doctor Gregory. I—"

"It ain't her fault, Doc," Rowdy mumbled. "It ain't nobody's fault, Miss Calliope. Things just happen sometimes, that's all. And I'm fine. I'm a tough old dog." He glanced over to her, grinning with encouragement. "You best run on home, before your family starts to worry."

"I will…when I'm certain you'll be well," she countered.

"Well, I've got this head wound stitched up nice and tight, Rowdy," Doctor Gregory sighed. He was a young man for a doctor—tall and lean, with sandy-colored hair and green eyes. "We'll bandage up your head and then shave off that beard to get to the one on your face there."

Rowdy exhaled a heavy sigh. "All right, Doc. But—"

"Calliope?" Judge Ipswich exclaimed, bursting into the room and giving everyone in it a start. He was frowning, and Calliope recognized it as his worried frown. "What's happened? Fox

Montrose came plowing into the courthouse like the whole town was on fire. He said you'd been hurt! Are you all right?"

Calliope smiled as her father dropped to his knees before her, taking her face between his strong, warm hands and brushing her wet hair back as he studied her face.

"I'm fine, Daddy," she assured. "Mr. Gates saved my life out by the mill. I…I was walking, and I slipped on some moist soil and—"

"You're covered in blood, sweetheart! How can you be fine?" Lawson interrupted, however.

"It's not my blood, Daddy," Calliope began to explain. "I told you, Mr. Gates saved me. And in the course of doing so, he was terribly, horribly wounded, suffering a gash to his head, and it bled on me when—"

Her words were lost as her father gathered her into his arms and against his trembling body. Kissing the top of her head, she heard him say, "Thank you, Rowdy. I don't know yet what happened, but I'm sure I owe you a debt I can never repay."

"No, sir, Judge," Rowdy said, however. "It's probably my fault for startlin' her. I came up behind her, and she started to slip."

"But he grabbed me, and we sailed off the edge of the high bank by the mill…landing in the water," Calliope interrupted. "Otherwise I would've been pulverized on the rocks of the bank when I fell, Daddy." She paused a moment, wiping another tear from her cheek. "He saved my life, Daddy—he did—and now he's all bloodied up and hurt. And he lost so much blood on the way back to town!"

Calliope collapsed against her father then, sobbing as overwhelming guilt engulfed her.

"I'm fine, Judge Ipswich," she heard Rowdy say. "Ask the doc here. I'm just a bit banged up—no more than usual, really."

"I can see by your condition, Rowdy, that you are more banged up than usual," Judge Ipswich humbly argued, however. "And I thank you for putting my daughter's well-being above your own."

"Judge, I swear—" Rowdy began.

But Lawson interrupted, "Please, Rowdy. I know you're not comfortable accepting any sort of praise or thanks. Therefore, I'll say thank you again, and we'll leave it at that…as long as you don't try to put off my gratitude, all right?"

"Yes, sir," Rowdy sighed.

"Thank you, Rowdy," Calliope's father said then. "Thank you for returning Calliope safely back to me."

"Yes, sir," Rowdy mumbled.

"Good man," Lawson said. He released Calliope, taking her face between his hands and wiping her tears with his thumbs. "Now, let's get you home, cleaned up, and into bed."

"I'm fine, Daddy," Calliope assured him.

"And so is Rowdy, Miss Ipswich," Doctor Gregory assured her. "You get on home to your family now. I'll make sure Mr. Gates is all patched up good as new before I send him on his way."

"Forgive me, Mr. Gates," Calliope began—unable to look at her rescuer at first for the guilt and humiliation she was feeling entirely thwarted in her usual confidence. "I'm so sorry to have caused you so much trouble…and discomfort."

"Nothin' to be sorry for, Miss Calliope," Rowdy reiterated. "I'm just glad you weren't hurt."

It was then that Calliope finally looked to him again—and when she did, an audible gasp escaped her. While she'd been embraced in the consolation of her father—had her head buried against her father's chest—Doctor Gregory had roughly shaven Rowdy Gate's face. The result was a revelation of just how intensely handsome Rowdy Gates was. He was more handsome without his beard and mustache than even Calliope had imagined—shockingly so!

She felt her mouth hanging agape in awed wonderment but could not seem to command it to close. Without his hat and heavy beard, the purely perfect, sculpted contours of his face were blessedly exposed. Square-jawed and cleft-chinned, Rowdy had high cheekbones that gave him the look of something akin to European aristocracy. He looked like some mythical, warrior prince! Further mesmerizing, his green eyes flashed with light, undimmed by the brim of his hat as they usually were.

Naturally, there was no ignoring the large wound at his right cheek that Doctor Gregory now worked to stitch, but even it did not detract one smidgen from the fact that the rather unmasked face of Rowdy Gates was stunning—literally breathtaking!

"Come on, sweet pea," Lawson said then, rising to his feet. Taking Calliope's hands in his own, he pulled her from her seat in the chair in Doctor Gregory's office and to her feet. "Let's get you home."

At last Calliope was able to close her gaping mouth, but she blushed, knowing she'd been staring at Rowdy as if gold were spilling from his ears.

Somehow she managed to stammer, "Th-thank you, Mr. Gates," to Rowdy.

He grinned at her and nodded, saying, "My pleasure, Miss Calliope."

Looking to Doctor Gregory—who stood, offering a blood-smeared hand to her father—Calliope said, "And thank you, Doctor Gregory."

"Of course, Miss Ipswich," the doctor said as Lawson accepted his handshake.

"Yes, Nelson," Lawson said, careless of the blood on the doctor's hand. "Thank you."

"I'm just glad it was Rowdy that sustained the lacerations," Doctor Gregory said. "I'd hate to have had to stitch up Miss Ipswich here." He smiled at Calliope, adding, "You're such a lovely young woman, Miss Calliope."

"Thank you," Calliope mumbled. She looked to Rowdy again, and again he grinned at her, nodding his reassurance that he was fine.

"And, Rowdy," Lawson continued, "I'll take care of lighting the lamps tonight...and putting them out in the morning."

"Oh, no, Judge!" Rowdy began to argue. "It's no problem. I'll just—"

"I'll take care of it, Rowdy," Lawson interrupted, however. "Please, allow me that one small task, as part of my thanks for your rescue of my daughter. All right?"

Rowdy frowned, and Calliope knew he was not a man to allow anyone to help him—let alone do his job for him—no matter what the circumstance.

"I think it would be wise to let it go for one night, Rowdy," Doctor Gregory confirmed. "You've lost more blood than you think because of that head wound. You really should head home to bed, at least for tonight."

Calliope could see the man's struggle. It was obvious he had no intention of allowing anyone to help him.

Therefore, quickly she said, "Please, Mr. Gates, I won't sleep a wink tonight for worrying if you don't do as the doctor suggests. Please, just go home and rest tonight, and let Daddy take care of the lamps. Please?"

Shaking his head, Rowdy rather grumbled, "Well, all right, Judge. But just light them tonight. I can put them out in the mornin' well enough."

Calliope knew her father was a wise man. She'd always known it.

But when Judge Ipswich agreed, "All right, Rowdy," his wisdom was even more evident. He knew Rowdy Gates's pride could only take so much—and so he'd agreed with Rowdy.

"Now let's get you home," Lawson said then. Putting a strong arm around her shoulder, Calliope's father pulled her close against him.

As much as she hated to leave Rowdy—as guilt-ridden as she felt over what had happened to him—she knew that Doctor Gregory was capable. After all, hadn't she already done enough? Hadn't she ruined his day, caused him pain and injury? What more could she do but leave him to his peace? Most likely he was relieved as she and her father stepped out of Doctor Gregory's physician's office.

"Did you see how much blood there was, Daddy?" Calliope asked as she walked toward home with her father still holding her close against him.

"I did," Lawson admitted. "But head wounds, they bleed quite fiercely, and Rowdy seemed otherwise well."

"It's my fault," Calliope whispered.

"It's no one's fault, sweetheart," Lawson assured her in a low, soothing voice. "Now let's just get you home, cleaned up, and comfortable. Kizzy's got stew simmering on the stove, and it should be just the thing to settle you down."

But Calliope doubted that anything would ever settle her down again. Rowdy Gates was so terribly wounded! How would she ever handle the guilt of knowing that, because of her, he'd been hurt? And not just because he'd saved her by jumping into the millpond with her. The only reason she was even there—and stepped on the soft soil on the high bank—was because she'd been spying on him. It really was all her fault—all of it!

❦

"Now you take it easy gettin' home, Rowdy," Doc Gregory said as Rowdy mounted his horse, Tucker. "Get home and eat somethin', and then get right to bed. You'll most likely feel like hell in the mornin' too. So don't overexert yourself tomorrow either."

"Thanks, Doc," Rowdy said. He already felt like hell, but there was no reason to let on. His head and face, and pretty much every other part of him, throbbed and ached something awful. But he'd been through worse—much worse. Therefore, he determined not to let a couple of little scrapes and bruises and a dip in the millpond drag him down too far. He was tired, however. Home, supper, and bed were sounding mighty inviting.

Reining Tucker toward home, Rowdy's attention fell to a chestnut and white appaloosa tied to a hitching post in front of the diner across the street. For just a moment, Rowdy's heart leapt inside his chest with an awful anxiety—for the appaloosa looked exactly like one he'd known from years past. Still, what were the odds that appaloosa from the past was even still alive—and still ridden by the man who'd owned it back then? Slim to none, Rowdy figured.

Shaking his head, he mumbled, "Get on home, Tucker. My head's poundin' like there's a drum pent up inside it." Tucker whinnied and started for home.

Glancing back once more at the appaloosa tied up in front of the diner, Rowdy shook his aching head and sighed. The day had been long, fatiguing, not to mention injurious, and Rowdy figured the culmination of a day the like he'd had was causing him to imagine things in the end.

Still, as he rode home, keeping Tucker's pace slow and steady to combat the dizziness that began in his head every time he tried to hurry things up, Rowdy figured it made sense that any chestnut and white appaloosa would put him in mind of Arness. And even for the remarkable resemblance between the appaloosa tied up in front of the diner and Arness's horse, Pronto, he figured old Pronto would be near to five years old by now. And even if Pronto hadn't broken a leg or died of some other ailment or injury, Rowdy knew the horse wouldn't look as fresh and fine as the one in front of the diner did. Arness never took good enough care of his horses, and Pronto had been no different.

Yet as Rowdy dismounted Tucker, unsaddled him, brushed him, and gave him a bucket of oats in his stall, the sight of that chestnut and white appaloosa in town nagged at his mind. The fact was it had brought back too many memories—bad ones. Rowdy figured that was what was eating at him. He was tired, banged up, and hungry. No wonder the appaloosa in town had turned his head a moment.

At last, however, Rowdy sat down next to Dodger's pile of rocks and exhaled a heavy sigh.

"I had me quite a day today, boy," he spoke aloud to his friend's remains. Rowdy lay down on the grass next to Dodger's grave and gazed up at the dusk-dusted sky. "First off, I had to keep from smashin' both Fox Montrose and that Tate Chesterfield in the face when I come upon them in town, tugging Calliope back and forth like they was fightin' over a piece of meat. But I got through that without any incident." He sighed, tucked his hands under his head, and continued, "Then them damn pigeons crapped all over me again, and I went outside to wash off and came upon the pretty Ipswich girl out for a walk along the high bank. Now that's a tale to tell you! But I'm tired, so I'll give you the short of it—which is, holdin' that piece of heaven in my arms was well worth a couple of lumps on the head, I'll tell you that!"

Rowdy closed his eyes and just breathed for a moment. Even for the cool aroma of the evening air, he could still smell the sweet fragrance of Calliope Ipswich. Somehow her fragrance had imprinted itself forever in his brain. He'd only had a whiff of it—just a whiff—the instant he'd wrapped his arms around her and jumped them off the high bank. But he'd never forget it. Calliope Ipswich smelled like warm bread and butter, lavender, and mint, all rolled together in one beautiful perfume.

"I ain't gonna lie to you, Dodger," Rowdy whispered. "I'd take three more cuts in the head just to have her in my arms again…even for a second." He chuckled. "Of course, I think three more cuts on the head mighta done me in. I've been dizzy all the rest of the afternoon from bleedin' out. Even thought I saw Arness's horse in town a while ago."

Rowdy exhaled another heavy sigh of fatigue. He reached over with one hand and laid it on top of the large rock in the middle of Dodger's grave. "I wouldn't have made it that day, Dodger. If it hadn't been for you, I woulda died out there for sure." He paused awhile. Then an instant before Rowdy Gates began to drift off to sleep under the old willow tree, stretched out next to the best friend he'd ever had in all the world, he mumbled, "I sure do miss you."

As sleep overtook him, he imagined he could hear Dodger's happy bark calling to him from off somewhere in the distance. "I sure do," he breathed.

"Are you sure you're feelin' all right, honey?" Kizzy asked as she handed Calliope a glass of warmed milk.

"Yes," she assured her worried stepmother and friend. "I'm just worn out. It's not every day I fly thirty feet off the millpond's high bank to go for a dive in the water," she said, smiling at Shay.

Shay had hardly left Calliope's side since the moment she and her father had arrived home with the harrowing tale of what had happened out at the millpond.

"Well, I've finished the pattern for the flower girls' dresses," Evangeline announced as she spread pieces of muslin out on the parlor floor.

"Maybe we should make sure we can convince Mr. Longfellow to let Mamie and Effie actually *be* the flower girls before we go making up their dresses, don't you think?" Calliope teased.

But Evangeline was undaunted. "Oh, he'll agree to it," she said, waving her hand as if dismissing a triviality. "But I think their dresses should be lavender...and the bridesmaids' and maid of honor's yellow. What do you think? Or should we just go yellow all the way around? Hmmm?"

Calliope's brow furrowed as she considered Evangeline's question. "I don't know, Evie. If we do all the dresses in yellow, then the lilacs and greenery will contrast so beautifully. But we could do lavender flower girl dresses and have yellow roses as their flowers. That would contrast nicely as well."

Evangeline frowned too. Then shaking her head, she said, "No. No, I agree. Let's do all yellow dresses. I think that will look much more soft and sweet. And then with the lilacs and greenery—"

"Here comes Daddy!" Shay exclaimed then.

Kizzy giggled as she gazed out the parlor window into the street as well. "Oh, doesn't he look handsome?" she mumbled. "I just love it when he's all dressed down like this."

"You mean instead of in his judge's robes and all?" Calliope teased.

Kizzy blushed. "Yes. Your father is such a handsome man, and those drab old judge's robes do nothin' to let everyone see his muscles."

"Mama!" Shay giggled, feigning astonishment.

Evangeline and Calliope smiled and exchanged glances of contentment. They were always pleased when Kizzy's adoration of their father was more obvious than usual. In town or at social gatherings, Kizzy played the calm, proper little wife of the judge. At home, especially when they were in private (or thought they were in private), Kizzy and Lawson Ipswich were as affectionate and passionate as any two lovers ever were.

"I'm so glad you love Daddy, Kizzy," Calliope said, suddenly feeling more grateful than ever that her father had Kizzy to love—and to love him in return. "You're so beautiful and vibrant, and you love him passionately—just the way I want to love one day."

Kizzy's eyes filled with moisture born of unexpected and intense emotion. "Well...well, thank you, Calliope," Kizzy breathed. "I never have felt worthy of capturin' his affections, you know."

"I do know," Calliope said, smiling at her. "But you are far more than worthy of him." She reached out, embracing Kizzy a moment. "Thank you for that...and for Shay."

"Look, Mama!" Shay exclaimed then. "Daddy's lightin' our lamp right this minute!"

Evangeline got up from her place on the floor, abandoning the muslin pattern pieces and gazing out the window with her sisters and stepmother.

"Hello, Daddy!" Shay called, gently knocking on the window. She squealed with delight as Lawson looked to the window, smiled, and waved. "He sees us! He sees us!"

As the Ipswich women watched Lawson continue on his way to light the remaining street lamps of Meadowlark Lake, Evangeline giggled.

"What's so amusing?" Calliope asked her sister.

"I was just thinking...isn't it funny that we all are so much more excited about Daddy being the lamplighter for the evening than we ever were for one minute about him being a judge?" she explained.

Calliope smiled. "That's because a lamplighter is a mysterious, romantic type of character, and a judge is just...well, severe in appearance, I suppose." Calliope's smile faded almost instantly, however. "I wonder how Mr. Gates is faring tonight," she mumbled.

"I'm sure he's just fine, Calliope," Kizzy encouraged. "He's a very strong man. I'm sure that after a night's rest, he'll be back to work at the mill in the mornin' as usual."

"Calliope, why don't you and me make a pie for Mr. Gates tomorrow?" Shay suggested with youthful exuberance. "Then we can take it over to him after the mill closes down for the day, and you can thank him proper for savin' you!"

"W-well, I…I don't know if we should," Calliope stammered.

"I think it's a wonderful idea, Shay!" Kizzy agreed, however.

"You do?" Calliope asked—rather surprised by Kizzy's collaborative opinion.

"I most certainly do," Kizzy answered. "Why, I bet Rowdy Gates hardly ever gets a pie brought to him."

"I think it's a good idea, as well," Evangeline chimed in.

"Then it's decided," Shay said. "Tomorrow you and me will make Mr. Gates a pie and take it to him so he can have it for his supper."

Calliope frowned. "He'll probably look at me and wish I'd never been born."

"Oh, don't be so dramatic, Calliope," Evangeline lovingly scolded. "He will not."

"But you didn't see his injuries, Evangeline!" Calliope argued as tears filled her eyes. "You didn't see the blood everywhere! It was all over him, draining from his head down over his face to those broad, broad shoulders of his."

Calliope stopped her dramatics almost at once, however. "Oh my!" she whispered to herself as a vision of Rowdy Gates, shirtless and wet and hovering over her with concern on his face, leapt to her mind.

In all the chaos of her slipping—of their fall and plunge into the water—with all the bedlam of the other men from the mill coming down to help them—of Rowdy's profuse bleeding—it was only then, in that calm moment at home, that the vision of Rowdy so wonderfully disrobed and muscular lingered in her mind.

"Oh my, what?" Evangeline prodded.

"Oh my, I…I…" Calliope stammered. But her mouth could not form words, for as her memory leapt from Rowdy hovering over her on the bank of the millpond to the way he'd appeared when Doctor Gregory had finished shaving him, she was rendered speechless.

Suddenly all she could think of—all she could see in her mind's eye—was the dazzling deep green of his eyes, his square jaw and cleft chin, his perfect nose.

"What's the matter, Calliope?" Shay asked with concern. "Are you all right?"

"Y-yes," Calliope managed, forcing another smile. "I'm just a bit tired, I suppose."

"Well then, you best get to bed," Kizzy said, taking the glass of milk from Calliope. "Sleep in a bit in the mornin', darlin'. You had quite a day."

"Yes, I did," Calliope agreed.

Once she'd kissed each member of her family good night—including her father, for she waited for his return before retiring—and lay comfortably tucked into bed, Calliope stared out the window of her bedroom, gazing up into the clear night sky. As she lay there, she wondered at Rowdy Gates's well-being. Had he eaten supper? Was he comfortable? Was he warm? Had the bleeding of his wounds finally stopped completely? Was he in pain?

Desperate to find sleep and thereby a reprieve from worry, Calliope began to count the stars twinkling like tiny flakes of frost in the dark night sky. And the activity did cause her eyelids to grow heavy and her mind to empty. Yet even as slumber overtook her, it wasn't images of stars twinkling in the sky that prevailed in her mind but the image of the masterful work of art that was Rowdy Gates's shaven face.

"His eyes…his green eyes," Calliope whispered to herself as unconsciousness overtook her. "They take my breath from me."

CHAPTER SEVEN

"Good morning, Calliope," Lawson greeted as Calliope stepped into the kitchen the next morning. The rest of the Ipswich family was already sitting down to breakfast.

"Good morning, Daddy," Calliope said in return. She pressed a loving kiss to his cheek, and then to Shay's, Evangeline's, and Kizzy's cheeks as well. "Forgive me for dawdling this morning."

"There's nothin' to forgive," Kizzy assured her as she placed another plate on the table. "The biscuits are even still warm," she said.

"Oh good!" Calliope said, smiling.

"And we saw Mr. Gates puttin' out the lamps this mornin' already, Calliope," Shay offered. "Daddy says he looks awfully robust for a man who nearly cracked his head open yesterday."

Looking anxiously to her father, Calliope asked, "Does he really, Daddy?"

Lawson nodded at her, smiled, and winked with reassurance. "Yes, he does. I ventured out to speak with him a moment, and other than the bandage around his head—which is well hidden by his hat—he looks none the worse for wear." Lawson shook his head with obvious admiration. "I'd have to say Rowdy Gates is one of the strongest men I've ever known. I can't say for certain that I'd be back to work the day after such an incident."

Although she was very relieved to hear Rowdy seemed well enough, the guilt that had plagued Calliope all night welled up in her again.

"I can't believe...I can't believe I hurt him like that," she said. She felt tears brimming in her eyes and struggled to keep them from spilling over her cheeks.

"You didn't hurt him, Calliope," Evangeline corrected firmly. "You know that. And I for one am just profoundly grateful that he was nearby when you began to fall."

"Me too," Kizzy interjected.

"All of us are," Lawson said. He reached out, cupping Calliope's chin in his strong hand, forcing her to look directly at him. "And don't diminish the incredible service Rowdy did for you by letting guilt envelop you, all right, darling?"

Calliope nodded, and her father released her chin and straightened in his chair. "Shay tells me the two of you are going to bake a pie today and take it over to Rowdy this evening as an offering of gratitude," Lawson began. "I think it's a wonderful notion. I'm sure Rowdy doesn't get many fresh-baked pies. Or many expressions of gratitude. It will be a well-deserved gift of thanks."

Calliope looked to her little sister. Shay sat smiling with triumph. Shay knew that Calliope would never bow out of baking a pie for Rowdy now—not when their father already knew about it and thought it was a good thing.

"I told him," Shay confessed, "before you woke up this mornin'...about the pie, I mean."

"So I gather," Calliope said, smiling. Shay was an angel with an angelic heart.

Smiling with joy in a new, sunshiny day, Calliope retrieved a biscuit from the plate in the middle of the table and slathered it with warm butter. "Mmmmm!" she sighed as she took a bite of it. "Kizzy, you make the best biscuits in all the world! I always feel so happy in a morning that begins with your biscuits."

Kizzy smiled and said, "Why, thank you, Calliope. I'm glad I can help start your mornin' off with some happiness."

"They really are the best biscuits I've ever had," Evangeline added. She sighed and quirked one pretty eyebrow. "No matter how hard I try, mine never come out as fluffy and light as yours."

"That's because Mama puts some gypsy magic into her biscuits, Evie," Shay explained.

Evangeline giggled and said, "Oh, that's right! I always forget about that part." She winked at Calliope. Although Shay constantly wanted to be reassured that she was as much an Ipswich as Evangeline, Amoretta, and Calliope, she was always reminding herself and everyone else that she and her mother had gypsy blood running through them.

"Well, do you think you'd be willing to put some of your own gypsy magic into the pie we bake for Mr. Gates, Shay?" Calliope asked.

Shay's smile of delight and gladness stretched nearly from ear to ear. "Of course, Calliope!" the little girl exclaimed. "Then he'll be sure to like it!"

Everyone at the table exchanged amused glances a moment before returning their attention to breakfast.

Calliope exhaled a sigh of calm. She felt a bit better. Knowing her father had spoken to Rowdy Gates, who seemed to be recovering quickly, she was glad that she truly hadn't been the cause of any worse damage to him. Furthermore, she was sure he would enjoy a pie. Calliope made excellent pies. She'd even won the first-place ribbon at the county fair the autumn before. Surely a delicious pie would help Rowdy to feel better. Surely it would help lessen any animosity he owned toward her for having nearly cracked his skull open like an egg. Anyway, she hoped it would.

"How're you this mornin', Rowdy?" Lou Smith asked Rowdy as he entered the livery. "I heard you had quite an afternoon yesterday," the friendly man said, smiling.

"Yep," Rowdy admitted. "I took me a tumble into the millpond from up on the high bank."

Lou nodded, still smiling. "Yeah, I heard you got a pretty bad bump on the head." He chuckled a little then, adding, "And a pretty good hold of Miss Calliope Ipswich."

Lou was a kind man, with an above average sense of good humor. Therefore, Rowdy wasn't at all irked by his teasing.

"Why yes, indeed I did," he said, smiling himself. "On both accounts."

Lou laughed again, studied Rowdy for a moment, and said, "Why, I ain't never seen you without a beard, Rowdy. You're a mighty good-lookin' feller!"

Rowdy's smile broadened as Lou winked at him. "Thank you, Lou. That means a lot comin' from a good-lookin' feller like you."

In truth, Lou was pushing sixty at least, with a belly that hung over his belt quite a bit. But his blue eyes sparkled with the same bright light Rowdy figured they had had when he was a boy. His hair was white now, but Rowdy imagined it was once as dark as his own.

Lou nodded, continued to smile, and asked, "What can I do for you today, boy? It ain't often you come into the livery."

Rowdy nodded. "Yeah...well, I just had a question for you."

"Ask away," Lou urged.

"Last evenin', on my way home from Doc Gregory's, I seen a mighty fine-lookin' appaloosa tied up outside the diner," Rowdy began. "At least I think I did. My head was still spinnin' a bit from the fall into the millpond. But I was wonderin'—you don't happen to know who it belonged to, do you? I mean, if the owner even stayed the night in Meadowlark and all."

Lou nodded. "Yep. I know just the horse you mean," he confirmed. "A couple of fellers did stay the night last night, stayed over at the inn. They boarded their mounts here, and one of them was that appaloosa. They left before sunup this mornin' though. Why do you ask?"

Rowdy shrugged, feigning indifference. "I just thought it was nice horse. Thought maybe the owner might be willin' to sell it to me. I always wanted a chestnut and white appaloosa. Did you...uh...did you catch the feller's name by chance?"

But Lou shook his head. "Nope. But him and his compadre looked a bit on the rough side. Can't really say I was sad to see them ride outta town, you know what I mean?"

A sick feeling began to smolder in the pit of Rowdy's stomach. Still, he nodded and said, "Yeah, I do. I sure wish I coulda got a better look at that appaloosa before it left town though."

"I hear you," Lou agreed. "A feller don't see many appaloosa anymore, especially around these parts."

"Well, I thank you, Lou," Rowdy said, bending the brim of his hat in thanks to Lou. "You have yourself a good day, all right?"

"I will, Rowdy," Lou said. "You too. And you keep outta that millpond, boy," he teased.

"Oh, I plan to," Rowdy said, forcing an amused grin.

Once outside again, Rowdy paused, exhaled a heavy sigh, and gazed up into the bright blue sky of morning. His head still ached, and his cheek, not to mention his back. The evening before, he'd fallen asleep next to Dodger under the willow tree and hadn't woken up for several hours, and it had left a crick in his neck and a twinge in his back. Still, he figured he'd loosen up after a couple of hours at the mill.

He mounted Tucker and headed down the road leading toward the mill. He tried not to frown as he rode, tried not to think of the appaloosa he'd seen the evening before—the one a stranger had put up at the livery for the night. Maybe the horse did look like Arness's Pronto, but it was gone now, and Rowdy figured worrying over it wouldn't get anything done.

He was surprised when he arrived at the mill to find Fox, Dex, and Tate had beaten him there. In fact, it looked to Rowdy like they'd already been there a while.

Securing Tucker's reins to the hitching post, Rowdy entered the mill and asked, "What're you boys doin' here so early?"

The three men smiled, and Dex held up two dead pigeons he was holding by the feet in one hand.

"We figured we'd get here a might early, Rowdy, and take care of these dang pigeons the way you asked," Dex explained.

Rowdy smiled—chuckled even. "Well, thank you, boys," he said. "Thank you indeed."

"You feelin' all right, boss?" Tate asked. "Fact was, we weren't sure you'd be comin' in to the mill to work today, bein' that you lost so much blood and all yesterday."

Rowdy shook his head. "Naw, I'm fine." He reached up, rubbing his freshly shaved chin. "I gotta few less whiskers than I did yesterday, but that's all."

Fox walked to Rowdy then. He offered a hand to Rowdy and said, "I want to thank you, Rowdy."

Rowdy accepted Fox's handshake, asking, "For what, Fox?"

"For savin' Calliope for me," Fox explained.

Somehow Fox's thanks—his obvious feelings of possession over Calliope Ipswich—ruffled Rowdy's feathers much more than he would've expected.

He was so annoyed, in fact, that he answered, "I saved Calliope for Calliope's sake...not yours, Fox. Any man woulda done the same, I'm sure."

Fox's smile faded. "Well, thank you, anyhow. I expect after this evenin', I'll have even more reason to be grateful to you."

Rowdy's eyes narrowed. Even though he full well understood Fox's implication, he asked, "Why's that?"

"Fox is gonna ask the judge if he can court Calliope official—with serious intentions, that is," Dex answered.

"Is that so?" Rowdy asked.

"Yep," Fox confirmed. He smiled, adding, "By this time tomorrow, I'll have staked my claim on the prettiest girl in town, and all you boys can envy me even more than you already do," he laughed.

"Maybe the judge ain't ready to let go of his baby girl," Tate suggested.

Rowdy looked to Tate, recognizing the obvious jealousy in his countenance.

"Any father would be happy to give his daughter over to me, Tate Chesterfield," Fox gloated. "But I'll tell you what. If Judge

Ipswich turns me away—and mind you, he won't—but if he does, you're welcome to try yourself for Calliope. Hmm?"

"Deal," Tate said.

"Same goes for you, Dex," Fox added. "But you boys are only dreamin'. Judge Ipswich ain't got no reason to say no to me. Ain't that right, Rowdy?"

Rowdy shrugged. "He's a judge. I expect he's said no to many a man in his day."

Fox scowled a bit but undaunted said, "He won't say no. Calliope's sweeter on me than a kid to candy. She wants me to start courtin' her."

"She's said that to you?" Tate asked. "She's told you she wants you to ask her father if you can court her?"

Fox smiled, arched a conceited eyebrow, and said, "She didn't have to tell me. I know she does."

"Get them pigeons outta here, Dex," Rowdy rather tersely ordered then. "We got work to do here, boys. We ain't got time to stand around chattin' about women."

The truth was, however, that Rowdy felt overheated with irritation and anger. Fox Montrose thought he was put on earth by God himself just for women to look at—and it peeved Rowdy that he was so sure Judge Ipswich would allow Fox to begin officially courting Calliope. Calliope Ipswich was far too good, kind, beautiful, and humble a young woman to end up with the likes of the self-admiring Fox Montrose. She was too good for Tate Chesterfield or Dex Longfellow for that matter.

But even though Rowdy felt like stopping in at the courthouse during midday meal and letting Judge Ipswich in on what a self-loving idiot Fox Montrose really was, he knew it wasn't his place. And besides, Judge Ipswich was the wisest man Rowdy had ever encountered. Chances were he already knew what a fool Fox was. Maybe he would deny Fox's request to court Calliope. Still, whatever the outcome, Rowdy knew it was none of his nevermind.

Yet all day long the memory of the pretty perfume that was Calliope Ipswich's fragrance seemed to linger in Rowdy's memory.

Warm bread and sweet cream butter—lavender and mint. It was near all he could think about—that and the fact that the blue of Calliope Ipswich's eyes was exactly the color of the bright spring sky.

❧

"Just knock on the door, Calliope," Shay urged in a whisper.

Calliope still paused, however. "But what if he's having his supper…or he's resting…or working. I don't want to interrupt him or to be a bother. I'm not sure we should—"

Exhaling a sigh of impatience, Shay reached out and rapped on the front door of Rowdy Gates's house as loudly as her tiny fist could.

"Shay!" Calliope exclaimed. "I'm not sure I'm ready to face him! He was almost killed because of me and—"

But it was too late. The front door opened, swinging in to reveal Rowdy Gates standing just inside the house.

"Good evenin', Mr. Gates," Shay greeted.

Calliope, however, paused in greeting the man—for his appearance had rendered her breathless. Not only was he so very, very, very handsome now that his face was free from the thick beard and mustache he'd always worn before, but he stood before her wearing only his trousers and boots.

"Good evenin', Miss Shay," Rowdy said, smiling at Shay. "And to you, Miss Calliope," he added, nodding to Calliope.

"Good evening, Mr. Gates," Calliope managed. "I…I hope we didn't disturb you."

"Nope," Rowdy assured. "Not at all."

Calliope gulped and pulled her gaze away from the broad shoulders and smooth, muscular torso standing in the doorway. Concentrating on looking Rowdy directly in the face, she began, "I wanted to thank you, Mr. Gates…to properly thank you for your service to me yesterday."

Rowdy chuckled a bit. "No mistakin' it, you certainly are your father's daughter." He continued to smile, adding, "It wasn't a service, Miss Calliope. Just a matter of being in the right place at the right moment. I'm just glad I could help."

"Well, I see it as a great service…a life-saving service, Mr. Gates," Calliope explained.

"That's why we baked you a pie, Mr. Gates," Shay chimed in. She held the still-warm pie, protectively covered in a square of cheesecloth, toward him. "It's a peach pie from the peaches Mama and me bottled last summer."

Rowdy's smile broadened as he reached out, accepting the pie as Shay handed it to him. "My goodness!" he exclaimed. "If I'da known there was a warm peach pie at the end of it, I woulda jumped into the millpond with your big sister long ago, little Miss Shay."

Shay giggled with the delight born of pleasing another human being.

"I hope you really do understand how truly grateful I am to you, Mr. Gates," Calliope reiterated.

"I do," he said, looking directly into her eyes—directly into her eyes with the mesmerizing green eyes of his own. "But I think you've done plenty of thanking. So no more worryin' about it. Agreed?"

"Agreed!" Shay answered for Calliope.

"Mmmmm!" Rowdy moaned as he held the pie closer to his face and inhaled. "Peach pie for supper. I can't tell you the last time I had peach pie for supper."

"And the good thing is, you don't have to share it with anybody!" Shay exclaimed. "You can just get a fork and sit down to the table and eat the whole thing all by yourself, Mr. Gates."

"Yes, I certainly can," Rowdy agreed.

Calliope blushed, embarrassed that, in her innocence, Shay had pointed out that Rowdy Gates was always alone for supper.

"Well, we just wanted to bring the pie by…and to thank you once more," Calliope stammered. "We should be on our way now."

"Let me put the pie on the table, and then I'll walk you ladies a ways down the road," Rowdy said.

"Oh, you don't need to—" Calliope began. But Rowdy had already turned and walked back into his house, leaving the door open.

"Let him walk with us a ways, Calliope," Shay whispered. "I think he could use some company."

Rowdy returned and stepped out of the house and onto the front porch.

"Even though I'm seein' you just now, Mr. Gates," Shay began, "I'm still gonna watch for you and wave when you come lightin' lamps tonight."

"That's mighty kind of you, Miss Shay," Rowdy said, grinning as he looked at Calliope.

She knew Rowdy was as charmed by Shay as everyone else who owned the blessing of knowing her, and it said a lot about the man's good character—the way he treated children, especially little girls.

"Is somebody buried here, Mr. Gates?" Shay asked as they neared an old willow tree thriving near Rowdy's house.

Calliope looked to see a grave-sized mound covered in large stones. She hadn't noticed it on their way to Rowdy's house. She'd been too anxious about facing him.

"Yep," he answered. "That's where I buried old Dodger after he was…after he passed on last fall."

"Who was old Dodger?" Shay asked. "Your grandpa or somethin'?"

Calliope smiled when Rowdy chuckled with amusement.

"No, honey," he answered as he stopped walking when they reached the grave and hunkered down next to Shay. "Dodger was my dog."

Calliope watched as Rowdy placed a hand on a large stone that topped the mound of rocks of the grave. Her heart pinched with empathy, for she could see in his demeanor that the dog had been a most precious thing to him.

"He was a good friend," Rowdy explained. "I had him for almost three years. He found me one day. He'd been abandoned or somethin' out in the middle of nowhere. I took him home, and Dodger and me were the best of friends ever since." He paused a moment, smiled, and closed his eyes. "Sometimes if I close my eyes like this and listen real hard, I can almost hear him barkin'…hear him welcomin' me home in the evenin'." Rowdy grinned. "I can see his face clear as day in my mind."

"What did he look like?" Shay asked.

"Oh, he was a big ol' black-and-white dog," Rowdy said. "He stood about yay high," he explained, leveling one of his hands near Shay's shoulder.

Calliope felt tears well in her eyes as Rowdy patted the large stone on top of the grave. "I sure do miss him. He was a good dog. He was my best friend."

"Why, that's the saddest thing I ever heard of, Mr. Gates," Shay mumbled. Calliope looked to see Shay's eyes brimming with tears as well. "I just don't know what I'd ever do if Molly up and died! I think I'd probably die along with her. How can you stand it, Mr. Gates?"

Rowdy reached out and took Shay's hands in his own. "Death is a part of life, Miss Shay Ipswich—a part we all have to face at one time or another. But it helps me to know that there's a place in heaven for everything, even ol' Dodger. And when I get too sad over missin' him too much, I just think of him up there in heaven where there ain't no pain and nobody can harm him ever again. I'm guessin' he's found an old willow tree to nap under up there and that he's just as happy as can be."

Shay smiled a little. "Maybe he's eatin' cake. That's what would make me happy if I was in heaven."

Rowdy laughed, wholeheartedly amused. "Maybe he is," he concurred. "Or bacon. It was his favorite treat, after all. And I certainly can't imagine heaven bein' heaven if it didn't have cake and bacon, can you?"

"No, sir!" Shay agreed emphatically. She looked up to Calliope and asked, "May I go pick some flowers for ol' Dodger's grave, Calliope? I promise I won't tarry. I'll be quick. I saw some pretty wild daisies just a ways up the road."

"Of course," Calliope said with a smile and a nod. "But do be quick, all right? It's almost suppertime."

She wondered how she would ever manage to be a good mother; she couldn't even refuse her little sister anything. How in the world would she manage to tell her own children no?

"I will," Shay agreed as she hurried off toward a beautiful cropping of wild daisies.

As Rowdy stood up once more, Calliope nervously warned, "She'll probably take to leaving flowers on the grave every few days or so now. I hope you don't mind. I'll tell her not to bother you— just to leave the flowers and leave you in peace. But now that she knows the story, she'll worry over your poor dog's little grave forever."

"She's a tenderhearted little soul, isn't she?" he commented.

"Yes, she is," Calliope confirmed. "I'm thinking that's why her cat Molly puts up with all the nonsense Shay showers over her."

Rowdy chuckled. "Yeah, the poor cat. I've seen little Shay draggin' that poor cat around town on a leash." He looked to Calliope, his handsome brow puckered with astonishment. "A leash, mind you! I never did hear of a cat that would tolerate a leash."

Calliope giggled. "Oh, Molly tolerates a lot that most cats wouldn't." She watched Shay picking flowers for a moment and then added, "And I think it's because that sweet old marmalade cat knows a good heart and soul when she sees them in Shay."

"It must," Rowdy agreed.

Calliope studied Rowdy as he watched Shay gathering flowers. She wondered if any of the other young women in town had seen him since he'd been shaved. Blanche, Winnie, Sallie, and all the others would swarm around him like moths to a lamppost once they saw just how handsome Rowdy was. The thought entirely disheartened her all of a sudden. Up until the millpond incident the day before—up until Doctor Gregory had had to shave Rowdy in order to stitch the wound on his cheek—Calliope had had Rowdy Gates all to herself. The other girls in town never paid him much mind. In fact, they were all a little scared of him, in truth—his being so solitary and all. But now—well, if there was one thing Calliope understood about her friends, it was how fast their attention was arrested by a handsome man. Calliope's secret bliss of being in love with Rowdy Gates—the secret that only Shay knew—was about to be brutalized by jealousy and competition with other young women.

In fact, the sudden realization that the other young women in town might actually begin to try and win Rowdy Gates's heart for their own caused a sense of urgency and near panic to rise in Calliope. If anyone ended up winning Rowdy's heart, she wanted it to be her! Couldn't endure it if it weren't her!

Thoughts of all the possibilities regarding Rowdy and the other young women of Meadowlark Lake converged into a tangled clump in Calliope's mind—so tangled that she couldn't even sort them all out.

Therefore, thinking of the day before—when she'd nearly been caught spying on Rowdy and ended up in the millpond with him after he saved her—bundled her feelings of powerful emotions for him, and before she even realized what she was doing, Calliope acted on the one impulse she could determine.

Raising herself on her tiptoes and placing her hands on his shoulders to steady herself, Calliope placed a lingering kiss to Rowdy's cheek just below his wound. As she kissed him, she slowly inhaled—relishing the scent of him, the feel of his whiskers and skin against her lips.

"Thank you, Mr. Gates…for saving me," Calliope said in such a quiet, timid voice that it was almost a whisper.

"Thank you for the pie," came his response.

To her great, great, nearly devastating disappointment, Rowdy seemed entirely unaffected by her gesture of thanks—by her pitiful attempt at allure. He hadn't touched her in return—hadn't been tempted to kiss her in return. He'd simply accepted her thanks and thanked her for the pie.

Calliope tried not to blush as she stepped back from him, just as Shay raced up to Rowdy holding a lovely bouquet of daisies, buttercups and poppies.

"Here you go, Mr. Gates," she said, offering the flowers to Rowdy.

"Oh, you go on and put them there, little miss," he said, smiling, however. "Ol' Dodger would rather a pretty girl paid him some attention than me anyhow."

Shay giggled and gently arranged the flowers at the head of the dog's grave. She exhaled a heavy sigh and said, "Rest well, Dodger. And don't worry. I'll be back with more flowers another day."

Calliope looked to Rowdy to find him looking at her with a smile conveying that he understood she had been right in her prediction that Shay would want to place flowers on the dog's grave regularly from that day forward.

"I told you," she whispered.

Quickly then, for she found her blush of humiliation at having kissed Rowdy's cheek so spontaneously was fast returning, she said, "Let's go, Shay. We've taken up enough of Mr. Gates's time this evening."

"All right, Calliope," Shay agreed. "But you go on ahead for a moment. I have somethin' private I'd like to say to Dodger here at his restin' place."

"Well, I…maybe you should ask Mr. Gates if that's all right with him, honey," Calliope suggested. "After all, it is his dog, and he's a very private man, and—"

"You say anything you want anytime you want, Miss Shay Ipswich," Rowdy said to Shay, however.

"Thank you, Mr. Gates," Shay said with a giggle. Looking to Calliope then, she gestured that Calliope should start home by shooing her little hand at her big sister. "You go on, Calliope. I'll catch right up to you."

"Um, all right, Shay…but don't dilly dally," Calliope said. She didn't want to leave Shay behind with Rowdy—not for a moment. Who knew what she was liable to say to him?

But with no choice before her—for she didn't want to make an issue of it in front of Rowdy—Calliope said, "You have a good evening, Mr. Gates."

"You too, Miss Calliope," he said with a nod.

Calliope turned then and started toward home, praying that Shay would use the good sense of tact Kizzy had been trying to instill in her.

Shay Ipswich shook her head with obvious disapproval as she looked up to Rowdy. She exhaled a heavy sigh, planted her hands on her hips, and quietly asked, "Do you have oatmeal for brains, Mr. Gates?"

"I beg your pardon?" Rowdy asked, astonished by the girl's scolding manner.

Shaking her head again, Shay answered, "She wanted you to kiss her, you big, silly goose! What do you think she kissed your cheek for?"

"Um…uh…to thank me for yesterday at the millpond," Rowdy stammered, still astonished at being scolded—and now further astonished by what he was being scolded for.

Shay Ipswich rolled her dark eyes with exasperation. "She kissed your cheek because she wanted *you* to kiss *her*, oatmeal brain." She leveled a small index finger at him, adding, "Next time you kiss her back, do you hear me?"

"Oh, she wanted me to kiss her, did she?" Rowdy chuckled, amused by the child's assumption. "And just how do you know that?"

"Because I'm a gypsy, Mr. Gates," Shay informed him. She shook her head with renewed aggravation.

"Well, I happen to know, Miss Ipswich Gypsy, that Fox Montrose is plannin' on askin' your daddy if he can court your sister Calliope," Rowdy baited. "What do you have to say about that?"

But Shay again rolled her eyes. "Oh, she told Daddy some time ago to tell Fox Montrose *no* if he ever comes askin' to court her, so I know that…"

The little girl gasped, covering her mouth with both hands. "Oh no! I'm not supposed to tell anyone that, Mr. Gates! Mama and Daddy will give me such a talkin' to if they find out, and Calliope might never, never tell me another secret!" She lowered her voice even further so that Rowdy could hardly hear her. "Please promise you won't say a word about what I slipped up and told you, Mr. Gates! Just promise me you won't let on."

"Even torture couldn't drag it from me, Miss Shay," Rowdy assured her with a smile. "I swear it to you."

"All right. All right then," Shay said, obviously feeling better. She looked to Rowdy again and said, "Just don't be an oatmeal brain next time my sister gives you a chance like she just done."

"Shay!" Calliope called.

Rowdy looked up to see a rather worried Calliope motioning for her little sister to join her.

"I gotta go," Shay said. "Remember what I said, okay?"

"Oh, I will," Rowdy chuckled as Shay ran to catch up to her sister.

He watched them clasp hands and start toward home. The fact was he watched them because he was too stunned to move for a second or two.

Was it true, what Shay had told him? Had Calliope wanted Rowdy to kiss her? Surely not. The child simply misunderstood. Calliope was still feeling guilty for the little bumps and scrapes Rowdy had gotten the day before when he jumped with her into the millpond. That was all. That was why she had kissed his cheek—to thank him.

Yet then there was the other part of it—the accidental revelation that Calliope wanted her father to deny Fox permission to court her. Could it be true? Rowdy knew it could, for in all his time in admiring Calliope from afar, it was always Fox coming after Calliope, never the other way around. Rowdy had always just assumed that Calliope wasn't as flirtatious as other women her age. But could it really be that she didn't like Fox Montrose as much as everyone in town seemed to think?

Rowdy finally came to his senses and returned to the house. He had a peach pie waiting for supper, after all. A peach pie made and delivered by the one girl in town who had managed to put her mark on his heart—and her little gypsy sister, of course.

CHAPTER EIGHT

"I still can't believe he denied me," Fox growled. "The almighty Judge Ipswich denied *me* permission to court Calliope!"

Fox's ranting was wearing on everyone else's nerves. Fox had done nothing but fume most of the day over the fact. Yet Rowdy had begun to wonder if Fox wasn't a bit more upset over the fact that he'd been denied something than over *what* he'd been denied.

"Give it a rest, Fox," Dex grumbled. "We know, we know—there's no good reason on earth for Judge Ipswich to have told you no. But he did. So shut up and get on with the day. My ears are achin' over your whinin' about it all mornin'."

"Mine too," Tate agreed.

Fox's eyes narrowed. "I know what the two of you are thinkin'. I ain't stupid. You're both thinkin' that since I got turned down by Calliope's father, then that leaves her for the two of you to have a go at. But it doesn't! She's still my girl. You hear me?"

"She was never your girl," Dex argued. "Did Calliope even want you to talk to her daddy about courtin' her?"

Fox straightened his shoulders indignantly. "She didn't have to. Every girl in this town wants me to ask her daddy if I can court her."

Dex and Tate both shook their heads with disgust. Even Rowdy's eyebrows arched with his wonder at Fox's conceit.

"You might want to simmer down that ego a bit, Fox," he began, "before that swelled head of yours explodes."

Fox glared at Rowdy, but Rowdy just exhaled a sigh of annoyance and said, "Let's get back to work here, boys. We're fallin' behind."

"All right, boss," Tate agreed. Dex nodded as well.

Fox, however, stood glaring at Rowdy a moment. Finally he asked, "Don't you think the judge was wrong to refuse me?"

Rowdy looked Fox straight in the eyes and answered, "I think a good man who's also a good father knows…well, I figure he knows what's right for his daughter and when."

Fox huffed a breath of frustration.

"Settle it down, Fox," Rowdy encouraged. "Things have a way of workin' themselves out for the best." He cleared his throat, adding, "But next time, maybe make sure the girl *wants* you to ask her daddy to come courtin' her…*before* you go askin'."

Glaring at Rowdy a moment, Fox eventually turned and stormed off to move some sacks of flour.

"That's what he gets for thinkin' he's the sweet cream in every milk bucket," Dex whispered to Rowdy as he passed him.

Rowdy didn't respond with more than a mild, almost imperceptible nod—but he wholeheartedly agreed with Dex. Fox Montrose was way too fond of himself—and if the truth be told, Rowdy was elated that Judge Ipswich had refused his permission for Fox to court Calliope. For one thing, it verified to Rowdy the truth of what little Shay Ipswich had told him the day before—that Calliope herself had actually asked her father to refuse Fox's proposal of courtship. It might also have proved that the youngest Ipswich gypsy wasn't completely loco when she'd told him that Calliope had wanted Rowdy to kiss her.

Rowdy shook his head, rattling his brains back to reality. His thoughts where Calliope was concerned were as foolish as Fox's assumptions had been.

Still, one thing he couldn't lie to himself about—and that was the fact that he was purely jubilant in knowing that Fox Montrose had no real claim to Calliope. Therefore, as Fox continued to mope around the mill, muttering angrily to himself, Rowdy unconsciously took to whistling a happy tune.

❦

"Ladies," Calliope said as she stood in the center of Dora Montrose's parlor, "I'd like to make an announcement."

"Oh, for Pete's sake, Calliope," Evangeline mumbled, blushing with humiliation.

But Calliope was undaunted. "I'm pleased to tell you all that my own very sweet sister Evangeline here…well, she's managed to convince Floyd Longfellow to allow Mamie and Effie to take part in our Tom Thumb wedding as the flower girls!"

Every woman in the room applauded and squealed with delight.

"Oh, however did you manage it, Evangeline?" Winnie asked.

"Yes, I can hardly believe it! Mr. Longfellow is so severe," Blanche chimed in. "I'm afraid to even look him in the eye, let alone ask him anything…especially somethin' the likes of this!"

But Evangeline shrugged. "I-I don't quite know why he agreed," she admitted. "I did take the time to explain everything to him, all the details and things. I noted that I thought it would be a good experience for Mamie and Effie—you know, something to help them get to know the other children in town." She shrugged again and added, "And before I knew it, he'd agreed to allow the girls to participate."

"Maybe Mr. Longfellow is a bit sweet on you, Evangeline," Pauline suggested.

"Oh, don't be ridiculous, Pauline," her sister Callie laughed. "Mr. Longfellow is old enough to be Evangeline's father, for heaven's sake!"

"My father married Kizzy," Calliope kindly pointed out, "and he's old enough to be her father."

"But that's different, Calliope," Callie suggested.

"How so?" Dora Montrose asked.

Callie shrugged. "Well…because Judge Ipswich is so wildly handsome! It makes sense he would win the heart of a younger woman."

"Well, I think Mr. Longfellow is quite nice looking," Evangeline said.

Callie seemed to ponder the statement for a moment. Then she nonchalantly shrugged and said, "I suppose he is. But I still wouldn't want to marry a man old enough to be my father."

"I find that older men are quite often far more attractive than younger ones," Blanche's mother, Judith, said. "Why, Mr. Gardener is a full ten years older than I am."

"It's not such a bad idea, now that I think about it," Josephine Chesterfield commented. "You'd make a fine wife to a man in need of a woman to raise two little girls, Evangeline."

Evangeline blushed, and Calliope leapt to her rescue.

"Anyway," Calliope began, "the point of it all is…we have our little flower girls assured us."

Everyone smiled and nodded with satisfaction.

"Now, Mrs. Ackerman," Calliope began then, addressing Sallie's mother, "what did Warren say when you explained the *entire* script to him? You simply *must* convince him to kiss the bride at the end of the ceremony!"

Ellen Ackerman exchanged amused glances with her daughter, Sallie. "Oh, don't you worry a bit, Calliope," she said. "When I told Warren that he was expected to kiss Shay—to kiss the bride, so to speak—his response was, 'Good! I can't wait!'"

Everyone burst into laughter once more, and Calliope and Evangeline clasped hands with excitement.

"It's going to be so wonderful, Evie!" Calliope sighed with glad anticipation.

"Wonderful!" Evangeline agreed.

"And Evie really convinced Mr. Longfellow to let Mamie and Effie be in the play?" Shay asked as she and Calliope sat on the old fallen log that spanned the stream.

"Yes!" Calliope confirmed. She shook her head in awed disbelief. "I don't know how Evangeline managed it, but somehow she persuaded him."

Shay smiled. "It's because Mr. Longfellow is sweet on Evangeline," she stated.

Calliope looked to Shay in astonishment. "Why do you say that, Shay Shay?"

Shay shrugged. "Because I can see it. Mr. Longfellow stares at Evangeline anytime she's around him…like every Sunday in church. I'm surprised no one else has noticed."

Calliope considered what Shay was saying. Was it true? Did Floyd Longfellow stare at Evangeline whenever he was in her presence? The truth was that at church Calliope was always too distracted trying to catch every glimpse she could of Rowdy Gates. Could it be that she'd been so preoccupied by Rowdy every Sunday that she'd never noticed Mr. Longfellow staring at her own sister?

"Hmmm," she sighed suddenly. "Maybe you're right, Shay. Maybe Mr. Longfellow is sweet on Evangeline. After all, it wouldn't be the first time a man had his eye on a woman quite a lot young than himself, now would it?" She giggled and nudged Shay with her arm.

Shay laughed. "You mean like Daddy and Mama," she noted.

"That's just what I mean," Calliope said.

Calliope and Shay sat quietly for a few moments, dangling their toes in the stream's cool water babbling beneath the log on which they sat.

They each heard a tiny splash, and Shay exclaimed, "There goes another one! Oh, I just love baby frogs."

"Me too," Calliope agreed. "By the time you get married in a few weeks, all the baby frogs will be big, slimy toads. Let's catch a few now, while they're little. What do you say?"

Shay nodded with enthusiasm. She paused for an instant, however, and then said, "You know that it's just a pretend weddin', right, Calliope? I'm not really marryin' Warren Ackerman."

Calliope smiled. She understood that Shay needed reassurance that the Tom Thumb wedding was simply a play—that nothing at all about it was real or binding.

"Of course, Shay," she assured her little sister. She giggled, adding, "The only *real* thing about it is the kiss you'll receive from Warren Ackerman!"

Shay blushed and grinned. But her smile faded as she asked, "But what if Warren won't kiss me at the weddin'? Oh, I'll be so embarrassed if he won't!"

Calliope put her arm around Shay's slight shoulders. "Don't worry, my angel. He will kiss you. I happen to know for a fact that he can't *wait* to kiss you!"

Shay's eyes widened. "How do you know that for a fact?"

Calliope arched one eyebrow and answered, "I have my ways." She giggled. "Now, let's go catch some baby frogs before they turn into big, slimy ones, all right?"

Again Shay nodded with emphatic agreement.

Taking Shay's hand, Calliope helped her to stand on the log and then followed suit. Carefully they walked across the log back to the bank of the stream.

"I've seen so many jump into the water from just here," Shay said, dashing to a spot on the bank near a grove of cattails.

"Well, then that's where we should start looking," Calliope said, following her.

Rowdy continued to observe Calliope as she hunted for frogs with her little sister. All day the reality had bounced around in his mind—the fact that Judge Ipswich had not granted his permission for Fox Montrose to court Calliope. Unlike Fox, who was still seething with indignation when he left the mill to ride around a bit and clear his head during the midday break for lunch, Rowdy had wandered to the meadow—to the hill that overlooked the stream.

When he'd seen Calliope and her sister sitting on the fallen tree that spanned the stream, allowing their toes to skim across the water's surface, he'd found himself a comfortable place to sit down in the grass. There he'd eaten his baked potato as he'd listened to their giggling and watched them talking to one another.

Evangeline wasn't with them this day, and they'd apparently traded their pretending at being ponies for hunting for frogs. It made Rowdy happy to think that the lovely, graceful Calliope Ipswich still enjoyed such things as dangling her toes in the stream and catching frogs.

"So...Fox ain't gonna be courtin' Calliope, hmm?" Rowdy mumbled to himself. He remember what Fox had told Dex and Tate at the mill earlier in the day—that they better not think they could be throwing their hats in the ring for Calliope's affections just because the judge had refused to let Fox court her. But Rowdy Gates had a hat too—didn't he? And didn't he also have the revelations of a cute little gypsy girl to guide him along as well? What if Calliope really had wanted him to kiss her when she'd kissed him the day before? What if there was even the smallest idea of a chance that she could care for him? Shouldn't he pursue her as earnestly as he knew Dex and Tate no doubt planned to do?

Before he could think to stop himself, Rowdy had stood and mounted Tucker and was riding down the hillside toward the place where Calliope Ipswich and her sister were hunting frogs.

He was nearly upon them when his courage began to fail. In fact, he reined Tucker to a stop and planned to turn the horse around and ride toward the mill. But it was too late, for Shay Ipswich had spied him and was now waving her little arm and hand frantically in motioning that he should ride to meet her and her sister.

What had he been thinking? As Rowdy reined in near Calliope and Shay, he wondered if he hadn't momentarily lost his mind. But he was there now—right there with them. He couldn't just ride away. What would Calliope think of him if he did?

"We're catchin' baby frogs, Mr. Gates," Shay announced. "Calliope says she'd rather catch them now when they're cute little babies, instead of later in the summer when they're big and slimy."

Calliope blushed all the way from her forehead to the tips of her toes when Rowdy Gates chuckled at what Shay had told him.

She was surprised, however, when he said, "Well, that's a good idea. 'Cause even if the slime don't bother you, you can't sail frogs when they get big."

"Sail them?" Calliope heard herself ask in unison with Shay.

"What do you mean you can't sail them when they get big?" Shay asked. The curiosity gleaming in her eyes was as bright as a summer sunrise.

"Well," Rowdy began as he dismounted his horse and secured the reins to a nearby tree trunk, "here. Let me show you."

Calliope watched as the ruggedly handsome man reached into one saddlebag, retrieving a small pad of paper. Next, he reached into one back pocket of his blue jeans and produced a small pocketknife. Tucking the pad of paper under one arm, Rowdy then used the knife to cut a few long strands of hair from his horse's tail.

"You hold onto these a minute," he said, offering the hairs to Shay.

Shay giggled, and Calliope smiled, curious as to what the man was up to.

"Now then," he said, closing the pocketknife and returning it to his pocket, "give me just a minute or two here."

As Rowdy sat down in the grass on the bank of the stream, Calliope and Shay sat down as well.

"When I was a boy," Rowdy began, "we used to head down to the crick in the summers and do this all the time."

Calliope watched, entirely intrigued as Rowdy tore a page from the back of the small pad of paper and proceeded to fold it into the shape of a small boat. She glanced at his face a moment—his handsome, handsome face. She realized that she adored the cleft in his chin. She was glad Doctor Gregory had had to shave Rowdy. Of course, the still stitched and healing wound on his cheek caused her heart to plummet to the pit of her stomach with guilt. Yet as she continued to look at him—to stare at him in studying every detail of him—the smile returned to her face, for she did love him so thoroughly. Inexplicable as it was, she did love him!

As Rowdy tore a second page from the pad, he nodded to Shay and then the bucket she'd brought along when she and Calliope had decided to walk to the stream. "Give them horsehairs to your sister here, and then take your bucket and see how many baby frogs you can catch real quick for me, will you, darlin'?"

Again Shay's eyes lit up with wild anticipation. "You bet, Mr. Gates!" she giggled, handing the horsetail hairs to Calliope. Hopping to her feet, Shay snatched up her bucket and headed to the grove of cattails nearby.

"Do you have a hairpin I could borrow here for a minute, Miss Calliope?" Rowdy asked.

"Of course," Calliope answered. Quickly she removed one of her hairpins, careless of the long, flaxen curl it released to cascade down her back.

She handed the hairpin to Rowdy. She watched him use it to poke a hole in the back of each of the three little boats he'd created by folding pieces of paper.

As he handed the hairpin back to her, he instructed, "Now give me one of them horsehairs, Calliope."

Calliope's heart leapt inside her at the sound of her name on his lips—the marvelous way his deep voice made it echo through her mind as if it were the most beautiful name in all the world. She felt butterflies fluttering in her stomach—and simply because he'd said her name without a "Miss" preceding it!

Rowdy looked up to her, for she'd quite forgotten to hand him a horsehair, being that she was so mesmerized by the way he'd addressed her by her first name.

"A horsehair, if you please," he repeated, grinning at her.

With a rather trembling hand, Calliope separated one of Rowdy's horse's tail hairs from the rest, holding it toward him.

"Thank you," he said.

She watched then as Rowdy carefully threaded one end of the horse's long, black tail hair through the small hole he'd made in the back of the paper boat using Calliope's hairpin. He then knotted the hair several times.

"There we go," he said, smiling as he studied the small paper boat with the length of horsehair tied to it. "Go on and give me another hair," he said.

Realization washed over Calliope as she handed him another hair and watched him repeat the same process of tying it to a small paper boat.

"You're gonna sail frogs down the stream!" she giggled with delight.

Rowdy's smile broadened. "*We're* gonna sail frogs down the stream," he playfully corrected. "The horsehairs will keep them from gettin' away from us. Well, they'll keep the boats from gettin' away from us. I can't make any promises about the frogs."

Calliope laughed and exclaimed, "How charming you are!"

"Charmin'?" Rowdy asked, quirking one eyebrow.

Calliope's smile broadened. "Clever then…if charming offends you."

"Oh, charmin' is fine. I've just never been called charmin' before now," he said, winking at her.

As butterflies again caused her stomach to feel dizzy, she said, "Well, I can't imagine why not. I find you very charming." Blushing with a sudden bashfulness for having spoken so freely, Calliope hurried on. "And these little boats are just so adorable. Shay is going to love them!"

"I've got six so far, Mr. Gates," Shay announced as she plopped down beside Rowdy in the grass. "Is that enough?"

"Are they tiny?" Rowdy asked.

"Very tiny," Shay responded.

"Then they oughta give us a good start," he assured her.

Though she didn't think it possible, Calliope fell even more in love with Rowdy Gates when he smiled and offered one of the small paper boats to Shay.

"Mr. Gates!" Shay exclaimed. "It's…it's just the perfect size for a baby frog!" Her sweet, pretty brows furrowed into a frown then. "But won't a frog hop out the moment we try to put him in the boat? And why is this horsetail hair tied to the boat?"

Rowdy nodded. "Oh, the frogs will hop out eventually, but for some reason, it takes them a while. You'll be surprised how long they'll sit on a paper boat. And the horsehairs…well, that's so we can hang onto the boats as long as we can."

Shay squealed and threw her arms around Rowdy's neck in an affectionate hug. Calliope laughed, wishing all the while she could throw her arms around the man's neck and hug him with appreciation as well. She remembered how wonderful he'd smelled the day before when she'd dared to kiss him on the cheek. Rowdy Gates smelled just as a man should—of grain and grass, ham, potatoes, and leather. She wondered if Shay would notice the way Rowdy smelled, and she wished again that she could hug him.

"You are so smart, Mr. Gates!" Shay giggled as she released him and reached into her bucket to retrieve a baby frog. "Show me how. Show me how to sail him in this boat you made."

"All right," Rowdy agreed. "Let's go over by them cattails where the water is calmer."

Calliope gathered up the remaining paper boats as Rowdy took hold of the bucket handle. And before long, Shay was holding tight to the free end of the horsetail hair while a tiny frog sat perched on the bow of a small paper boat as it floated on the surface of the water.

"Keep him movin'," Rowdy explained. "If you let him sit still in one spot too long, he'll jump out quicker."

Shay nodded and manipulated the horsetail hair so that the little sailboat bobbed back and forth and back and forth.

Shay's giggles were like the chimes of heaven, and Calliope could no longer remain a spectator.

"May I try?" she asked Rowdy.

"Of course," Rowdy said. "Pick yourself a frog outta the bucket, and go to it."

Calliope reached into Shay's bucket and retrieved a very small frog. "Oh, look how cute he is! Isn't he just the cutest little thing?"

Rowdy laughed. "Why do you girls keep referring to these frogs as hims? There's girl frogs in there too, I'm sure."

Calliope smiled and explained, "Because I think we assume that all frogs are really handsome princes that have been turned into frogs by some wicked witch or fairy," she explained. "Haven't you been reading your fairy tales, Mr. Gates?"

"I guess not," Rowdy answered, smiling at her.

Carefully Calliope placed her little frog in one of the tiny boats and cast it adrift. The excitement that traveled through her as the horsetail hair almost slipped through her fingers was startling, but she held tight and sailed her frog the way Rowdy had instructed Shay to do.

"You're gonna sail a frog too, aren't you, Mr. Gates?" Shay asked.

"You bet," Rowdy assured her.

Calliope watched as he reached into the bucket, retrieved a frog, and very adeptly set it to sailing.

He chuckled. "Me and my brothers used to spend hours sailin' frogs," he remarked.

"So you have brothers?" Calliope asked.

But Rowdy's smile faded. "I did...when I was boy," came his rather unhappy sounding answer.

"I don't have any brothers," Shay sighed. "At least yet. But maybe the baby Mama has in her tummy right now will turn out to be a brother."

Calliope exchanged expressions of surprise with Rowdy.

"What do you mean, Shay?" Calliope asked. "Did Kizzy tell you she's going to have a baby?"

Shay rolled her eyes with exasperation. "Goodness sakes, no, Calliope!" the little girl exclaimed. "She hasn't even told Daddy yet. Why do you think she would've told me?"

Rowdy Gates smiled a smile of amusement at understanding mischief. "You did know that your little sister here is a gypsy, didn't you, Miss Calliope? The child claims to know things others don't."

"I *do* know things other don't," Shay corrected Rowdy emphatically but kindly. "And I know my Mama is gonna have a baby. She'll tell Daddy and the rest of us when she's ready." Turning to Calliope, she wagged a small, scolding index finger at her. "Now don't you go tellin' Mama that I told you, Calliope. There are some secrets sisters have to keep. Aren't there?"

Calliope blushed when Shay nodded toward Rowdy, implying that she knew Calliope's secret concerning her feelings for him. It was an unspoken reminder that some secrets needed to be kept.

"And don't you tell nobody either, Mr. Gates," Shay said, returning her attention to her sailing frog. "This is a family matter, so keep it to yourself."

Rowdy frowned with confusion for a second but eventually agreed, "Yes, ma'am, little miss."

There was the sound of a tiny splash, and then Calliope gasped, "Oh no! My frog jumped out!"

Shay put a hand on her sister's knee as a gesture of reassurance. "That's all right, Calliope," she soothed. "We have more in the bucket."

"Whoops…and there goes mine," Rowdy chuckled.

Shay smiled. "Mine is still on my boat! I'm a good frog sailer, ain't I, Mr. Gates?"

"The best I've seen in many a year, Miss Shay," Rowdy assured her.

Calliope sighed with contentment as she watched Rowdy take another frog out of the bucket and send it sailing. She watched as he laughed and talked with Shay—thinking of what a good father he would make to his own children.

Naturally she started to inwardly scold herself for thinking of Rowdy Gates having children—of she and Rowdy having children together. But then Calliope glanced around her, noting the loveliness of the day, the warmth of it, and the matchlessness of the moment in which she was lingering. She figured it was almost expected to daydream ridiculous things on such a wonderful day.

And so, for an instant, she let herself imagine that she and Rowdy were married, that Shay was one of their own children, and that they'd be sailing frogs on paper boats together every summer forever.

❦

Rowdy sat down next to Dodger. He exhaled a heavy sigh of worry. Closing his eyes for a moment, he thought back on the pretty parts of the day—the fact that Fox Montrose wasn't going to have

Calliope Ipswich for his own anytime soon, as well as the hour or so he'd spent with Calliope and her little sister sailing frogs in the stream.

Still, no matter how hard he tried not to think of it—to push it from the forefront of his thoughts and into the corner of his mind—he couldn't.

Opening his eyes once more, he stared up into the starry sky. "It's Pronto, Dodger. I'm sure of it," he said. "A man doesn't forget a horse like that, and I saw it outside the diner again tonight." He nodded with determination. "In the mornin', I'll ask Lou Smith if he caught the owner's name this time. But even if he didn't…I know that's Arness's horse. I know it is!" He exhaled another heavy sigh. "And I know why it's here."

He glanced over to the grave of his faithful friend. The sight of the fresh flowers sticking out of an old medicine bottle filled with water at the head of it made him grin.

"She told me her little sister would worry over you all the time now, Dodger," he said. "I suppose it's nice for you to have someone besides me to come visitin', hmm?"

Rowdy lay back in the grass under the old willow, tucked his hands under his head, and continued to gaze up into the night sky.

"What do you think, boy?" he asked. "You think Judge Ipswich would turn me down cold too? That is, if I ever got up the gumption to ask him for a chance at his daughter." He frowned again. "I suppose I best talk to the sheriff tomorrow…maybe the judge too. It'll put the nail in my coffin where Calliope's concerned, of course. But it has to be done…because I know that's Arness's horse, and there's no way I can let that go."

Rowdy closed his eyes once more. He simply breathed in and out for a moment or two, and as images of Calliope flittered around in his mind, he mumbled, "I amused her a bit today, Dodger. She even said I was charmin'. Can you imagine that?"

But once more, his joy was stripped away and his smile replaced with a frown. "Why the hell did Arness have to choose this town, Dodger?"

CHAPTER NINE

Anxiety pulsed thick in Rowdy's veins as he dismounted Tucker in front of the livery early the next morning. He had hardly slept a wink—worrying about having seen the appaloosa in town again, thinking on the fact that Judge Ipswich had sent Fox Montrose packing, leaving Calliope free from an entanglement with him. Angst and worry had mingled with hope and gladness all night long, and now Rowdy felt ill-tempered from lack of rest.

"Mornin' there, Rowdy," Lou Smith greeted as Rowdy stepped into the livery. He smiled. "I figured I'd be seein' you today, bein' that the appaloosa you was wonderin' over was stabled here again last night."

Rowdy nodded and said, "Yep. That's why I stopped in on you, Lou. I was wonderin'…did you happen to get the owner's name this time?"

Lou nodded his affirmation with pride. "I sure did, Rowdy. The man's name is Arness. That's all he give me. I'm not sure if that's a first name or a last name. He just said his name was Arness. I got the distinct feelin' he didn't care to let on anything else about himself."

As nausea welled up inside him, Rowdy nodded once more. "I see," he mumbled. "And I don't suppose he was interested in sellin' that horse neither."

Lou shook his head. "No, sirree, he was not. Gave me the stink eye for even askin'." Lou shrugged. "Guess you'll have to run on up to Denver or down to Santa Fe if you're still wantin' to buy yourself an appaloosa, Rowdy."

Rowdy exhaled a nervous sigh. "I guess so," he said. "Thank you all the same, Lou. I appreciate it." He offered a hand.

Lou struck hands with him and said, "You have yourself a nice day, all right, Rowdy?"

"Same to you, Lou," Rowdy countered. "And thanks again."

"Anytime, Rowdy."

Outside the livery, Rowdy paused in mounting his horse. Leaning against Tucker's belly, he folded his arms along his saddle and rested his head on them a moment. He felt as if he would vomit.

It was well he knew Arness and his appaloosa, Pronto—too well. Furthermore, he knew that where Arness Morrison went, so went Carson and Walker Morrison as well. The Morrison brothers were infamous for their thieving and murdering ways. They were outlaws—through and through outlaws, and as evil as outlaws came.

But why was Arness riding through Meadowlark Lake? The fact was that Rowdy already knew the answer; he just didn't want to face the truth of it. If Arness had been to Meadowlark Lake twice already—spent the night at the inn and stabled Pronto in the livery both times—Rowdy knew Arness was looking for a new town to hole up in.

Over the past couple of years, Rowdy had wondered how long it would take the sheriff of Cochise County, Arizona—Texas John Slaughter—to run the Morrison brothers out of Tombstone. He'd heard that when Texas John Slaughter told an outlaw to leave, they left. Sheriff Slaughter was said to be judge, jury, and executioner in Tombstone. And with Arness riding out from Arizona, Rowdy guessed John Slaughter had had his fill of the Morrison brothers and given them the boot.

Yep, Arness was looking for another town to hole up in—a town where he could promise the local lawmen that he'd help protect the town, and mostly keep out of trouble, on the condition that the lawmen turned a blind eye to the fact that Arness and his brothers were murdering outlaws.

Glancing across the street to the county courthouse, which stood next to the jail and Sheriff Montrose's office, Rowdy knew what he had to do.

He noticed little Warren Ackerman coming down the street toward him then and called, "Hey, Warren."

The boy stopped and looked at him. "Yes, sir, Mr. Gates?" Warren asked. It was obvious by the way the color drained from the boy's face that he thought he was about to be scolded for something.

"I was wonderin' if you'd do me a favor," Rowdy began to explain. Reaching into his front pocket, he fumbled around until he found a nickel. "I'll give you a nickel if you run on out to the mill right quick and let the men out there know I'm gonna be a bit late gettin' there this mornin'."

Warren's eyes lit up like fireworks in a Fourth of July night sky. Rushing to Rowdy, he said, "You bet, Mr. Gates! A whole nickel? Really?"

Rowdy handed the boy the nickel and smiled. "Yep. Just run on out and tell the men I'll be in as soon as I take care of somethin' here in town, all right?"

Warren nodded as he stared at the nickel like he'd never seen one before. "I'll do just that, Mr. Gates! And thank you for the nickel!"

"You're gonna earn it, boy," he said. "Thank you for bein' willin' to help me out."

Warren was off at a dead run toward the mill then, and Rowdy couldn't help but smile, even for the sinking feeling in the pit of his stomach over the Morrison brothers. He knew just how much candy a boy could get over at the general store with a shiny nickel to spend. He figured that once Warren Ackerman delivered Rowdy's message to the men at the mill, the boy would probably eat himself sick on licorice laces and butterscotch.

Inhaling a deep breath of acceptance, Rowdy patted Tucker's neck and said, "I might as well leave you tethered up here, Tucker. I shouldn't be long."

Reconciled to doing what he must, no matter the consequences, Rowdy strode across the street toward the jailhouse and Sheriff Montrose's office.

❦

"Why, thank ya kindly, Miss Calliope," Sheriff Montrose said as he took a muffin from the basket Calliope held out to him.

"You're welcome, Sheriff," Calliope chirped. She turned to her father then. "Daddy?" she asked, holding the basket out to him. "You might as well have another one. They're not warm like they were at breakfast this morning, but they're still delicious."

"Oh, don't I know it," Judge Ipswich said, smiling as he took a muffin from the basket as well.

"Mmm, apple!" Sheriff Montrose mumbled. "I love anything made with apples."

"Oh, I'm glad," Calliope giggled. She looked to Blanche a moment, adding, "Blanche and I are on our way to the Ackermans' house to measure Warren for his groom's suit, and we thought you deserved a little treat today, Sheriff. And we've still got plenty of muffins."

"Groom's suit?" the sheriff asked. "Ain't Warren a little young to be gettin' fitted for a groom's suit?"

Calliope and Blanche both giggled.

"Oh, surely Mrs. Montrose has told you about the Tom Thumb weddin' we're all puttin' together," Blanche commented.

"Oh yes!" Sheriff Montrose exclaimed. "Dora did say somethin' about that to me. I guess I didn't realize that Warren Ackerman was the…the, uh…the lucky fellow gettin' married at it."

Calliope arched one eyebrow with suspicion. "Oh, I know what you're thinking, Sheriff," she said. "You're thinking this is all just silly female nonsense. But I promise it will be so much fun for everyone in town! Even you'll enjoy it."

"Oh, I'm sure I will," Sheriff Montrose chuckled. "As long as it's half as good as these muffins of yours, I'll enjoy it."

Calliope smiled as Sheriff Montrose reached into her basket, snatching out a second muffin.

"Well, you gentlemen have a nice day now, all right?" Blanche said. It was obvious Blanche was anxious to leave the jailhouse and get to the Ackermans'.

"We will, Miss Blanche," Sheriff Montrose said.

"And you young ladies have a fine afternoon as well," Judge Ipswich added.

Raising herself on her tiptoes, Calliope placed a loving kiss on her father's cheek. "We will, Daddy," she assured him.

"Come along, Calliope," Blanche said, linking arms with her friend. "There's so much to do today. Best get at it."

Calliope frowned a little, puzzled. Blanche seemed uncharacteristically impatient.

"What's got you in such a hurry, Blanche?" Calliope asked in a whisper.

"I have somethin' to tell you, Calliope," Blanche whispered in return. "And I can't tell you anything about it until we're outside."

"All right...but does it warrant being nearly rude to Sheriff Montrose and my father?" Calliope giggled.

Yet no sooner had Calliope and Blanche stepped out of the jailhouse than Calliope found herself standing face to face with Rowdy Gates.

"Oh!" she gasped with astonishment. She'd nearly plowed him over! Blanche had been pulling her along so quickly that she'd almost bumped right into Rowdy.

"Pardon me, Mr. Gates," Calliope said, suddenly breathless. The sight of Rowdy always took her breath away, but to come upon him so unexpectedly—why, she was nearly panting with gladness.

"Good mornin', ladies," Rowdy said, tugging at the brim of his hat and smiling at Calliope. "Miss Calliope," he said as his gaze seemed to linger on her. At last he looked to Blanche, saying, "Miss Gardener."

"Good mornin', Mr. Gates," Blanche chirped.

The sweetness in Blanche's voice gave cause for Calliope to look over at her. Blanche was smiling as if someone had just handed her a chest full of silver! Furthermore, she was blushing.

Calliope sighed with aggravation, for none of the other young women in town had ever given Rowdy Gates a second look—not until Doctor Gregory had had to shave him. Now it seemed every one of Calliope's friends turned to eye-batting coquettes whenever she saw him.

"Would you like a muffin?" Calliope asked. She lifted the cheesecloth that was covering the muffins in the basket she held. "They're apple, and I baked them fresh this morning."

Rowdy did grin a little then. "Thank you, Miss Calliope," he said as he took a muffin from the basket. He nodded, said, "You ladies have a nice day now," and stepped passed them into the jailhouse.

Calliope sighed with admiration of her heart's desire.

"He is so handsome!" Blanche sighed as well. "I envy the woman that captures his heart one day."

"Me too," Calliope admitted aloud. She sighed with longing. Quickly, however, she remembered that Blanche had hurried her outside in order to tell her something. And so she inquired of her friend, "And what is it that you want to tell me? For pity's sake, Sheriff Montrose is going to think we're up to some kind of mischief or something! You pulled me out of there like my bloomers were on fire, Blanche."

"Oh, that," Blanche said. "I swear, those deep green eyes of Rowdy Gates's nearly chased it from my mind. But I had to ask you...are you aware that your daddy refused Fox when he asked to come courtin' you?"

"What?" Calliope exclaimed in astonishment. Oh, she wasn't at all astonished that her father had refused Fox's request to court her—just that Fox had really, truly asked in the first place.

Blanche nodded emphatically. "It's true! Winnie told me that she heard her folks talkin' just yesterday...talkin' about how Judge Ipswich wouldn't give his permission for Fox to court you. Blanche said her parents weren't upset at all because they think Fox is too young to get serious with a young lady. But I guess Fox was pretty angry with your daddy. Winnie said his folks settled him down and suggested he move on—you know, think about other girls in town for a while."

When Calliope said nothing in response—for she was quite stunned that Fox had finally gone to her father to ask permission to court her—Blanche urged, "So…you didn't know? I mean, you didn't know Fox had gone to your father?"

Calliope shook her head. "I didn't," she answered.

"And…well, I'm guessin' you're not too upset that your father told Fox no—bein' that I don't think you ever liked Fox as much as he wanted you to," Blanche prodded.

Calliope smiled at her friend. "No. I didn't."

Blanche blushed a bit and ventured, "Then you don't mind if the rest of us available girls toss our lures in Fox's direction?"

Calliope giggled. "Not at all, Blanche," she answered. "You, of all people, know that I wouldn't have minded if you'd tossed your lures at him long ago."

"Oh good!" Blanche sighed. "I mean, I already told Sallie, Pauline, and Callie that I didn't think you'd mind at all. But I wanted to make sure I asked you first." Blanche paused a moment, seeming thoughtful. "I do think it's odd though…that Fox would go to your daddy without even askin' you if you wanted him to."

Calliope nodded and sighed. "I know. But unfortunately Fox Montrose thinks he's the sugar in every cookie on the face of the earth and that no other man might even begin to turn a woman's head."

Blanche laughed. "Oh, I know it! His head is as big as the Ackermans' barn!"

Calliope laughed too, though she felt guilty for doing so. "Poor Fox," she said. She shook her head.

"Come on," Blanche said, again linking arms with Calliope. "Let's go take some measurements so we can give Warren Ackerman a proper swallowtail suit coat for his weddin', shall we?"

Again Calliope giggled with delight. "Yes. Let's do just that!"

"Mornin', Rowdy," Sheriff Montrose greeted as Rowdy stepped into his office in the jailhouse.

At first, Rowdy was a little uncomfortable that Judge Ipswich was with the sheriff. But then he figured it was better to kill two birds with one stone—not to mention less time consuming.

"Mornin', Sheriff," Rowdy greeted in return. He nodded to the judge. "Mornin', Judge."

"Good morning, Rowdy," Judge Ipswich said, offering Rowdy his hand.

Rowdy struck hands with the judge and then Sheriff Montrose.

"What brings you by?" the sheriff inquired.

Rowdy inhaled a deep breath, exhaling as he said, "Well, I might as well get right down to it, Sheriff. And I'm glad you're here too, Judge…because I think we're about to have some trouble here in Meadowlark Lake."

Sheriff Montrose frowned, and so did Judge Ipswich.

"Have a seat, Rowdy," the sheriff said, nodding toward a nearby chair.

Sheriff Montrose leaned back against his desk, and Judge Ipswich remained standing.

Almost collapsing into the chair, Rowdy suddenly realized how tired he really was.

"Why do you say that, Rowdy?" Sheriff Montrose asked.

"I've seen a horse in town. A couple of times now I've seen it," Rowdy began. "It's an appaloosa."

Sheriff Montrose nodded. "Yep. I've seen it too. It's a nice mount. Very distinctive."

Judge Ipswich folded his arms across his chest. He nodded in the direction of the diner across the street. "Chestnut and white, right?"

"Yep. That's the one," Rowdy said, encouraged that Sheriff Montrose and Judge Ipswich were such watchful, wary men. "It belongs to an outlaw. Arness Morrison."

Sheriff Montrose stood straight then. "Arness Morrison? He's one of the Morrison brothers outta Tombstone, ain't he?"

"Yeah," Rowdy confirmed. "And the fact that he's been comin' through town...I'm thinkin' he's lookin' for someplace to hole up."

Judge Ipswich frowned. "He's looking for a town with lawmen who will allow him to tarry amongst good people while he does his outlawing elsewhere," he stated.

"I think so, yes, Judge," Rowdy admitted. "I talked to Lou Smith this mornin'. Seems he asked the fellow with the appaloosa...well, he asked his name this time around, and the man said his name was Arness. And I...well, I know for a fact that Arness Morrison owns a chestnut and white appaloosa named Pronto. And I know that appaloosa we've been seein' in Meadowlark Lake is it."

Sheriff Montrose exhaled a heavy sigh, removed his hat, and raked his fingers back through his hair.

"Arness Morrison. He rides with two of his brothers, ain't that right?" he asked.

"Yes, sir," Rowdy answered. "Carson and Walker Morrison."

"So we're expecting three outlaws to ride into Meadowlark Lake and ask the sheriff to give them asylum then?" Judge Ipswich inquired.

"At least three," Rowdy confirmed. "Maybe more. Arness and his two brothers, they're just the ringleaders. Sometimes they have two, maybe three other men ridin' with them."

"I don't like to hear this, that's for dang sure," Sheriff Montrose grumbled.

But it was Judge Ipswich who asked the question Rowdy expected to be asked.

"Tell me, Rowdy," the judge began, "why do you know so much about Arness Morrison and his brothers?"

Rowdy inhaled a deep breath of courage. Then he answered, "They tried to kill me once."

CHAPTER TEN

Lawson Ipswich arched his eyebrows, astounded, while Sheriff Dennison Montrose's mouth hung agape for a moment.

"They tried to kill you once?" Dennison finally managed to ask.

"Yes, sir, they did," Rowdy confirmed. "They gave me a hard beatin', tied me up, drug me behind a horse for about a mile, shot me twice, and left me to die in the desert."

Lawson exchanged glances with the sheriff. An unspoken understanding passed between them, both accepting that Rowdy had told them all that he wished to tell them about how he recognized Arness Morrison and his horse—at least for the time being.

Sheriff Montrose nodded and then asked, "When do you think they'll come askin' to hole up in Meadowlark Lake?"

Rowdy shrugged. "I don't really know. But since he's been here twice already that we know of, I'd expect it would be pretty soon. And he won't approach you alone, Sheriff. He'll have his men with him...for purposes of intimidation."

"Well, they ain't gonna hole up in my town," Dennison Montrose strongly affirmed. "I won't have them even ridin' through."

Rowdy nodded, and Lawson saw the relief in his expression.

"You're a good man, Sheriff," Rowdy said. "I figured you wouldn't want to have nothin' to do with it."

"But how do we prevent it?" Lawson inquired. "I'm assuming Morrison and his men will plan to use more than mere intimidation to secure their wishes."

Again Rowdy nodded, saying, "Yes...they will."

Sheriff Montrose was undaunted, however. "Then we deputize every able man in town and have them ready for a confrontation."

"Maybe," Rowdy agreed, though halfheartedly. He frowned, sighed, and shook his head. "Of course, maybe Arness is truly just travelin' through. Maybe he just went one way, stopped here for the night. Then when he went back...he stopped again."

Lawson's eyes narrowed as he studied Rowdy for a moment. The fact that Rowdy referred to the leader of the Morrison brothers' gang of outlaws by his first name was disconcerting. Rowdy Gates seemed to know a wealth of detail concerning Arness Morrison's horse as well.

Yet Lawson's instincts told him that Rowdy Gates was just what he appeared to be—a good, hard-working man who had seen a bit of trauma in his past.

"But then again, you might be correct that Texas John Slaughter finally had his fill of the Morrison brothers and banished them from Tombstone, and they're looking for some other town to loiter in," Lawson suggested.

Rowdy nodded. "Yes, sir. Maybe."

Sheriff Montrose exhaled a heavy sigh of discouragement. He removed his hat, tossed it on his desk, raked his hand through his hair again, and said, "Let me think this through for a bit. I don't want to alarm the entire town. But I need to be prepared too."

Lawson nodded. As disturbed as he was—as worried as he suddenly felt over his own family's safety, as well as the safety of the other citizens of Meadowlark Lake—he knew the sheriff needed some time to take a breath and strategize.

The sheriff looked to Rowdy then, offering a hand and saying, "Thank you, Rowdy. If you hadn't had your eyes open and your wits about you...well, I surely would not have been prepared if Arness Morrison and his men do come callin'."

Rowdy shook the sheriff's hand and said, "I hope I'm wrong, Sheriff."

"I do too," Sheriff Montrose agreed. "But my gut tells me you're probably not."

"Rowdy," Lawson said, offering his own hand to Rowdy then, "you're a good man. A man to be admired and emulated. I'm grateful to you as well."

Rowdy accepted Lawson's hand, giving it a firm shake. Lawson smiled. He could tell a lot about a man from the way he shook another man's hand. Rowdy's grip was strong, straightforward, and confident. It was the handshake of a good, honest man with a clear conscience, and Lawson was further assured that Rowdy Gates could be thoroughly trusted.

"Well, as much as I hated to be the harbinger of bad news, Sheriff, I feel a might better knowin' that the lawmen of the town are aware of things," Rowdy said. "I best get on with my day. Let me know if there's any way I can help."

"I will, Rowdy," Sheriff Montrose assured the man. "I most surely will."

Rowdy turned to leave but paused. Looking back to the sheriff and Lawson, he said, "I might as well tell you now…I'm a good shot. A *very* good shot. So if there comes a need, I'll do what I need to in defense of our town."

Sheriff Montrose nodded. "That's good to know, Rowdy. I appreciate your willin'ness, where all this is concerned."

"As do I," Lawson said.

Rowdy nodded then and left.

Lawson looked to Dennison. "Now that I think about it, Dennison—was he offering to be deputized, or warning us that he would do whatever needed to protect Meadowlark Lake regardless of the lawfulness of it?"

The sheriff shook his head. "I don't rightly know. But if Arness Morrison and his brothers mean to corrupt Meadowlark Lake, I gotta be honest. Shootin' them all dead might be our only option."

"I know," Lawson agreed—dishearteningly.

Judge Lawson Ipswich had sentenced outlaws before—many of them to hang. But somehow he imagined that an outlaw gang like the

Morrison brothers would choose to go out shooting rather than to be captured and stand before a judge. His anxieties over the safety of his family heightened.

"So…what do you think, Judge?" Sheriff Montrose asked, nodding in the direction of Rowdy's exit. "Former lawman? Or former outlaw?"

Lawson considered Dennison's question. Rowdy Gates was a good man; and least he was in the present time. Lawson really couldn't imagine Rowdy running with outlaws.

"Former lawman," Lawson answered at last. "Why else would the Morrison brothers try to kill him?"

Sheriff Montrose sighed. "Well, in my experience, outlaws like Arness Morrison are capable of anything…even killin' their own men." He paused a moment, however, and then added, "But I think you're right. Rowdy Gates strikes me as a man with a sound mind as well as a sound moral character." He nodded. "Yep, I'm with you on thinkin' ol' Rowdy Gates was a lawman at some point in his past life."

"Well, I'll get back to the courthouse and to my own work for the day, Dennison," Lawson said. "I know you have a lot to consider. Just let me know what you decide when you decide it."

Lawson struck hands with his friend, and the sheriff said, "I will, Judge. As soon as I figure it all out."

"Thank you, Sheriff," Lawson said.

Leaving the jailhouse then, Lawson headed back to the courthouse. Off in the distance, he could see Rowdy Gates riding in the direction of his home—not toward the mill.

"After all, Dodger," Rowdy said as he sat under the willow next to Dodger, "I own the mill, don't I?" He shrugged, adding, "Of course, no one but me and Ben Mulholland know it. Still, as the owner, I oughta be able to take a mornin' off to catch up on some sleep, right? I did send that Ackerman boy over to the mill to tell the boys I'd be tardy. So why not have me a little rest here in the shade, right, boy?"

Dodger didn't answer, of course. But Rowdy looked over to where he lay resting in peace all the same. He chuckled when he saw fresh flowers had already been put in the old medicine bottle at the head of the grave.

"That little Ipswich girl…she sure gets out early in the day, doesn't she?" he chuckled. He laughed out loud and then said, "That poor cat of hers! I ain't never seen a cat go through what that feline does. I wonder how that leashed-up cat feels about walkin' out here to put flowers on a dog's grave."

Rowdy closed his eyes, a smile lingering on his face. Thoughts of Shay Ipswich always led to thoughts of Calliope Ipswich. He could see her in his mind at that moment—the way she'd looked the day before when he'd shown her and her little sister how to sail frogs. She'd been barefoot, and several blades of meadow grass still lingered in her beautiful hair here and there, evidence she'd been stretched out on the ground at some point. Calliope's smile had been as bright as the summer sun and her eyes as blue as the summer sky. And Rowdy Gates decided to let the loveliness of Calliope Ipswich linger in his mind, instead of thinking about the fact that Arness might be back.

"Calliope," Rowdy mumbled as he began to drift into a light slumber. "Even your name is pretty."

"Oh, for Pete's sake, hold still, Warren!" Sallie ordered her little brother. "I swear you're as wiggly as a worm in a rainstorm."

But Warren frowned. Looking to Calliope, he asked, "You sure I ain't gonna look like a fool in this getup, Calliope?"

Calliope smiled at Warren, stroking his cheek with the back of her hand with reassurance. "I'm certain of it, Warren. Why, you're going to be the handsomest groom anybody has ever seen!"

Warren blushed and asked, "Do you think Shay will think I'm handsome?"

Calliope's smile widened. She exchanged amused glances with Sallie.

Leaning closer to Warren where he stood on the stool being fitted for his suit coat, Calliope whispered, "She already does," and winked at him. His blush deepened, and Calliope was delighted.

"Calliope," Evangeline called from nearby.

Calliope turned to face her sister, who was busy fitting Mamie and Effie Longfellow for their flower girl dresses.

"Yes?" Calliope asked as she strode to where her sister stood with Mamie Longfellow standing on a chair.

"What do you think about the neckline here?" Evangeline asked. She draped the pretty butter-yellow fabric that would soon be Mamie's dress across Mamie from shoulder to shoulder. "I'm thinking just a wisp of a sleeve, with a lower neckline and a light swag of fabric across the front. What do you think?"

"Hmm," Calliope pondered as she studied Mamie. She glanced for a moment to Floyd Longfellow. But his attention was rapt by Evangeline, and Calliope did wonder if maybe Mr. Longfellow agreed to allow his girls to participate in the wedding simply because he was charmed by Evie. "I like that," Calliope concluded at last. "I think you're right. It'll give the girls a somewhat angelic appearance." She laughed as Evangeline nodded. "And you needn't ask me my opinion on things like this, Evie. You're the best seamstress in the family!"

"No, I'm not," Evangeline countered. "And I want to be sure we capture the vision in your mind."

"Well, these dresses will be lovely on the girls," Calliope said. Taking little Effie's hand in her own—for Effie stood looking rather neglected as Mamie was being fitted—Calliope knelt down in front of her and said, "You and Mamie will be just so adorable and lovely, Effie! And we'll make sure you have some lovely flowers to carry along with you."

Effie smiled at Calliope, grateful for the attention.

"Miss Evangeline will fit your dress just after she's finished fitting Mamie's, all right?" Calliope asked the toddler.

"Yes, ma'am," Effie answered.

Calliope stood once more, turning to Floyd Longfellow. "Oh, thank you so much for letting the girls help us with the play, Mr.

Longfellow. They're just what we needed to make everything else so perfect."

Mr. Longfellow, who looked just like an older version of his son, nodded to Calliope. "Well, I just couldn't make myself refuse your sister…bein' that Evangeline asked so nicely and all."

Calliope smiled at him, for his eyes had fairly twinkled when he'd spoken of Evangeline.

"Well, thank you again," Calliope told him. "I'm sure you'll enjoy watching them at the performance."

"Oh, Kizzy," Calliope heard Dora Montrose exclaim, "that beadwork on the bodice of Shay's dress is marvelous. How lovely!"

Kizzy smiled and said, "Thank you, Dora. I've been workin' on it for so long now that I can't believe I've almost finished."

"Shay's dress is beautiful, Kizzy," Calliope exclaimed, moving to stand by her stepmother.

"Well, whether it's for a play or in years to come the real event, I want my daughter's weddin' dress to be perfect for her," Kizzy laughed.

Dora sighed. "Sometimes I wonder if Winnie will ever settle her mind on a young man and get married." Lowering her voice so that only Kizzy and Calliope could hear, Dora added, "I'm afraid my daughter is a fickle fanny when it comes to young men. One day she swears she's in love with Dex Longfellow; the next she swears to be in love with Tate Chesterfield. Why, just yesterday, she'd determined that Rowdy Gates was the man she wanted to marry." Dora sighed and shook her head.

Calliope felt nausea rise from her stomach all the way up into her throat. It burned so sour that she couldn't have begun to speak in that instant, even if she could've thought what to say.

Still, Kizzy soothed Calliope's anxiety a bit when she said, "Somehow I see Winnie with someone like Tate more than I do Rowdy." Calliope felt the color drain from her face when Kizzy looked up to her then, inquiring, "Don't you, Calliope?"

"Um…y-yes," Calliope stammered. "I think Tate and Winnie would make a lovely couple."

Did Kizzy know? Did she know that Calliope hoped to win Rowdy one day? Had Shay broken her promise and told her mother of Calliope's secret bliss? But then Calliope remembered that Kizzy was a gypsy—more gypsy than even Shay—and Shay had guessed at it. Thus, it stood to reason that Kizzy had guessed at it as well.

"Warren Ackerman, you behave yourself!" Mrs. Ackerman screeched, startling everyone.

"I just wanna practice on her a bit, Mama," Warren laughed.

Calliope and the others looked up to see Warren chasing Shay around the inside of the Ackermans' barn. He still wore his half-sewn swallowtail suit coat, and Shay was giggling with delight.

"You do *not* practice a weddin' kiss, Warren!" Mrs. Ackerman scolded. "And get back here and let your sister finish fittin' that coat proper!"

But Warren had already caught up with Shay. As the little boy took hold of Shay's shoulders, spinning her around to face him, Calliope giggled with delight when the boy planted a kiss right on her lips.

Shay blushed and pushed herself out of his grasp. "I oughta slap you, Warren Ackerman!" Shay exclaimed—although it was obvious she was elated about Warren's having kissed her. "And I bet you can't catch me again," Shay giggled, offering further proof to everyone in the barn that she was enchanted by Warren's attention.

"I am so sorry, Kizzy," Mrs. Ackerman apologized as she came to stand near Calliope. "That boy just about runs me ragged most of the time. I hope you're not too upset that he's a bit sweet on your Shay."

Kizzy smiled. "Not at all, Ellen," she assured her friend. "Lawson and I adore Warren! And I'll venture to say my Shay does too. And after all, there's no harm in a little game of kiss-and-chase at their age."

Calliope smiled, glad that both Kizzy and Mrs. Ackerman understood children's infatuations. She thought back on something Amoretta had told her just after she and Brake were married. Amoretta had told Calliope that Brake had once chased Amoretta into Mr. Ackerman's hayfield last autumn. Naturally, Amoretta had swiped Brake's hat from his head and had run as fast as she could for the hayfield. But once Brake had caught her—and Amoretta sorely wanted him to catch her—he'd pushed her into the belly of a haystack and kissed her something fierce! Amoretta had confessed that kissing Brake in the haystack that evening had been one of the most marvelous experiences she had ever had.

Calliope sighed, wishing Rowdy Gates would chase her into a haystack and kiss her—wishing Rowdy Gates would chase her anywhere and kiss her.

"Seems to me kiss-and-chase would be fun at any age," Calliope said. As everyone looked at her with wide, wondering eyes, she gasped. "Oh dear! Did I say that out loud?"

"You certainly did," Dora Montrose laughed. "And I'll say this: I'll confirm that kiss-and-chase *is* fun at any age." She continued to smile. "To this very day, I just love it when my Dennison chases me around the kitchen table and then catches me in his arms and kisses me."

"Oh, me too!" Kizzy agreed.

Ellen Ackerman quirked one eyebrow and smiled. "Well, how delicious is it to stand here and imagine both the sheriff and the county judge playin' at kiss-and-chase?" she asked.

"Very fun, if I do say so myself," Dora answered.

Everyone laughed then, and Calliope sighed with satisfaction. She knew a Tom Thumb wedding would bring the folks in Meadowlark Lake closer together. And the proof sat all around her in the Ackermans' barn.

CHAPTER ELEVEN

The last lamp was lit for the night. Most nights he rode right home to an empty house, a bland supper, and retiring to bed early. But this night—this night Rowdy was already so tired he just sat right down under the last street lamp near the Ipswich house. He wasn't ready to leave town for the isolation of his own house.

He was wound up about the fact that Arness might turn up again. But he'd checked the diner and the livery when he'd lit the lamps and found no chestnut and white appaloosa—and no Arness.

The other reason Rowdy didn't want to hurry home was a feeling that had begun to grow in his chest—an emotion. He was beginning to become attached to the folks in Meadowlark Lake. He'd found, of recent, that he was starting to feel amused in the company of the men at the mill. He liked talking to Sheriff Montrose and Judge Ipswich whenever his path crossed theirs. He enjoyed discussing horses with Lou Smith and hearing Mrs. Perry go on and on and on about the commodities she'd managed to procure for the general store—whether or not Mr. Perry agreed that they were necessary.

Rowdy was beginning to realize that more than just his stiff knee had healed over the past few months; his soul had begun to heal as well. Glancing back to the Ipswich house, standing in the dark with bright-lit windows and beckoning like the essence of heaven, Rowdy admitted to himself that Calliope Ipswich had a hand in his healing.

The moment Judge Ipswich had moved his family to town, Rowdy had started to feel like maybe life wasn't so miserable and hopeless after all. Oh, the other Ipswich girls were pretty too, but there was something different about Calliope. It was as if a bright, radiant ray of sunshine had been sifted into her eyes—into her heart and soul. Her eyes were the color of the noonday sky but sparkled like stars had fallen into them.

Furthermore, there was a sincerity about Calliope that Rowdy had learned was a rare thing in a person. She meant it when she smiled and said she was happy; she meant it when she smiled at *him*.

"Are you just plum tuckered out tonight, Mr. Gates?"

Rowdy startled a bit at the sound of Shay Ipswich's young voice.

He looked to his right to see her standing there, holding onto the handle of her cat's leash. The old marmalade cat sat down on its haunches, blinking slowly as if being led on a leash to a streetlamp at night were the most normal thing in all the world for a feline.

He grinned at Shay, noting the sincere compassion in her expression.

"I am plum tuckered, darlin'," he admitted. "And what are you and Molly doin' out so late?"

Shay sighed and glanced to her cat. "Well, Molly saw you sittin' out here all alone, and she figured we best come out and check up on you...you know, make sure you're feelin' all right and things."

Rowdy's smile broadened. "Well, thank you, Molly, for your kind concern," he said, addressing the cat. The cat simply looked at him and produced another slow blink.

"I got my first kiss today, Mr. Gates," Shay announced in a whisper.

"You did?" Rowdy exclaimed as the girl blushed and smiled with joy.

"Mm hmm," she affirmed. "Warren Ackerman chased me around in his daddy's barn 'til he caught me! Then he kissed me...right on the lips!"

"And did you like it?" Rowdy chuckled. "Is Warren Ackerman a good kisser?"

Shay shrugged, still blushing—still smiling. "Well, I don't have anything to compare it with…but I liked the way he kissed me, so I guess so."

Rowdy nodded. "Then I'd say ol' Warren's a good kisser all right."

Shay Ipswich cocked her head to one side. "Are *you* a good kisser, Mr. Gates?"

Rowdy blushed a bit. He rubbed the whiskers on his chin and answered, "I ain't never had any complaints…so I guess I am."

"Hmm," Shay hummed. "Well, it just so happens that my sister Calliope is about to go stargazin' tonight out in the grassy space behind our house. Maybe you could sorta wander on out there and look at the stars with her. Then maybe you could give her a kiss like Warren gived me today. And then maybe Calliope can tell you for sure that you're a good kisser."

Rowdy took off his hat and raked a hand through his hair. He chuckled then and asked, "What kind of mischief are you up to exactly, Miss Shay Ipswich?"

Shay smiled. "I'm up to usin' my gypsy magic to make people's dreams come true, Mr. Gates. That's all," she answered plainly.

"Makin' people's dreams come true, huh?" Rowdy teased.

But Shay was undaunted. "Go on, Mr. Gates," she told him. "Go on out there and look at the stars with Calliope." She smiled at him, winked, and then turned and started to walk away. "Come on, Molly. We best be gettin' inside before Mama starts to worry about us."

Rowdy shook his head as mingled disbelief and curiosity rattled around in his head. The little Ipswich girl sure was something. Surely she didn't expect him to just saunter out to the grassy expanse behind the Ipswich home, scoop Calliope Ipswich up in his arms, and get to sparking with her.

He sighed as he leaned back against the lamppost once more. But as his thoughts immediately turned to the possible impending trouble with Arness, an interesting idea washed over him.

"Why not?" he mumbled to himself. "If Arness tries to kill me again, he might just do it this time. So why not take a chance on a little girl's fancy?"

Before he could think better of it, Rowdy was on his feet. Making sure Tucker was still tied up well enough to the hitching post nearby, Rowdy straightened his posture and headed for the grassy expanse behind the Ipswich home that separated the woods from the town.

The moment he rounded the corner of the Ipswich house, he could see the flicker of a lantern light a ways off in the grasses.

"Well, I guess that would be Calliope out there," he muttered under his breath. His courage was wavering. But once again he remembered Arness and his brothers might well get the better of Rowdy Gates in the end. So why let fear of rejection stop him from seeing whether Shay Ipswich really was a little gypsy who was trying to make people's dreams come true? After all, Rowdy had been dreaming of kissing Calliope Ipswich since the day he first saw her.

Calliope spread the blanket she'd brought with her out on a space of shorter grass. Setting the lamp to one side, she stretched out on the blanket.

She crossed her feet at her ankles, tucked her hands behind her head, and sighed, "Ahhh! Serenity...sweet serenity."

"Evenin', Miss Calliope."

The sound of Rowdy's voice startled her but only for a moment. As she looked up to see him approaching through the grass, she smiled, her heart swelling with such complete joy that she thought it might burst from her chest.

"Why, Mr. Gates!" she greeted. "What brings you out here tonight?"

Rowdy smiled at her and asked, "I'm not botherin' you, am I?"

"Oh, my goodness, no!" she assured him.

"I just saw your little sister out by the last lamppost this side of town, and she told me you'd come out here to look at the stars tonight," he explained. "And bein' that I'm somewhat of a stargazer myself, I thought maybe you wouldn't mind if I joined you."

"Oh, I can't think of anything more delightful," Calliope chirped. She knew she was too obvious in her excitement, but she couldn't help it! She was so overjoyed to see him—so surprised—so blissful in the fact that he meant to join her—that she could hardly contain her emotions.

She blushed as Rowdy stretched out on the blanket next to her. He tucked his arms beneath his head and sighed. "I hope I'm not spoilin' your serenity."

"Not at all, Mr. Gates," she truthfully told him.

Calliope bit her lip to keep from squealing with elation. Rowdy Gates was right next to her! He was so close she could feel the warmth of him—smell the scent of leather and grasses and grain that was his.

"I do like to look at the stars," he said. "I take a bit of time almost every night to look up at them—unless it's cloudy and a body can't see them at all, that is."

"I love them too," Calliope agreed. "I do know a few constellations, but I prefer just to watch them wink at me individually or as a whole. It's too much work to try and chart out the constellations."

"Yeah, it kind of takes the relaxation out of lookin' at the stars if a body spends the whole time tryin' to be smart about it," he concurred. "I do like the Big Dipper though. It just sorta jumps out at you. You don't have to work at seein' it."

Calliope smiled. "Me too." She looked over to Rowdy. "I didn't know you liked the stars, Mr. Gates."

He looked over to her, and when he did, Calliope was fairly certain she'd begun to melt. Even for the darkness of the night, the green of his eyes was apparent—apparent for they captured the light of the stars perfectly.

"I expect there's a lot of things I like that you don't know about, Miss Calliope," he said in a low, enthralling tone.

He grinned at her then—an alluring, seductive sort of grin—and Calliope held her breath for a moment. She sensed something emanating from him, but she wasn't quite certain what it was. She did know, however, that she felt breathless, overly thrilled somehow.

Letting her instincts guide her, she asked, "Like what? What's something else you like, besides the stars?"

Rowdy looked back up into the sky, exhaled, and said, "I like you. That's somethin' I like besides the stars, Miss Calliope. You."

Calliope gulped and looked away from Rowdy and back up to the stars. "I expect you like most people in town, Mr. Gates."

"I like some people in town, yes," he admitted. "But not the way I like you."

"Are...are you just teasing me, Mr. Gates?" she asked, rendered more breathless than ever by the hope suddenly flaming inside her.

"Not at all, Miss Calliope," he answered without pause. "In fact, Fox Montrose told me that he went to see your daddy...asked him if he could come courtin' you with serious intentions. When I heard your daddy said no, I was mighty relieved."

Calliope squeezed her eyes shut for a moment. Was she dreaming? Opening her eyes, however, she turned her head to see that Rowdy Gates was indeed lying next to her on the blanket.

"Now tell me about this Tom Thumb weddin' you ladies in town are plannin' out," he said.

Calliope giggled. "Oh, you don't really want me to tell you all about that, do you?" she asked—still euphoric over his saying he liked her, that he was relieved when her father had denied Fox.

"I most certainly do," he assured her. "From what I understand, it's really gonna be somethin' to behold."

Calliope smiled and said, "I certainly hope so. Everyone is working so hard on getting everything ready. We've almost got the clothes all made for the boys. We finished up Warren Ackerman's suit today. All the boys will have them—swallowtail suits, all matching—and bow ties for each boy too" she explained. "Naturally, the girls' gowns are taking quite some time, but they're going to be so lovely. Of course, Shay is pretending that she is quite disturbed about marrying Warren Ackerman. But I know that, in truth, she's over the moon for him. I mean, imagine it—you're sweeter than honey on somebody, and you get to pretend to marry him? I would've savored such a thing for years to come if I'd had that opportunity at her age."

"It seems like a whole lotta work, just for a bit of fun," Rowdy suggested.

Calliope sighed and nodded in agreement. Yet the smile never left her face. "It is a lot of work. But just imagine how everyone will enjoy it! Nothing like this has ever happened in Meadowlark Lake, I'm quite sure of that. And folks need something fun, entertaining, and carefree to look forward to. It helps make work, struggle, and disheartening events seem tolerable...if a body has something to look forward to."

Rowdy nodded, for what she said was true.

"I mean, consider this," she went on. "Even for all the terrible, frightening, tragic events of last All Hallow's Eve...even for all of it, I can't *wait* for the town gathering at the Ackermans'. And that jack-o'-lantern festival...I'm simply giddy with anticipation! And that's why I thought we should have a Tom Thumb wedding here in Meadowlark Lake—to give us all something to look forward to."

Rowdy glanced over to Calliope for a moment. He could've sworn there was a radiance about her—a light that encircled her beautiful blonde head like a halo. He thought then that Calliope Ipswich made everyone feel important, happy, and hopeful the way she made him feel.

"I've never been to a Tom Thumb weddin'," he commented. "Is everythin' just like a normal weddin'?"

Calliope answered, "Yes and no. The bridesmaids and groomsmen, the lavish clothing, the flowers, and the cake at the reception afterward are made to mimic a real wedding. But the vows..." She interrupted herself with a giggle. "The vows certainly are not!"

"They're not?" he asked.

"Oh, heavens no!" she answered. "They're quite ridiculous—things like making the bride promise to close her eyes to the groom's faults and failings and only open her lips every moment of the day in praise of his virtues…or making the groom tell the bride her mother may only visit once every quarter of the year." She paused a moment and then sighed. "Evangeline, Amoretta, and I have written darling little vows for the children to exchange. And of course, we *are* going to have the bride and groom kiss. That usually is omitted in many Tom Thumb weddings. But we want the kiss." She giggled again, adding, "And Shay was not at all averse to the suggestion…which is only further evidence that she's sweet on the Ackerman boy. Oh, it's going to be so fun! You'll enjoy it so much more than you think you will, Mr. Gates. I can promise you!" Calliope laughed wholeheartedly, adding, "Oh, I can't wait to see the faces of everyone when Sallie Ackerman's little sister performs 'Oh, Promise Me'!"

"Why? Doesn't she sing well?" Rowdy asked.

"Oh, but she does!" Calliope exclaimed. "Like an angel. But no one knows it because she's never sung in front of anyone before…well, other than her parents and me and Evangeline. It's bound to be one of the highlights of the event. I simply cannot wait for it all to come together and for everyone to smile for days and weeks afterward just thinking about it."

Rowdy chuckled. The young woman was enchanting! It was, of course, the longest conversation he'd ever had with her—and he enjoyed the fact that it was about something she was so happy about.

"You will attend, won't you, Mr. Gates?" she ventured. He looked over to see her staring at him with an expression of worry.

He smiled and answered, "Of course I'll attend, Miss Calliope. I wouldn't miss it for anything."

He saw her visibly gulp, even for the fact that the only light around them was moonlight, starlight, and a little lantern's flicker.

"W-will you be attending *with* anyone, Mr. Gates?" she ventured.

He smiled at her, wholeheartedly smiled. "Well, maybe if I can muster up the courage to ask the judge's permission…maybe I could attend with you, Miss Calliope."

Her face lit up with so much radiance and obvious pleasure, Rowdy's heart warmed instantly.

"Really?" she asked in a whisper.

"Well, if you'd have me for your escort, I surely would like to be him," he answered.

Calliope didn't know whether to faint from bliss or scream with rapture. Rowdy Gates liked her—he did! She could see it in his eyes. All the weeks and months she'd spent dreaming about him, wishing she could capture his attention—could it be that she'd held it captive all along?

"I'd be honored if you'd be my escort, Mr. Gates," she said breathlessly.

"Thank you, Miss Calliope," he said. "Now all that's left for me to do is see if your daddy will allow me to be your escort."

"I'm certain he will!" she exclaimed.

But Rowdy looked back up into the sky then and mumbled, "Well…we'll have to see."

His smile faded, and Calliope wondered why on earth he would think her father would deny him permission to escort her to the Tom Thumb wedding.

He sighed then and said, "I suppose I should be headin' home. Tomorrow comes faster than I always think it will."

Calliope felt sorry. She'd kept him far too long. He worked hard at the mill and didn't have the luxury of sleeping in a bit longer if he had the mind to, as she did.

"Oh, I'm so sorry to have kept you!" she apologized, sitting up.

Rowdy rose to his feet, offering a hand to assist her to standing. She smiled, delighted at the thrilling sensation that traveled through her at the feel of his warm, callused palm as she placed her hand in his.

"I lose track of time when I'm out looking at the stars," she said—even though they hadn't been stargazing for very long in truth.

"Me too," Rowdy said, grinning at her. She was disappointed when he released her hand—thought she felt more chilled than she had a moment before.

"Oh, I almost forgot the blanket," she mumbled, turning and beginning to stoop to pick up the blanket she'd brought.

"I'll get that," Rowdy said, however. He swooped the blanket up with one hand, tossing it over his shoulder.

Calliope picked up the lantern, and it cast its bright light out over the grassy expanse. She gasped a little, astonished when Rowdy took the lamp from her, puffing into the top and extinguishing the flame inside.

"Oh, I don't think we need that," he said.

Calliope glanced up to him, awed at how well her eyes had adjusted to the darkness, for she could see him quite clearly. Naturally, the full moon overhead lent its silver mist of shimmering luminance to the night, and coupled with the twinkle of the stars, Calliope fancied it would be quite easy to walk back to the house without the lantern. After all, starlight was always preferable to lamplight when one was out for the purpose of admiring the stars.

"You might should take my arm," he said, holding his crooked arm toward her. "Just in case you stumble on somethin'."

A quiet giggle of delight escaped Calliope's throat, even for all her efforts to keep it from doing so. Walking home arm in arm with Rowdy Gates? It was the stuff of fantasy! Taking his arm, she smiled up at him. He nodded and grinned at her.

They didn't speak as they walked toward the house. Calliope felt that, like her, Rowdy was enjoying the ambiance of the night—the crickets' soft song, the low croaking of frogs in the distance. A soft breeze caressed the blades of grass at their feet, and the scent of someone's hearth fire lent comfort to the air.

All too soon, they'd reached the back porch of the Ipswich home.

"Well, here you go," Rowdy said as he placed the lantern and blanket on the back porch.

Calliope felt as if her heart had suddenly dropped into the bottom of her stomach. She didn't want to part company with Rowdy—not in that moment—not ever!

"Thank you for looking at the stars with me," she ventured. "I know you probably had much more important things you needed to do at home this evening."

"Nope."

"Well, thank you all the same," Calliope said, smiling.

He was so handsome—sinfully handsome! And he was kind—so kind—and so strong. Yet all at once it seemed he looked a little downhearted. Calliope's instinct was always to try and cheer anyone who might not be feeling the happiest they'd ever felt. And Rowdy Gates certainly qualified as someone she didn't want to see feeling less than cheerful.

Thus, she rambled on. "I still don't feel like I'll ever be able to repay you for saving me at the millpond. Peach pie just doesn't seem to go far enough. And you were so kind to make the paper boats and spend the time down at the stream with Shay and me. I know it meant a lot to her. So…thank you, again."

Raising herself on her tiptoes and placing her hands on Rowdy's shoulders to steady herself, Calliope placed a soft, lingering kiss on the man's cheek—the way she'd done the day she and Shay had taken the pie to him.

Again she relished the feel of his warm skin and prickly whiskers against her lips. "Thank you," she whispered into his ear.

She promised herself she would always remember the way he smelled in that instant—of meadow grass and leather, of having lingered in the evening air stargazing with her. She inhaled the masculine aroma of his face once more, not wanting to give him up.

And then, the very moment she meant to release him, Calliope's breath caught in her chest as she heard Rowdy mumble, "You're welcome, Miss Calliope"—as she felt his lips press to her cheek in a tender kiss in return.

"I suppose if that little Ackerman boy can gather up the gumption to kiss little Shay," he began in a lowered voice, "I oughta be able to gather up enough to give you a proper 'you're welcome,' shouldn't I?"

Calliope blushed with the anticipation of paradise—with the thrill of possibility. Did he mean to kiss her again? To bless her cheek with another, perhaps more lingering, caress of his lips?

"Why would you need to gather up some gumption, Mr. Gates?" she whispered, although bashfully. "It's not like I wouldn't be accepting of...of a 'you're welcome' from you."

Was he understanding her correctly? Was she implying to him that she'd actually allow him to kiss her? By the glistening anticipation in her eyes, Rowdy knew that she would—that she wanted him to.

Maybe little Shay Ipswich really was as observant as she claimed to be. Of course, what girl wouldn't be a little sweet on a man who'd jumped into a millpond with her? Either way, Rowdy's mouth was watering for wanting to kiss Calliope so badly. And so he decided to risk it. After all, what did he have to lose? Arness might well kill him in the near future, so why not have a taste of heaven before he got there?

Calliope was again rendered breathless as Rowdy unexpectedly reached out, taking her face between his warm, strong hands.

"You're welcome, Miss Calliope," he said in a lowered voice.

He kissed her then; Rowdy Gates kissed her! Not on the cheek but square on the lips. Yet it was over too soon, and Calliope felt not only disappointment but also extreme inadequacy.

"But I wasn't ready!" she exclaimed in a whisper.

Rowdy grinned. "You weren't ready?"

"No, I wasn't," she said, shaking her head. "And what if...what if that was my only chance? My only chance to prove to you that...what if something happens, and you never—?"

"Shhh," Rowdy shushed.

"But...but..." she stammered.

"Shhh," he shushed again. Still grinning her, he asked, "Do you think you're ready now?"

Calliope exhaled with relief and nodded. "Yes. At least...I think I am. But what if I'm not, and you—?"

"Shhh," Rowdy shushed. "A body can't always be ready for everything, Calliope. Sometimes you just gotta jump right in when the opportunity presents itself."

Rowdy kissed her again then—pressed his mouth to her lips, sending her mind spinning, her skin rippling with goose bumps, and causing her limbs to feel limp as a dishcloth. Somehow Calliope managed to return his kiss, and it prompted him to kiss her again—and again.

They were kissing—standing under the starry, moonlit sky, kissing. Rowdy's kiss was consuming in its proficiency—in the way it made Calliope feel powerful and weak in the same moment. She hadn't even realized it when it happened—when the transition from a soft, purely simple kiss to that of a more fervent exchange occurred. She hadn't even realized she knew how to respond to such a kiss as Rowdy was applying to her mouth—warm, moist, demanding, and intensely passionate.

Somehow Calliope found herself bound in his strong arms—held securely against his firm, warm body. Somehow her arms had encircled his neck, her fingers having woven themselves through his hair at the back of his head.

Rowdy eased their affectionate exchange. With a heavy sigh, he released Calliope, and she sensed that he wanted her to step back from him.

"I best be gettin' on home," he said. His eyes were fixed on hers and filled with desire.

"Tomorrow always comes faster than you think it will," Calliope whispered. She grinned a little, hoping he would smile back at her—reassure her that he still liked her after kissing her.

Rowdy did smile at her, and Calliope began to breathe more easily.

"Yes, it does," he confirmed. He started to turn but paused, looking back at her. "Is it still all right with you if I ask your daddy if I can accompany you to your little sister's weddin'?"

"Of course it is!" Calliope softly exclaimed.

He nodded, bending the brim of his hat and saying, "Good night then, Miss Calliope Ipswich."

"Good night, Mr. Rowdy Gates," she said. And she watched him walk away until he'd rounded the corner of the house and she couldn't see him anymore.

CHAPTER TWELVE

When Calliope entered the kitchen the next morning, she was still enjoying the lingering euphoria of Rowdy Gates's kisses. She had spent most of her sleepless night convincing herself that it really *had* happened—that Rowdy had gazed up at the stars with her, walked her back to the house, and then kissed her. Yet she knew it hadn't been a dream. The way her lips tingled at the memory—the way her mouth warmed and her heart raced as she thought of it—if her mind still doubted she lived it for certain, her physical senses proved it.

"Good mornin', Calliope," Shay greeted.

"Good morning, Shay Shay," Calliope said, smiling at her little sister as she took her seat at the breakfast table.

"How were the stars last night?" Shay asked.

Calliope's eyes narrowed with suspicion as she looked to Shay. "Lovely as always. Why do you ask?" Calliope answered.

Shay shrugged. "I just thought maybe they were lovelier than usual last night, that's all."

Evangeline startled everyone when she burst into the kitchen by way of the back porch door.

"I've just been to the general store to check our post—" Evangeline began.

"And you got another letter from Jennie?" Shay interrupted.

"Well, no," Evangeline continued. "But this parcel came from Amoretta!" she squealed with delight, producing the brown parcel she'd been holding behind her back.

"The invitations!" Calliope and Kizzy exclaimed in unison.

"Amoretta has finished them already?" Calliope asked as Evangeline set the parcel on the table and began to untie the twine that bound it.

"It would seem so," Evangeline confirmed. "Of course, we want to make certain she hasn't forgotten anyone, so it's very good that she's sent them this quickly."

"Very good indeed," Kizzy agreed. "I would hate for anyone in town, or close around town, to be left out. We must make sure there's an invitation for everyone—every family or singular person."

"Yes," Calliope said, nodding. She frowned a moment and looked up to Kizzy, asking, "Are we quite sure we have the most complete list of citizens? I worry so that we've missed someone."

All the females in the room gasped, looking to Lawson in astonishment when he put his hand on the parcel to keep Evangeline from opening it.

"Before you girls plunge into all this wedding preparation, again," he said, "I have something I'd like to share with you."

Shay leaned close to Calliope and whispered, "Remember... pretend to be surprised."

"What?" Calliope asked.

"Of course, Daddy," Evangeline encouraged her father, however. "What is it?"

Kizzy's scarlet blush tumbled Calliope's memory back to the secret Shay had inadvertently revealed the day she and Shay had sailed frogs with Rowdy Gates.

She smiled as her father took Kizzy's hand, winked at her, and then announced, "Well, come November we'll be having a new addition to the family, my girls. Kizzy's carrying a baby." He smiled at Shay, cupping her chin in one strong hand as he said, "I'm afraid you won't be the baby in the Ipswich family for much longer, my angel."

But Shay giggled, leapt from her chair, and ran to where her mother stood, holding a plate of breakfast ham. "Oh, Mama! You know I've been wanting a baby for so long!" she said, throwing her little arms around her mother's waist. Turning to where Lawson sat, she hugged him about the neck and chirped, "And I don't mind not bein' the baby anymore, Daddy. It's about time I grew up a little bit. After all, I *am* gettin' married in a few weeks."

Everyone laughed as Lawson's strong arms enveloped his youngest daughter in a loving hug. "You may be getting married in a few weeks, my Shay," Lawson said, kissing her cheek, "but you'll always be my little girl. All right?"

"I know, Daddy," Shay sighed.

Calliope felt her eyes brimming with tears of happiness. How wonderful it was that her father and Kizzy were going to have a baby. Babies always brought more joy and love into a home than even there existed in it before.

She looked to Evangeline to see that her eyes were filled with tears as well. And then an unspoken understanding passed between them, and they both hopped up out of their chairs, racing to Kizzy and flinging their arms around her.

"Oh, Kizzy!" Calliope exclaimed as tears spilled over her cheeks. "How wonderful it will be! A new baby to cuddle and love? You're heaven-sent to us, Kizzy. Heaven-sent!"

As Evangeline wept over the joyous announcement—as the family exchanged hugs of happiness, hope, and glorious anticipation of new life—Calliope thought of Rowdy. She thought of Rowdy—thought of his handsome face and delicious kiss—and she couldn't keep from daydreaming of how wonderful it would be to one day hold a baby of her own in her arms—a baby that looked like his or her father—a baby who looked like Rowdy.

"I'm thinkin' we need to let the townfolks know, Judge," Sheriff Dennison said. He shook his head with discouragement. "I sent a telegram out last night, down to Tombstone."

Lawson knew what Dennison was going to say before he even said it. But he held his tongue anyway, hoping he was wrong.

But he wasn't.

"Seems the Morrison brothers left Tombstone about a month ago," the sheriff explained. "They've been causin' a bit of trouble here and there. Seems they can't find a town that will put up with them."

Lawson nodded. "They are looking for a place to hole up…as Rowdy feared," he said.

"It would seem so," the sheriff confirmed. "And it wouldn't be right to leave folks ignorant of what might happen. Anyhow, if there's a shootin' or anything that erupts, I want folks to know what to do…who should shoot and who shouldn't."

"You're a very wise man, Dennison," Lawson said. "And I agree. When people are frightened and unprepared, that's when the innocent are hurt…or killed. So what do you propose? A town meeting?"

"I'm thinkin' we tell the men first," Dennison answered. "We come up with a strategy, and then we tell the men, and they can prepare their families from there. I don't want a town meetin' where women are ruffled up into a panic over the safety of their children."

"I understand…and I agree," Lawson said. He thought of Kizzy and the baby growing inside of her—of little Shay and of Evangeline and Calliope. He even thought of poor Molly the marmalade cat, and his own protective nature suddenly outweighed his fear.

"Let's you and I make a list of men we know are good shots and keep their heads calm in any sort of circumstances," Lawson said. "Then might I suggest that those are the men you temporarily deputize or set up as watchmen?"

Sheriff Montrose nodded. "That sounds like a good way to go about it, Judge. I'll post a sign on the jailhouse door and start spreadin' the word about the meetin'."

"Let me know what I can do to assist you, Dennison," Lawson said. "Anything you need."

The sheriff grinned a rather anxious grin and asked, "Are you a good shooter, Judge?"

Lawson nodded and said, "Yes. A very good one."

"You feelin' all right, Rowdy?" Fox asked.

"What's that?" Rowdy asked in return. His thoughts had been so absorbed in Calliope that he hadn't really heard exactly what Fox had said.

Fox chuckled and exchanged amused glances with Dex and Tate. "I asked if you're feelin' all right," he repeated. "You seem a little preoccupied or somethin' today."

Rowdy grinned. "Well, I suppose I am. I didn't get too much sleep last night for some reason, and it's left me feelin' a step behind on everything, I guess."

It wasn't a lie; he truly had not slept much. What man could've slept much after spending time out gazing at the stars in Calliope Ipswich's company, let alone having kissed her?

The truth was, Rowdy couldn't think about anything else! He wanted to walk out of the mill, ride Tucker over to the Ipswich house, barge right in, take Calliope in his arms, and steal more of her incredible kisses. But knowing such an idea was pure fantasy—and probably a bit loco to boot—Rowdy was simply attempting to work as well as he could when his mind was so entirely elsewhere.

"Well, you let us know if you need to bed down for a nap sometime today," Dex said, patting Rowdy on the back. "After all, a foreman oughta be able to do somethin' once in a while that sets him apart from his workers, right?"

"I gotta tell you, Rowdy," Tate began, "I ain't never worked alongside a boss who works as hard as everyone else. I admire you for that."

Rowdy arched one suspicious eyebrow. "So...what you want, Tate?" he chuckled. "Seems like you're butterin' me up for something."

But Tate shook his head. "Nope. Just speakin' the truth."

Fox even nodded. "It's true. Remember when Mr. Mulholland owned the mill? He never worked with us—just stood around shoutin' orders and makin' sure we didn't slow down. Even his son, Sam, didn't work as hard as you, me, and Dex, Rowdy. But you do work hard."

"Well, I guess I'll thank you boys for the compliment," Rowdy said, "though it still puts me in mind that you're up to somethin'," he said, grinning with amusement.

Rowdy wondered whether the men who worked at the mill would still be offering compliments to him if they knew the truth about who he was. But they didn't—so he guessed it didn't matter a whit.

The men went back to work, and so did Rowdy, though he did find it a might harder to concentrate on his tasks than he had the day before—before he'd kissed Calliope. Rowdy figured he'd never be the same now that he had. No matter what happened, or whether he ever had the chance to kiss her again, he'd never be the same.

In fact, goose bumps broke over his arms for a moment as he thought of her—thought of her warm, sweet mouth and the way she'd melted into his arms and against him. He smiled, thinking of the way she'd told him she hadn't been ready when he'd kissed her the first time. She could certainly be amusing, there was no doubt about that, and it was another thing he'd always admired about her— her ability to make others laugh and feel happy, whether or not it was her intention.

"Good mornin', boys," Sheriff Montrose said as he entered the mill.

"Mornin', Sheriff," Dex and Tate greeted in unison.

"Mornin', Daddy," Fox greeted.

Rowdy nodded his greeting—for the sick feeling that suddenly bubbled up in his gut told him why the sheriff had come to the mill.

"What brings you out here, Sheriff?" Dex asked.

Rowdy watched as Sheriff Montrose exhaled a heavy sigh of discouragement. "I wanted to tell you boys that I've scheduled a meetin' of all the men in town for Thursday night, and I really would appreciate it if you boys would attend. In fact, you boys need to make sure that you do."

Rowdy glanced around to the men in the mill, noting the frowns that suddenly furrowed their brows.

"What's goin' on, Daddy?" Fox asked. "Is somethin' wrong?"

"No, no…at least not yet," the sheriff answered. "I'll be discussin' it at the meetin', and I want to make sure you mill boys are there."

"Then we'll be there, Sheriff," Rowdy stated. "All of us. Ain't that right, boys?"

"Of course," Tate agreed. He glanced to Dex and Fox, asking, "We'll be there, right, men?"

Fox and Dex both nodded.

"Well then, I'll let you fellers get back to work," the sheriff said. "You all have a good day now." And he left.

As soon as Sheriff Montrose was gone, Dex and Tate turned to Fox.

"What's that all about, Fox?" Dex asked.

But Fox shrugged. "I don't rightly know," he answered. "But if my daddy is callin' a meetin'…it must be important."

"Yes," Rowdy mumbled. "It must be."

All at once, Rowdy felt a sense of urgency where Calliope was concerned. He wanted her to know how he felt about her—how he'd always felt about her—and he wanted her to know before he missed the opportunity to tell her, for one reason or another.

He felt an increased urgency to ask Judge Ipswich's permission to escort Calliope to the Tom Thumb wedding, even if he weren't around to actually do it. Rowdy had told Calliope he'd ask her father for permission to escort her, and he meant to do it. If nothing else, he wanted her to know that he was serious in his intentions toward her. He'd do it; the moment he had a chance to do it, he would.

As Rowdy returned to the labor at hand at the mill, he wondered if Calliope might go stargazing again that very night. He determined he'd wait by the lamppost at the edge of town and watch for her lantern to begin bobbing around in the grassy expanse behind her house. His time in Meadowlark Lake might be coming to a forced end, and if it were, he wanted to steal as much time as he could to be in the company of the beautiful Calliope Ipswich.

Once more he thought of kissing her. He figured heaven itself could not be so wonderful as kissing Calliope. Then he wondered if he might know all too soon just what heaven was like. Yet he took a small measure of comfort in knowing that if he did end up dead, it might just be old Dodger who came to greet him again.

🍒

Delicious as it was, Lawson could hardly eat his supper. His stomach was churning with worry. As he studied each member of his beloved family sitting around the kitchen table enjoying supper, his worry and anxiety increased. He would not have outlaws lingering in town! He would not see his family subjected to the sorts of danger and influence loitering outlaws spread. He had three beautiful daughters and a beautiful wife—all of whom would capture any man's notice, but especially an outlaw's. He had a new baby arriving in November.

Thus, in that moment, Lawson reaffirmed to himself that he would do whatever was necessary to protect his family. Whatever was necessary. He'd always protected them, of course, but he'd never had to face the reality of killing men in order to do it.

"What's the matter, Daddy?" Shay asked, rattling Lawson from his ponderings.

He looked to Shay, forcing a reassuring smile. "Oh, nothing, sweet pea. Just thinking over things that need to be accomplished tomorrow."

Little Shay's lovely dark eyes narrowed. "All right. I'll believe you...for now."

Lawson had learned early on that Shay had a sort of sixth sense that was strong enough to almost convince him that she and Kizzy really did own supernatural gypsy powers. He knew that his littlest girl could read his countenance more easily than she could her children's books.

Therefore, he smiled, swallowing his worry and trying to hide the severity of his thought processes.

Feigning a carefree conscience, Lawson asked, "So? What are all my lovely ladies' plans for the evening, hmmm?" He chuckled, adding, "More wedding preparations?"

"Of course," Kizzy answered first. "There's still so much to do, Lawson—for our youngest daughter's weddin', you understand."

Shay giggled with pride and delight.

"Amoretta's invitations are so enchanting, Daddy!" Evangeline offered. "We're going to go over the guest list and make certain no one has been missed. Then tomorrow we'll be going over to the Ackermans' to discuss the decorations for the interior of the barn and to see if Mr. Longfellow has finished building the stage and stairs."

"Well, I'll say this," Lawson began. "You girls really have managed to draw everyone in town into an excitement over this Tom Thumb wedding of yours."

"And it was all Calliope's idea," Evangeline noted. "I don't know what inspired you that night we were all sitting out on the porch, Calliope," she said to her sister, "but whatever it was, I'm grateful for it! This wedding has all been so much fun for everyone who is involved. I know those who attend will remember it fondly forever!"

Calliope smiled. "Thank you, Evie. I hope everyone enjoys it." She paused a moment, and Lawson thought she appeared a little timid suddenly as she inquired, "Daddy…if someone asks you if he may escort me to the wedding, will you give him permission please?"

Lawson chuckled. "Are you asking me because you want me to give this *someone* my permission? Or because, as was the case with Fox Montrose, you wish me to withhold my permission?"

Calliope smiled. "This time I want you to give the *someone* your permission," she answered. "Please, please, please give this someone your permission."

Lawson quirked one curious eyebrow. Calliope's face fairly radiated with joy and anticipation.

"Oh, I see," he muttered. "And who is this someone who might ask to escort you? I mean, I'll need to be prepared in case more than one individual approaches me about the matter."

Lawson watched Calliope as she bit her lower lip—almost as if she were afraid to answer him.

"Rowdy Gates," she said at last.

"Rowdy Gates?" he asked, frowning. So many emotions sped through his mind that he wasn't sure at first whether he was glad to hear Calliope's answer or disturbed. "Rowdy Gates?" he repeated.

"Yes, Daddy," Calliope affirmed. "You've always said he was one of the hardest-working, most reliable men. In fact, you once said you admired him more than any other man in town. So there wouldn't be any reason for you to refuse him permission, right?"

Lawson slowly shook his head—even though he was still quickly mulling the matter over. Yet Calliope was right. Lawson had always admired Rowdy—had always held him in very high esteem. In fact, the only thought that gave him pause at that moment was his most recent experience with Rowdy—the man inexplicably having been a victim of attempted murder by the Morrison brothers and his knowing so much about them. Still, the only explanation for Rowdy's experience with and knowledge of the Morrison brothers' gang involved Rowdy having once been a lawman himself. Thus, Lawson felt no trepidation or mental warning when he considered Rowdy's escorting Calliope.

Therefore, he answered, "There isn't. If Rowdy Gates asks to escort you to the Tom Thumb wedding event, I will gladly grant him my permission."

Calliope squealed with delight, fairly leapt from her chair, and threw her arms around Lawson's neck. "Oh, thank you, Daddy! Thank you! Oh, I just hope and pray he really does ask to escort me. I might die if he doesn't!"

"Oh, I wouldn't worry, Calliope," Kizzy said, smiling. "I'm sure Mr. Gates will be by to talk to you father about it any day now."

"Really, Kizzy?" Calliope asked, hopefully.

"I'm certain of it," Kizzy reassured her.

Lawson frowned, for his young wife didn't seem at all astonished at Calliope's revelation that Rowdy Gates might ask to escort her to the wedding. Furthermore, neither Kizzy nor Shay seemed surprised at Calliope's desperation that Rowdy actually ask her.

Suddenly his dark, worrisome thoughts returned. He and Sheriff Dennison had agreed to inform the men in Meadowlark Lake of the possible danger from the Morrison brothers and to let each man prepare his own family. It was time to prepare *his* family.

"I do have something I need to tell you all," Lawson began. Leaning back in his chair and inhaling a deep breath, he began, "There is a possibility that a gang of outlaws is considering Meadowlark Lake as a place to hole up."

"What?" all the Ipswich women exclaimed.

"What are you talking about, Lawson?" Kizzy asked. "Why in all the world would outlaws want to hole up here? In our little town?"

"Because it *is* a little town," Lawson answered. "It has come to Sheriff Montrose's attention that the Morrison brothers have been driven out of Tombstone and are thus looking for a new place to spend their time. We don't know if they've chosen Meadowlark Lake for certain, but we have our suspicions. Therefore, until we can be thoroughly convinced that the Morrison brothers are not traveling nearby or considering our town as a place to rest after they've committed their crimes, I do not want any of you venturing far from the house without companions." He looked to Shay, knowing how she adored to take Molly out for long, meandering walks. "That means you need to have someone with you every time you leave the house, Shay. No more walks with just Molly with you, all right?"

Shay nodded. Lawson could see the fear in her eyes, and he felt sick at having to be the one who put it there.

Smiling at her, he reached out and gathered her into his lap, kissing the top of her head. "I don't want us all living in fear," he said strongly. "We just need to be more watchful for a while. Furthermore, if you ever see a chestnut and white appaloosa anywhere near Meadowlark Lake, you need to inform me or Sheriff Montrose at once. All right?"

"Yes, Daddy," Evangeline and Calliope assured him in unison.

"And what about you, my littlest angel?" Lawson asked his youngest daughter.

He felt Shay snuggle in more tightly against him. "Yes, Daddy," she answered—though fear was evident in her voice.

"Shay, why don't you come help Evie and I go over the guest list and invitations to make certain it's complete?" Calliope suggested. "With three of us checking the list, it will go faster."

"And we can sing some songs while we're working too," Evangeline added.

"Can we sing 'Three Little Girls Dressed in Blue'?" Shay asked. Lawson felt her relax a little.

"Of course!" Calliope and Evangeline exclaimed.

"Come on then, darling," Evangeline said, offering a hand to her littlest sister.

Hopping off Lawson's lap, Shay and her sisters left the kitchen then, leaving Lawson alone to talk with his wife.

"So," Kizzy sighed, resting her elbows on the table, "how much danger are we really in, my love?"

Lawson shook his head. "I'm not really sure we're in any danger. I just want us to be prepared if there happens to be any on the horizon." He reached out, taking one of Kizzy's hands in his own. "I've told you all I know about it at this point."

Kizzy nodded, exhaling a worried sigh.

Lawson frowned then, saying, "But I have a question."

"Yes?" Kizzy prodded.

"Rowdy Gates?" he asked. "Calliope seems a might sweet on him. When did this transpire?"

But Kizzy burst into laughter, shook her head with amusement, and said, "Oh, Lawson! Sometimes I wonder how I ever managed to capture your attention. You're so observant and wise about everything, and yet you've completely missed the fact that Calliope has been in love with Rowdy Gates since she first saw him!" Kizzy laughed again, rising from her chair and embracing Lawson. "You're such an adorable man!"

But Lawson frowned. "You're sure? Calliope's been sweet on Rowdy for a long time?" He sighed, however, chuckling at his own naïveté. "The Tom Thumb wedding epiphany she had that night we were on the front porch...Rowdy had just been visiting with us." He laughed. "Rowdy Gates stepped down off the porch and was hardly on his way before Calliope erupted with the inspiration to have a Tom Thumb wedding."

Kizzy giggled and nodded. "You see? You *did* know! Just not consciously."

Lawson nodded, wrapped his strong arms around his pretty wife's waist, and said, "It's because you're always distracting me, my little temptress."

Lawson kissed Kizzy then—savored the warm, sweet flavor of her mouth. After a moment he broke the seal of their lips, just long enough to chuckle. "Rowdy Gates, is it? Poor Fox Montrose never had a chance against a rival the likes of Rowdy Gates."

"No, Judge Ipswich," Kizzy whispered against his lips. "He did not."

As Kizzy instigated an impassioned kiss with him then, Lawson surrendered to her alluring ways. All thoughts of danger coming to Meadowlark Lake, or of Calliope being sweet on Rowdy for so long without her father knowing, were swept from his mind. There was only his beautiful Kizzy.

CHAPTER THIRTEEN

Rowdy stood near the last lamplight in town, glancing from the warm-lighted windows of the Ipswich home to the blackness of night veiling the grassy expanse behind it. He half expected little Shay to show up and urge him on, but she didn't, and Rowdy began to wonder whether perhaps Calliope had decided not to go stargazing that night.

But just as he was thinking he should abandon his post and hopes of seeing Calliope again, he heard the sound of a door closing. And then he saw it—a tiny lantern light bobbing along in the darkness like a Georgia lightning bug.

"Patience is a virtue, they say," Rowdy mumbled to himself, glad he'd had enough virtue to wait as long as he did at the last lamppost.

He'd already reined Tucker nice and tight to the nearest hitching post, and now Rowdy made his way toward the small flame skipping farther and farther away from the Ipswich house. As he stepped into the cool, new grass, he smiled at the tiny flame suspended in the air a ways in front of him. Everything about Calliope Ipswich seemed enchanted—even the way the light in her lantern moved through the darkness.

"Hello?"

The sound of his voice caused such a thrilling tremor to travel through Calliope that she actually quivered for a moment. Holding her lantern up a little higher and peering through the moonlit night, she smiled as she saw him coming toward her.

"Mr. Gates!" she quietly called. "Oh, I was hoping you'd join me again this evening."

"You were?" Rowdy said as he reached her.

"I was," she managed. Every inch of her was tingling with anticipation as she looked up into his handsome face. He was smiling at her—not just grinning, smiling—and it made her heart leap in her bosom.

"Well, here I am," he said. "So what're you gonna do with me?"

A nervous yet delighted giggle escaped Calliope's throat. He was flirting with her! It was wonderful. But she didn't quite know how to respond.

"Well, I have my blanket and was planning on watching the stars again tonight," she began. "But I'd much rather just sit and talk with you."

His smile broadened as he took the blanket from where it was draped over her arm, winked at her, and said, "I think that's a good idea."

Calliope watched as Rowdy spread the blanket out over the grass. Taking the lantern from her, he set it to one side of the blanket, took her hand, and helped her to sit.

"Thank you," she said, tucking her legs to one side.

Rowdy sat down across from her, resting his arms on his knees. "And how was your day, Miss Calliope?"

Calliope shrugged. "Uneventful," she answered. Then smiling at him, she added, "Until now."

Rowdy chuckled. "Uneventful, huh?" he asked. "Well, that's one of them answers that can be either good or bad."

Calliope nodded and agreed, "You're right. And in this case I thought it was bad, until Daddy talked to us at supper tonight. And after he told us what might happen, now I think it might be good."

Rowdy's smile faded. "Your daddy told you about the Morrison brothers?" he asked.

Calliope nodded. "Yes. And that's why I guess it's good today was uneventful, right?"

Rowdy nodded. Calliope did not miss how quickly his smile had faded at the mention of the Morrison brothers.

"I'm guessing you know about them," she ventured.

"What do you mean?" he asked, seeming almost defensive.

"I mean, I'm guessing you've heard of them…or maybe you even knew that there may be some reason they might pass through Meadowlark Lake," she explained. "Daddy seemed very concerned about it. Oh, he tried to pretend it wasn't anything too awful important…but I can tell when he's worried." Calliope tipped her head to one side and studied Rowdy for a moment. "I wonder where he came by his information? I never thought to ask him." She shrugged and sighed, "I suppose Sheriff Montrose received a telegram or something."

"*I* told him," Rowdy confessed. He didn't know why he'd felt such a strong impression that he should tell Calliope that he was the one who had told Sheriff Montrose, but he did, and so he continued. "I saw one of the Morrison brothers' horses in town one day. Actually, I saw it twice, on two different days. So I told your daddy and Sheriff Montrose that I thought the Morrison brothers might be lookin' for a town to hide out in."

He looked to Calliope to see her staring at him wide-eyed with astonishment. "But…but how did you recognize a horse that belonged to an outlaw?"

Rowdy almost reached out, grabbed her, and kissed her before she could run screaming from him. Yet she didn't look frightened of him—or suspicious. She only looked curious.

"I've seen that horse before," he answered. "It's a chestnut and white appaloosa, with very unique markin's."

Calliope nodded. "Daddy told us that if we saw that very horse, we should tell him or the sheriff immediately." She frowned and asked, "Where did you see that horse before? How did you know it belonged to an outlaw?"

Rowdy was surprised that she still looked calm. She was sincerely only interested in what he knew and how he knew it. So he decided to tell her the tale. He'd told her father and the sheriff that the Morrison brothers had tried to kill him—even told them *how* they'd tried to kill him (for the most part). Maybe he'd held back why they'd tried, but that fact wasn't relevant to the danger the Morrison gang posed to the folks in Meadowlark Lake. The same applied to Calliope. All that was important was that the Morrison brothers had tried to kill him, and that's how he recognized Arness Morrison's horse. At least, that was what was important at the moment. And so he did resolve to share his secret with someone besides Judge Ipswich and Sheriff Montrose. He decided to share it with the woman he was in love with. After all, secrets between lovers—it meant certain doom to their future. His mother had taught him that—and proved it to him with the loss of her own life.

"The Morrison brothers tried to kill me a while back," he began.

"What?" Calliope gasped. She was horrified at the thought that anyone in the world would want to kill Rowdy Gates, let alone *try* to kill him.

"It's true," Rowdy assured her, however. "It was a couple of years back. I was livin' in Texas, near my mama and daddy's place. And one day the Morrison brothers rode in lookin' to get me to join up with them...start outlawin'."

Calliope's eyes widened with terrified awe. "They did?"

Rowdy nodded. "They did," he answered. "My mama...she was killed that day. She jumped in front of my daddy when Arness Morrison tried to shoot him."

"Rowdy! I-I'm so sorry," Calliope said in a whisper. She wondered what had happened to the gladness she had felt only moments before. Where had the flirting between them gone? How had their conversation out under a lovely moonlit, starry sky turned to the murder of his mother at the hands of an outlaw?

But he was thinking back now—she could see it in his eyes—the pain of a tragic past. And so she listened as he continued, "Then

Arness told Carson Morrison to rope me, and he did. I was standin' there—watchin' my daddy leanin' over my mama and beggin' her to come back to him—so I didn't see the lasso comin' until it was already around me. The Morrison brothers gave me a beatin' that I thought was the end of me. But it wasn't. So they tied me tighter and drug me behind their horses for about a mile, I think, before Arness Morrison shot me twice. They rode off and left me to die. I remember bein' so hurt that I was almost numb to the pain. I remember the sun bein' so bright overhead and thinkin' that I hoped heaven would take the misery away."

He paused, and Calliope wiped tears from her cheeks.

"Oh, don't cry, pretty girl," Rowdy said, grinning with sympathy and reassurance. "It was a long while back."

Calliope continued to weep, however, for it was a horrid story. Furthermore, she well knew that Rowdy was only skimming the top of it. She knew that what he was telling her didn't begin to describe the terrifying truth of it.

"Your leg," she managed to sniffle, "the leg you started lighting the lamps to heal."

Rowdy nodded. "Yep. That beatin—or the draggin' afterward, I don't know which—broke a lot of things in my body. My stiff leg was the somethin' that took the longest to heal."

Calliope brushed more tears from her cheeks. "But...but how did you...how did you survive? Did your daddy come lookin' for you?"

But Rowdy's eyes narrowed. "Nope," he said. "The Morrison brothers had doubled back when they thought they'd killed me. They doubled back and..."

"Killed your daddy," Calliope finished for him.

Rowdy nodded. He swallowed hard, obviously struggling to keep his emotions in check. Then he said, "It was Dodger. It was ol' Dodger that saved me."

"Your dog?" Calliope asked. "So he was your dog before...before the Morrison brothers."

"No," Rowdy said, however. "I was lyin' there in that hot Texas sun, just parched and swelterin' and ridin' in and out of consciousness, when all of a sudden I felt somethin' rough and wet on my face. It woke me up a bit, and I saw it was this big old mutt of a dog. He was lickin' my face and my wounds and whimperin' somethin' awful." Rowdy paused and chuckled a bit at the memory.

He looked to Calliope and said, "It was Dodger. I'd never seen him before that day. Not around town, not on any nearby farms...nowhere. He just appeared outta the desert and started lickin' my face."

"Maybe he was an..." Calliope began. But then she realized how ridiculous what she was about to say would sound.

Nevertheless, Rowdy grinned at her and finished her thought, "You mean, an angel?"

Calliope blushed and nodded her confirmation.

Rowdy nodded as well and said, "It's an interestin' notion that I've considered many times myself."

"So Dodger found you, and...and he...he what? Led you home?" Calliope prodded.

"Actually, he run a couple a miles up the way to another farm and managed to cause a big enough ruckus that an old farmer followed him back to me." Rowdy paused and smiled at Calliope, though his eyes remained sad. "It's another reason I wondered for a while if Dodger was an angel. What man in his right mind would follow a stray, barkin' dog for two miles just to see what the fuss was? Most folks woulda just shot him, thinkin' he was loco with rabies or somethin'."

Calliope didn't know what to say. She was stunned—nearly in a state of shock by what Rowdy had just revealed. She well remembered the day her mother and little infant brother had died. Even though she'd been very young when her mother was lost, the excruciating pain still pierced her heart whenever she thought of her mother's death. How could a man endure such a thing as Rowdy had endured? Seeing his mother shot before his very eyes? Being beaten by outlaws? Dragged for a mile through the desert, shot twice? And then to return home to find his father had been killed as well?

It was surreal! Did such horrible things really happen? Yet she knew they did. And she didn't need to witness those horrors with her own eyes, for the stories her father told of experiences of his profession were proof enough.

Calliope stared at Rowdy. "H-how did you come through it all?" she whispered.

Rowdy shrugged. "God," he answered. "And that stray dog of an angel he sent to me."

Calliope straightened her posture. She brushed more tears from her eyes and sniffled. She was determined not to completely melt into a puddle of sympathetic despair. "And that's how you recognized the outlaw's appaloosa in town," she stated.

"Yep."

Calliope, still determined not to burst into sobbing, did manage a confession of her own. "I'll never get over that story, Rowdy," she said. She looked to him, forcing a comforting grin. "Thank you for telling me."

Rowdy quirked a doubtful eyebrow. "Why on earth would you thank me for tellin' you all that mess, Calliope?"

It had happened. In the space of one sharing of a deep, painful secret, Calliope noted that she and Rowdy had ceased in referring to one another as Miss Calliope and Mr. Gates. The fact of it warmed her heart more than he could ever know—even for the pain she felt at what he had endured and overcome.

"Because…because I like to think it means you trust me," she told him.

"Why wouldn't I trust you?" he asked. The pain was evaporating from his beautiful green eyes to be replaced by mischief and gladness as he looked at her.

"Well, you don't know me too well yet, now do you?" she asked.

"I know you much better than you think," he said, grinning at her.

"Oh really?" she challenged.

He nodded. "Yes, really. In fact, I know much more about you than you know about me," he stated.

But Calliope giggled. "Oh, believe me, you most certainly do not."

"I'll wager that I do," he countered.

Calliope's eyebrows arched in amused disbelief. "You'll *wager* that you do, is it?"

"I will," Rowdy insisted. "Name your price, pretty Ipswich girl," he said. "Name your price…and then we'll get to it."

For some reason, Calliope found herself staring at the man's mouth—studying the shape of his lips—lingering on the memory of his kiss.

"All right, Rowdy Gates," she said. "I'll trade you one of my secrets for one of yours. If you already know my secret, then I lose. And if I already know the secret you choose to reveal, you lose."

He smiled. "And what do I get when I win?"

Calliope giggled. She liked the smoldering expression of desire she could see in his eyes as his attention lingered on her mouth.

"When *I* win, then I'll tell you what I want from you," she countered.

"Deal," he agreed.

"All right then, tell me your secret, Rowdy," Calliope flirted. She leaned closer to him.

"I'm kinda gettin' the short end of the stick here, now that I think about it," he said, however. "I mean, I already told you one secret that you didn't know. So now let me think a minute, 'cause I gotta come up with somethin' else."

"Take your time," she said, once more allowing her gaze to settle on his mouth.

Rowdy could hardly control himself! He wanted to kiss Calliope with every thread holding him together. In fact, he wanted to do more than kiss her; he wanted her completely!

Reining in his desires, however, he said, "All right, here I go. Did you know this about me—that I own the gristmill?"

He chuckled when her bright blue eyes widened, perfectly catching the moonlight and looking like two radiant sapphires.

"What?" she exclaimed. "You bought the gristmill from Mr. Mulholland?"

Rowdy's smile broadened. He had her! She hadn't known that he'd been the one who had gained ownership of the mill when Ben Mulholland had to leave Meadowlark Lake.

"I did," he confirmed triumphantly. He knew so much about Calliope—for he'd been watching her and studying her for months! "I bought it and kept the fact to myself, so I could still work there as the foreman and so the townsfolk wouldn't know I had enough money to buy it."

Calliope's pretty brows furrowed. "How did you have enough money to buy it?" she asked.

"Ah ah ha," Rowdy scolded, wagging an index finger at her. "That would take me revealin' another secret about myself. And we agreed to one secret for one secret. And besides, you already have two on me now."

Calliope giggled. "All right. I'll admit that I did not know you owned the mill," she said.

"So I get to tell you what I want now that I won our wager?" he teased.

"No, not yet," she needlessly reminded him. "I still get to tell you one secret and see if you know it about me."

"Fine," Rowdy said. "Try me, pretty girl. But I'm warnin' you— I've been watchin' you for a long, long time."

"Really?" Calliope sighed, overwhelmed with sudden bliss at Rowdy's revealing he'd been watching her.

Rowdy nodded, answering, "Yes, ma'am. Try me."

Calliope bit her lip. It was a rather difficult task. After all, Calliope didn't keep a whole lot of secrets; it just wasn't in her nature. The only one she could think of was the one she'd been keeping about Rowdy—that she loved him—and had loved him for a very long time.

But then it struck her—a secret she could share with him that she knew he would never have guessed at. Furthermore, it would begin to reveal to him the depth of her feelings for him, without her having to say out loud that she loved him.

"Very well," she began. She found that it was hard to confess the fact to him, for she did feel foolish in having brought him harm. "You remember when you saved me…when we fell from the upper bank of the millpond?"

"Of course," he said.

Calliope frowned as she glanced to the wound still healing on Rowdy's cheek. She figured that she owed him what she was about to tell him. After all, he'd risked his life to save her.

"Well, I wasn't just out walking that day," she confessed. "I went to the mill with the sole intention of getting a glimpse of you. I was looking through a loose board when the pigeons did their business on your shirt. It was only when you took your shirt off in planning to rinse it out that I realized you might see me, and I tried to hurry away…pretending that I was out for a walk and—"

She didn't even know how she'd ended up there, but in an instant, Calliope was cradled in Rowdy's arms as his mouth claimed hers in such a driven kiss that it nearly smothered her. Over and over he kissed her. And over and over she returned his kisses—drowning in bliss, swept away in euphoria!

For a moment, Rowdy broke the seal of their mouths, still holding her in his arms as he gazed down into her eyes. Calliope saw the depth of emotion in him—the green windows that opened to reveal his soul as he looked at her.

"Y-you already knew what I was going to ask for when I won the wager," she whispered. "I-I wanted you to kiss me again."

He grinned at her—*lovingly* grinned at her, and her bliss was multiplied a hundredfold.

"But you didn't win the wager," he mumbled against her mouth. "*I* did. And now I'm collectin' my winnin's while I can."

Calliope's heart was pounding so hard within her chest! Her breath was labored as she pushed herself from the cradle of Rowdy's arms only long enough for him to follow his own instincts and pull her to her feet with him.

As his arms entwined about her, Calliope melted to Rowdy even more completely than she had the night before when he'd kissed her. Any tentative, careful way he'd held or kissed her the previous night had vanished. Likewise, something in Calliope felt free of restraint. She found that there was no timidity left in her where Rowdy Gates was concerned—for she knew by the way he held her, as if she were a rare possession, that he truly cared for her. She knew by the way he kissed her—as if he thirsted for her somehow, or could never satisfy his hunger for her—that he cared for her.

In the midst of their exchange of affections, it came to her mind that he had confessed to having watched her for months, and she wondered—had he dreamed of her the way she'd dreamed of him?

He took her face between his strong hands and gazed at her a moment. "You know, I think I'll ask your daddy for permission to do more than just escort you to that weddin' you're plannin'."

Calliope's heart leapt in her chest. Did he mean to ask her father his permission to marry her?

"Y-you do?" she managed.

Rowdy nodded. "I do. I plan to ask your father if he'll let me do what he refused to let that idiot Fox Montrose do. I want to court you proper, Calliope. Would that be all right with you?"

A slight whiff of disappointment traveled through her at his not wanting to ask her father for permission to wed her. But she quickly realized that courting was only the necessary precursor to marriage—wasn't it?

"It would be far more than all right with me, Rowdy," she whispered. "I think you know that by now."

"Well then, would it also be all right if I kissed you the way I'm thinkin' of kissin' you right now?" he asked.

Calliope frowned, puzzled. "What do you mean?"

But her question was answered in a heartbeat as Rowdy's kiss was even more affecting than it had been, for his mouth descended to hers—open, warm, and intimate. Every other thought, every other vision was forced from Calliope's mind as Rowdy Gates kissed her the way he'd apparently been thinking of kissing her—and it was extraordinary in the rapturous sensations it sent bursting through her!

As she'd dreamt all those months past of kissing Rowdy, she'd never imagined it would be such thoroughgoing ecstasy as it was. His arms around her, the feel of his firm torso against her, the warm flavor of his kiss that she knew was unique to only him—all of it was far more than she'd ever conceived possible!

Calliope caressed his square, whiskery jaw and thrilled at the feel of it moving to work a kiss that so affected her as to sending thoughts through her mind of surrendering to him wholly. Rowdy was kissing her! It couldn't be real!

But it had been real. Hours later as Calliope lay in her bed tossing and turning for want of being in Rowdy's arms again—of being in his arms forever—she knew their time in the grassy expanse between her home and the woods beyond was real. The lingering sensation of his mouth melded with hers proved it to her over and over again, and it was now another secret bliss Calliope Ipswich owned. A secret that she shared with Rowdy Gates.

CHAPTER FOURTEEN

"Oh, these invitations are beautiful!" Dora Montrose exclaimed. "Amoretta certainly does have lovely penmanship."

"Yes, she does," Evangeline confirmed. "I'm so glad she was willing to write out all the invitations."

Calliope handed the Gardeners' invitation to Blanche's mother, Judith. "We thought we'd hand them out right away. Most people in town already know we're having the event, but we want everyone to have their pretty invitation as soon as possible." She offered the Ackermans' invitation to Ellen. "After all, they're so wonderful, and Amoretta worked very hard. They're meant to be enjoyed as well as to invite."

"Oh, this is gonna be so much fun!" Ellen exclaimed, accepting the Ackermans' invitation as Calliope handed it to her. She glanced around the barn for a moment, adding, "And the barn will be simply transformed by the time we're all finished decorating it."

"Yes," Josephine Chesterfield agreed. "I can already imagine. And Mr. Longfellow did such a wonderful job buildin' the stage platform." Josephine exhaled a sigh of satisfaction as she then looked to Calliope and Evangeline and said, "Thank you girls so much! I was so worried when we first moved here—that we wouldn't be happy for some reason or other. But you Ipswich girls..." She paused, glancing to everyone in the barn in turn. "All of you, you've all been so welcomin' and so willin' to include us in everything. Thank you all so very much."

"We're just ever so glad your family moved to Meadowlark Lake, Mrs. Chesterfield," Calliope assured the woman. "We would never have been able to cast the Tom Thumb wedding so perfectly if your family hadn't moved here and provided so many character parts and help. You see? You were *meant* to be our friends!"

Calliope glanced around the inside of the Ackermans' barn. For a moment, she stood rather awed at how many people were so willing to help with putting on the Tom Thumb wedding performance— from all the women who had sewn and were still sewing so many dresses and suits to Mr. Longfellow, who was putting the finishing touches on the stage. It was so wonderful to see so many citizens of Meadowlark Lark working together and enjoying each other's company. She figured that even if the performance itself didn't go as smoothly as she hoped it would, there was no doubt the people would enjoy it—and that those who had prepared it would be delighted with the end result.

Glancing down to the stack of invitations she still held in her hands, Calliope smiled as she saw *Mister Rowdy Gates* elegantly written across the envelope at the top of her pile. Just the sight of his name caused her arms and legs to ripple with marvelous, tingling goose bumps.

Closing her eyes a moment, she allowed herself to bathe in the reverie of the thrilling bliss Rowdy had whisked her away to the night before. Had she known he would be so overjoyed about knowing she had been to the mill that day to see him, that he would've kissed her the way he did, she would've told him long before!

"Calliope?"

It was Shay's little voice of inquiry that finally drew Calliope's attention back to the moment at hand in the Ackermans' barn.

"Yes, darling?" she asked, smiling down at her sweet sister.

"Well, now that I'm not allowed to take Molly for a walk all by myself," Shay began. Lowering her voice to a whisper, she added, "You know, because of what Daddy told us about the Morrison brothers?"

"Yes, darling. I know," Calliope whispered in return. She glanced around to make certain no one had overheard what Shay had said. She knew the sheriff had asked all the men in town to attend a meeting that evening so that he could inform them of the concerns regarding the outlaws, but she didn't want any of the ladies or children nearby to hear Shay and begin to panic.

"Well, would you walk with me to Mr. Gates's house after supper, so that I can put some fresh flowers on his dog's grave today?" Shay asked. "I figured you could bring along Mr. Gates's invitation and deliver it to him then—so we get both of them important things done."

Calliope smiled. She could see the worry in Shay's eyes, and she didn't want the precious angel to have to give up all her adventures just because some mangy outlaws may or may not ride through town one day.

"Of course I'll go with you, Shay Shay," Calliope assured her. "And I do need to get Mr. Gates's invitation to him. So you were very smart to think of it."

Shay sighed with satisfaction and renewed hope. "Thank you, Calliope," she said. "I feel much better now. And besides, Molly was so worried that she wouldn't get her walk today! Now I can settle her right down."

"Yes, you can," Calliope giggled. "Now, you run on and play with the other children, and no more worries. We'll make sure Mr. Gates's dog has fresh flowers as often as we can, all right?"

"All right," Shay agreed. She hugged Calliope a moment and then ran off to join the other children, who were playing with a litter of new puppies that the Ackermans' were keeping in the barn until the wedding.

Calliope smiled with contentment. Leave it to Shay to give her an excuse to see Rowdy later in the day. And she couldn't wait to see him again! Oh, she knew this meeting, for Shay to put flowers on Dodger's grave and Calliope to deliver Rowdy's invitation, would be nothing akin their meeting out in the grassy expanse the night before. But it didn't matter. Any opportunity to see Rowdy—to simply gaze upon his handsome face and hear his low, alluring voice—was a blessing in itself.

And now that she had seeing Rowdy later to look forward to, Calliope returned her attention to helping with finishing up anything and everything that still needed to be taken care of before the Tom Thumb wedding performance in three weeks' time.

❧

"Afternoon, Judge," Rowdy said as he stepped into the courthouse.

Lawson Ipswich looked up, smiled, and nodded to Rowdy in greeting. "Good afternoon, Rowdy. What brings you into the courthouse today?" Naturally, Lawson already knew exactly what had led Rowdy to the courthouse—and that was Calliope.

"Well, I was wonderin' if I could have a few minutes of your time to talk over a couple of things with you, Judge," Rowdy answered.

"Of course," Lawson said. He nodded toward a seat at the table at which he was sitting. He'd been working on some documents but pushed them aside as Rowdy took a seat across from him. "Now, what is it you'd like to discuss?"

Rowdy cleared his throat nervously, and Lawson fought the urge to smile with amused understanding.

"Well, Judge, first of all, I was wantin' to ask your permission to be Miss Calliope's escort to this weddin' play the ladies in town are puttin' together," Rowdy began. "I'm a good man, Judge. I promise you that. I have only honorable intentions toward Calliope."

Lawson smiled. "Do you have more intentions toward Calliope than just this one occasion of being her escort, Rowdy?"

Rowdy cleared his throat again. "Bein' that you asked the question, I'll answer it. Yes, I do. I was hopin' to somehow manage to acquire your permission to court Calliope, officially. I realize that Fox Montrose recently asked for your permission as well...and that you denied him."

"I did," Lawson nodded. "And do you know why I denied him?"

Rowdy nodded. "Again, I'll answer honestly, Judge. Yes, I do. Calliope asked you to refuse Fox your permission. Young Shay let it slip when she was talkin' to me one day."

Lawson chuckled. His sweet Shay tried so very hard to keep secrets yet often failed miserably. It was something Lawson adored about his youngest daughter.

"That would be correct, Rowdy," Lawson affirmed. "And in like manner, Calliope herself asked me to grant you permission to escort her to the Tom Thumb wedding, and I told her I would. And so you have that. You may indeed escort Calliope to the event to be held at the Ackermans' barn." Lawson paused, however, studying Rowdy a moment. "But I will admit to you, Rowdy, that Calliope didn't say anything to me about you asking me to court her."

Rowdy frowned, seeming concerned. "Well, I asked her if it was all right if I came to you about that, and she said that it was."

Lawson's smile broadened. "Good man!" he complimented. "Good man, Rowdy. That is evidence to me that you care more for Calliope's wants and wishes than you do mine. And I like that. That's what I wanted to hear. So yes, Rowdy, I'd be happy and proud to have you pay court to Calliope. You're a good man, and I trust you."

Lawson saw the relief wash over Rowdy like a summer rain. "Thank you, Judge Ipswich," Rowdy said. "And I want you to know that I can take good care of Calliope…if one day she will have me for her husband. I own the gristmill, and I have other means of financial stability as well."

"I'm sure you do, Rowdy," Lawson said. "I know what a hard worker you are…what an honorable businessman you are. But my concern is Calliope's happiness as far as her being loved and respected the way she deserves."

"Oh, you have no need to be concerned about that, Judge, I assure you," Rowdy said.

Lawson smiled. "Well then, do you want to just make this our one and only meeting concerning Calliope's future with you? What end result do you hope for by courting my daughter, Rowdy?"

Rowdy's face brightened. "Well, to marry her one day, of course…if she'll have me."

Lawson nodded. There rose a pinching pain in his heart—the same pain that had accompanied him the day he'd given Brake

McClendon permission to marry Amoretta. One of his little girls was not so little anymore and would be leaving her father's home and protection soon. It was a bittersweet feeling: a gladness that Calliope would be so thoroughly loved by Rowdy, an excitement for her in knowing she would be starting her own family soon. Yet it was also a sense of overwhelming sadness, for another one of his little girls would be leaving him.

"Then if she'll have you, Rowdy," Lawson began, "you may have her. You may propose to Calliope when you and she both feel the time is right."

Rowdy sighed with satisfaction, and Lawson fancied for a moment there rose a bit of excess moisture in his eyes.

"Thank you, Judge," Rowdy said. "I know how much you love, care for, and protect your family, and I can only imagine how difficult it must be to see your three oldest daughters grown and beginnin' to leave the nest. So I take a great deal of pride in ownin' your confidence." He paused a moment, seemed to inhale a deep breath of courage, and said, "And that's why I'd like to tell you the whole of it, Judge—the whole story of how I so easily recognized Arness Morrison's horse and of what happened when the Morrison brothers tried to kill me."

Lawson frowned, though he didn't feel any less confident in Rowdy's being the man who most deserved and would most love Calliope.

"Very well, Rowdy," he said. "Go ahead and tell me everything and anything you think I need to know."

Rowdy nodded. "I did tell Calliope some of the tale, Judge, and I mean to tell her the rest the next time I have the chance. But for now, I do want you to hear it all."

"All right," Lawson said. "I'm listening."

Some time later, Lawson shook Rowdy's hand and watched the young man walk out of the courthouse. Truth be told, he was somewhat stunned. How could anyone endure what Rowdy Gates had endured? A man who could weather the kind of horrors Rowdy

Gates had, survive, and then rise up strong was a man to be admired indeed.

Exhaling a sigh of disbelief mingled with admiration and awe, Lawson Ipswich returned to the papers he'd been working on before Rowdy arrived.

"Well, one thing cannot be denied," he mumbled to himself. "My daughters certainly do not settle their hearts on men of mediocrity."

❦

"Thank you for comin' with me, Calliope," Shay chirped as she and Calliope meandered toward Rowdy Gates's house. "Molly really needed her walk today."

Calliope giggled as she looked over at the cat, who so patiently endured a leash for the sake of loving the little girl who owned her.

"Oh, I can see that," Calliope said. "But what do you say we let Molly off the leash for the walk home? She might feel like running a bit or chasing a mouse or something, as well as having had her walk."

Shay nodded and looked down to Molly. "Would you like that, Molly, hmmm?" she asked the uniquely tolerant marmalade cat. The cat meowed as if in answer to Shay's question, and Shay said, "Okay, Molly. You can run off and play while I'm gettin' Dodger's flowers today."

Being that they were nearly to Rowdy's house, Shay stopped, removing Molly's leash, and lovingly stroking her several times. "Now you have fun, Molly. But be careful all the same. I wouldn't want you to be the one who run into them outlaws while you're out by yourself, all right?"

Again Molly meowed, gratefully brushed up against Shay's leg, and scurried off into the grasses.

"Molly's such a good cat," Calliope noted. "I've never known a cat to love her little girl as much as Molly loves you."

Shay sighed with contentment and smiled when she took Calliope's hand as they began walking again. "I like it out here a bit out from town," Shay commented. "It's more quiet. Maybe that's why Mr. Gates lives out here…because it's so quiet."

"Maybe," Calliope confirmed. "It is lovely—the grass, the trees, and the wildflowers. Of course, you do realize that we just have to step off our back porch and we have a quiet, beautiful space as well."

"I know," Shay said. "But nobody could see you kissin' your beau out here…the way they can from our house."

"What?" Calliope giggled.

Shay looked up to her sister. "You and Mr. Gates," Shay began. "I saw him kissin' you last night *and* the night before from my bedroom window. But if he kissed you out here, nobody's around to see."

Calliope blushed and laughed, "You were spying on me and Rowdy?"

Shay shrugged. "No. I just saw you from my bedroom window while I was lookin' up at the stars." She smiled, adding, "He sure did kiss you a lot, didn't he, Calliope?"

"Well, I-I guess so, Shay," Calliope stammered. "I mean—"

"Oh look! Look at those wild daisies over there!" Shay interrupted, however. Pointing to a nice bunch of wild daisies growing not so far from Dodger's grave, Shay said, "I need those for Dodger today. You go on and give the invitation to Mr. Gates while I take care of Dodger's flowers."

In the next instant, Shay was off flouncing through the grass toward the daisies.

Calliope giggled, amused that Shay didn't seem surprised at all by the fact she'd seen Rowdy and Calliope kissing the two previous nights. In fact, it appeared as if Shay thought less of the kissing she'd witnessed than she did the bunch of daisies she wanted for Dodger.

Still smiling over her amusement when she knocked on Rowdy's front door, Calliope felt her eyes widen when Rowdy opened the door to greet her wearing nothing but his trousers and boots.

"Well, my, my, my," he said, grinning at her with an expression of something akin to hunger. "What a nice surprise it is to find you standin' on my doorstep, Miss Calliope Ipswich."

Calliope held up the invitation she'd brought. "Good afternoon, Mr. Gates," she began. "I've come to officially invite you to Meadowlark Lake's very first Tom Thumb wedding."

"Fancy!" Rowdy said, taking the invitation from her. "But you didn't have to walk all the way out here by yourself, Miss Ipswich."

Calliope giggled. "I didn't," she told him. Nodding toward the place where Shay was busily gathering flowers for Dodger's grave, she said, "Shay was ready to burst apart if she didn't get out here today to tend to Dodger's grave. She's working on making a tombstone for him, you know."

"A tombstone?" Rowdy chuckled.

Calliope shrugged. "Well, a marker, at least. She's got a big old rock she's whitewashed, and she's got some black paint from the general store. She's just waiting until Amoretta comes for the wedding so that she can have her paint Dodger's name on the rock with an appropriate amount of artistic flamboyance."

Rowdy laughed. "She's a cute little thing, ain't she? So tenderhearted and all."

"She is," Calliope agreed.

Rowdy stared at her a moment and then said, "Well, thank you for the invitation, Miss Ipswich. And since you did walk it all the way out here for me, I might as well confess that I talked to your daddy today, and he gave me permission to escort you to this weddin' thing you've brewed up."

"He did?" Calliope exclaimed.

"Yes, ma'am, he did," Rowdy affirmed.

Throwing her arms around Rowdy's neck, she squealed, "Oh, I'm so excited, Rowdy! How fun it will all be. And me on your arm at the wedding? It's another dream come true!"

"Another dream come true?" Rowdy asked, holding her securely against him.

The warmth of his skin penetrated Calliope's bodice, and she reveled in the feel of it—in the soft, smooth contours of his back as she hugged him.

"Yes," she whispered. "The first dream was that you would kiss me someday…and you already made that one come true."

"Oh, I'd be willin' to make that one come true over and over again, Miss Ipswich," Rowdy mumbled against her ear.

Calliope's entire body broke into goose bumps as she felt him press his mouth to her neck. A wave of warmth washed over her, and butterflies erupted into flight in her stomach.

"Mmm," Rowdy breathed against her cheek. "You taste like honey, Calliope."

Her mouth was watering for want of his kiss, and she thought she might faint of unquenched desire before he finally kissed her on the mouth. Rowdy's kiss was warm and driven one moment, gentle and somehow teasing the next.

"I asked your daddy if I could come courtin' you too," he whispered.

"You did?" Calliope asked a moment before he kissed her again.

"I did," he answered in a low, provocative tone. "And he said that I could."

"Did you ask him anything else?" she breathed between kisses.

"See what I mean, Calliope?" Shay said from somewhere very close.

Calliope unwillingly pulled away from Rowdy. Looking to her little sister, she asked, "And what's that, Shay Shay?"

"That you and Mr. Gates should be kissin' out here at his place, where nobody's likely to see you," Shay answered. "Well, other than me, I guess."

Shay smiled, and Calliope couldn't help but giggle. "I guess," she said to her sister.

"And you best put your shirt back on and head into town soon for the meetin' Sheriff Montrose is havin' this evenin', Mr. Gates," Shay said. "Daddy says every man in Meadowlark Lake is supposed to be there."

"Oh, that's right," Rowdy said. "I almost forgot about that, Miss Shay."

Shay smiled at him, patted his arm, and said, "That's 'cause you were kissin' on Calliope and didn't have your wits about you...so it's all right."

"Maybe we'll see you in town, Rowdy," Calliope mentioned. "I promised Evangeline I'd go with her to check the post at the general store once I'd delivered your invitation."

"I'd like that," Rowdy said. "And I sure am glad you delivered my invitation yourself, Miss Calliope."

Calliope blushed, and Shay rolled her eyes. "Sappy, Mr. Gates. Purely sappy," she giggled.

"Well, you ladies have a nice amble home," Rowdy said. "And maybe I will see you in town this evenin', Miss Calliope."

Calliope blushed with delight as he winked at her.

"And thank you, Miss Shay, for Dodger's flowers," he added. "I know he appreciates bein' attended by a pretty little girl like you."

Shay blushed then and said, "You're welcome, Mr. Gates. Now you have fun at the meetin' in town, all right?"

"I will," Rowdy assured her.

He gave Calliope one final wink before she and Shay turned and headed back toward town.

"Look at them goose bumps on your arms, Calliope!" Shay exclaimed as she took Calliope's hand. "That Mr. Gates really tickles your fancy, doesn't he?"

"Yes," Calliope admitted, exhaling a sigh of wonder in the emotions that had so quickly flamed between her and Rowdy. "Yes, he does."

CHAPTER FIFTEEN

"Here you go, Evangeline," Mrs. Perry said, handing Evangeline a letter. "I do declare that I've never seen two friends exchange letters back and forth as often or as quickly as you and your friend do! You two must be quite close."

Evangeline nodded. "We are, Mrs. Perry," she said. "I've known Jennie for as long as I can remember, and I'm so glad we've rejuvenated our friendship through correspondence."

"I can imagine," Mrs. Perry commented.

As Evangeline opened and began to read Jennie's most recent letter, Calliope held out an invitation to Mrs. Perry, saying, "And here's the invitation for you and Mr. Perry to the Tom Thumb wedding, Mrs. Perry."

"Oh, I'm so excited for this, Calliope, honey," Mrs. Perry exclaimed. "I've been gatherin' up little hints and details here and there, and it sounds as if it's gonna be somethin' to behold, indeed!"

"I certainly hope so," Calliope said.

"And just look at this handwritin' of Amoretta's," the woman gasped. "So lovely, just so very lovely! I'm assumin' she and Brake will be in town for the event."

Calliope nodded. "Yes! We're so excited to see them both. I just miss her so much sometimes that I can hardly bear it."

"I understand, dear," Mrs. Perry sighed. "I haven't seen my own sister for near to five years now." She nodded, saying, "We do exchange letters, but it's just not the same as a hug."

"No, it's not," Calliope agreed.

"Thank you so much, Mrs. Perry," Evangeline said then. "I hope you have an enjoyable evening."

"You too, dear," Mrs. Perry said. "And you have fun deliverin' the rest of your invitations there, Calliope. What fun!"

"Isn't it though?" Calliope agreed with a giggle as she followed Evangeline out of the general store.

As they started for home, Calliope asked, "How is Jennie, Evie?"

Evangeline frowned a little. "I'm not certain, for I haven't read the entire letter, but she's not feeling well."

Calliope frowned as well. "Oh dear! That's very worrisome. When is the baby expected?"

"October…late October," Evangeline answered.

"Good evenin', ladies," Mr. Longfellow greeted, stepping up in front of Calliope and Evangeline.

"Good evening, Mr. Longfellow," Evangeline said, forcing a smile.

Calliope could see how worried her sister was about her friend. She knew that Evangeline probably would rather Mr. Longfellow didn't linger in speaking with them.

Therefore, Calliope asked, "Are you on your way to the sheriff's meeting, Mr. Longfellow?"

"Yep. Dex is already there, so I best hurry. You ladies have a nice evenin'," he said.

Calliope did not miss the manner in which Mr. Longfellow's eyes lingered admiringly on Evangeline.

"You as well," Evangeline said with a nod.

"He's sweet on you, Evie," Calliope whispered once Mr. Longfellow had entered the courthouse where the meeting was to be held.

"Oh, hush, Calliope, he is not!" Evangeline giggled.

Suddenly the sound of horse's hooves pounding the ground startled Calliope and Evangeline. They looked up to see Fox Montrose and Tate Chesterfield riding into town. Both young men were as pale as the moon and winded as they reined in before the courthouse.

Fairly leaping from his mount, Fox asked, "Have you seen my daddy?"

"I-I think he's in the courthouse. Why?" Calliope responded.

"We seen them!" Tate said then, panting with exertion or fear—Calliope wasn't sure which. "We seen the Morrison brothers ridin' straight for town!"

"What?" Evangeline and Calliope exclaimed in unison.

"I gotta tell my daddy," Fox said, pushing past Calliope and Evangeline and heading into the courthouse.

"You ladies best step back inside the general store," Tate said. "There ain't time for you to make it to your house before they get here."

Calliope exchanged looks of terror with her older sister. Then, without another word, they turned and hurried back to the general store. Just as they stepped into it, however, Calliope looked back—in the direction from which Fox and Tate had ridden in. There, on the horizon already on the edge of town, were five men on horseback. And one man—the one riding in the middle—rode a chestnut and white appaloosa.

"Rowdy," Calliope breathed as panic began to consume her.

"What's goin' on? I'm on my way out to the meetin' the sheriff called for this evenin'," Mr. Perry said as Calliope and Evangeline hurried to the front window of the store. "What's all that ruckus I'm hearin' outside?"

"A gang of outlaws has ridden into Meadowlark Lake," Calliope answered simply.

"What?" Mr. Perry asked.

"It's why Sheriff Montrose and our daddy called the meeting in the first place," Evangeline began to explain. "The Morrison brothers' gang was recently driven out of Tombstone, and there were suspicions that they were heading toward Meadowlark Lake in search of a new place to hole up."

Mrs. Perry gasped, and Mr. Perry simply stormed across the room to the sales counter, reached down behind it, and retrieved a shotgun. Cocking it with determination, he returned to the window.

"You ladies best step back if bullets start flyin', all right?" Mr. Perry said.

"Of course, dear," Mrs. Perry agreed—though she was staring out the window into the street as intently as Calliope and Evangeline were.

"Here comes Sheriff Montrose and the judge now," Mr. Perry mumbled.

Calliope watched, terrified, as she saw Sheriff Montrose saunter from the courthouse and into the middle of Meadowlark Lake's main thoroughfare. Her terror mounted to an almost tangible point when she saw her father join him, both men armed with rifles.

"Daddy!" Evangeline gasped.

It was like witnessing the unfolding of a nightmare for Calliope as she watched the five outlaws ride into town and rein in a ways off from her father and Sheriff Montrose.

"Turn them horses around, boys," Sheriff Montrose shouted. "You ain't welcome here."

The middle rider—the man on the appaloosa—smiled and leaned forward, resting one arm on his saddle horn.

"Now, Sheriff, I know you must be aware of how this kind of thing works," the man said. "We come into your town, and we rest up and eat and have our baths. We play a little poker, and then we move on for a while. And as long as you allow us a bit of restin'-up time, everyone in your quiet little town here continues to live on safe and sound."

Calliope knew this man was the leader of the Morrison brothers' gang. Rowdy had referred to him as Arness. But there was something about Arness Morrison that Calliope had not expected. Rather than being a dirty, yellow-teethed, matted-beard sort of outlaw, Arness Morrison was fairly handsome. In fact, the longer Calliope studied Arness Morrison, as well as the two men on either side of him, the more she began to think they bore a nearly uncanny resemblance to…

"Ride on, Arness. You turn Pronto around and ride on to someplace else."

Calliope's mouth dropped open in horrified astonishment as she watched Rowdy walk out into the street wearing a gunbelt and pistol.

"You heard the man, Morrison," Sheriff Montrose said. "Ride on. You're boys ain't welcome here."

But Arness Morrison wore an expression exactly as if he were looking at a ghost as he stared at Rowdy.

"Rowdy?" Arness asked. "Is that you, boy? That can't be you! You're dead! I kilt you myself."

"Naw. You tried to kill me, Arness," Rowdy said as he stared down Arness. "You—all three of you—you and Carson and Walker. You tried to kill me…but you failed."

Arness laughed, looking back and forth between the two men on either side of him. "Boys, lookie here! Our baby brother…back from the dead."

"Brother?" Calliope heard Evangeline and Mr. and Mrs. Perry exclaim.

"Their brother?" Calliope herself whispered.

"Half brother," Rowdy corrected, however. "And I pause in even acknowledgin' that much to a man who killed his own mother…and mine."

Arness leveled an accusing finger at Rowdy, and Sheriff Montrose and Judge Ipswich leveled their rifles at him.

"That was her own fault, brother," Arness growled. "I didn't mean to shoot Mama. I was tryin' for that no-good husband of hers…your daddy."

"You killed my mama, and you killed my daddy," Rowdy said, however. He pointed to the two men on either side of Arness, whom Calliope had now determined were Carson and Walker Morrison. "And you two, you didn't lift a finger to stop him."

"You shoulda joined up with us, Rowdy," one of the other two Morrison brothers hollered. "But you were always mama's little saint, weren't you?"

"Ride outta here, boys," Rowdy said, "or die."

"You ain't the law, Rowdy," Arness laughed. "You don't speak for the sheriff here." Arness looked back to Sheriff Montrose then. "What do *you* say, Sheriff? You gonna give some innocent, tired men who been ridin' for weeks some rest here in town? Or would you rather see us take your town out from under you…leaving dead who knows how many of your sweet, kind townsfolk to bleed out in your street?"

"Ride on, Morrison," Sheriff Montrose said, however. "Ride on, or we shoot you in your saddles."

Arness straightened, puffing out his chest with the arrogance only an outlaw possessed. "You're makin' a mistake, Sheriff," he said. "If you don't let us—"

"Ride on," Calliope heard her father say. "The sheriff already warned you. Leave or die."

Arness looked at Lawson Ipswich and asked, "And who the hell are you?"

"Judge Lawson Ipswich," Lawson answered. "And I will kill you, Morrison."

Arness's brow furrowed in an angry, defiant frown. "You all are makin' a big mistake. Because we will ride on, for now—until the folks in this little town are all tucked in one night, sleepin' without a care in the world. And that's when we'll be back to kill the three of you." He nodded to Sheriff Montrose, then to Calliope's father, and then to Rowdy.

Then his eyes narrowed as he said, "Come on, boys. I don't want to stay in a town of idiots." He glared at Rowdy then, adding, "Or ghosts."

Calliope realized she'd been holding her breath, and she exhaled as three of the five outlaws turned their horses.

But she gasped once more when she heard Arness Morrison shout, "Mama's little saint ain't a saint no more!" He drew his pistol and leveled it at Rowdy.

Calliope screamed as she heard the gunshot ring out—though tears of thankfulness filled her eyes when she saw it was Arness clutching his chest with blood beginning to saturate the front of his shirt.

As Arness Morrison collapsed and fell from his saddle to hit the ground hard, the rest of the outlaws drew on Rowdy, her father, and the sheriff.

Gunfire began, and Mr. Perry shouted, "Get away from the window!" as he strode from the store, leveling his shotgun at the outlaws still sitting their mounts.

It was no more than a few moments—seconds or less—and all was quiet once more. Racing toward the window, Calliope looked out, tears of relief spilling over her cheeks as she saw Rowdy, her father, and Sheriff Montrose standing over the dead outlaws littering the street.

"Calliope! Don't!" Evangeline cried out as Calliope raced from the general store and toward Rowdy. She threw her arms around him, sobbing against his shirt, and then released him to hug her father.

"Oh, Daddy! You men could've been killed!" she cried.

Then she raced back to Rowdy, taking hold of the front of his shirt and crying, "What were you thinking? They could've killed you! This time they really might have killed you!"

She was still trembling with residual terror, weeping tears of fear mingled with relief.

"I'm...I'm sorry I didn't have the chance to tell you the whole truth of it, Calliope," Rowdy said.

All the men who had been waiting in the courthouse were now in the street investigating the bodies of the outlaws.

"I meant to tell you last night...but I..." Rowdy stammered.

"You could've been killed, Rowdy!" Calliope wept, however.

"I'm sorry, Calliope," Rowdy said. "I should've told you that the Morrison brothers…that they are my brothers." He frowned a moment, glancing over his shoulder to where Arness lay dead. "They were my brothers…my half brothers."

He looked back to her then, and she could see the pain in his eyes. "How do you feel about me now that you know who I really am…who my brothers are? How do you feel about me knowin' I just killed two of them?"

Straightening her posture, Calliope brushed her tears from her cheeks. "Come with me," she said, taking his hand.

Storming toward the livery with Rowdy in tow, Calliope could think of only one answer to give him. Therefore, once they were in the livery, leaving all the people of Meadowlark Lake out in the street to discuss what had happened and remove the bodies of five outlaws, Calliope took hold of Rowdy's shoulders and turned him to face her.

"How do I feel about you?" she asked him. "Knowing everything I do now?"

Taking hold of the lapels of the black vest Rowdy wore over his shirt, Calliope pushed him back against the livery wall and said, "*This is how I feel!*"

She raised herself on her tiptoes and kissed Rowdy square on the mouth. Again and again she kissed him, until he reached out, gathering her into his arms and taking command of their affections—kissing her with such fervent passion and promise that Calliope could hardly breathe.

CHAPTER SIXTEEN

It had been a mere three weeks since the Morrison brothers' gang had come to a fatal end in Meadowlark Lake. Normally, such an astonishing, frightening, and gruesome event would still have dominated the thoughts and conversations of the townsfolk. But as Willis and Albert Chesterfield ushered in the guests of the first Tom Thumb wedding ever to be held in Meadowlark Lake, it was clear that the sudden terror that the Morrison brothers had brought to the town had vanished nearly as quickly as the outlaws themselves were vanquished.

Everything looked perfect—or at least in Calliope's opinion. The inside of the Ackermans' large barn had been draped in festoons of lavender and yellow ribbon and bows. Each row of seats for the guests, filled with perhaps not matching chairs, owned its own

bouquet of lilacs, greenery, and yellow roses at the edge near the aisle. Candles were set hither and yon throughout the barn on nearly every surface available, and their tiny flames added an atmosphere of romance to the setting.

Eva Chesterfield proved to be a very accomplished violinist indeed and provided a lovely rendition of Johann Pachelbel's "Canon in D" while the guests were seated, and as Calliope entered the Ackermans' barn on the arm of her beloved beau, Rowdy Gates, such a thrill of delight ran through her that for a moment she thought she could not be any more excited if she were attending her own wedding.

"Follow me please, and I'll show you to your seats," Willis Chesterfield said as he met Rowdy and Calliope at the back of the barn, offering his small crooked arm to Calliope.

"Thank you," Calliope said, letting go of Rowdy's arm and taking Willis's.

Escorting Calliope to her seat, with Rowdy following him, Willis stopped before a row near the front, releasing Calliope, gesturing to his left, and saying, "Please take your seats."

After Rowdy had rejoined Calliope, Willis gave a low, very low bow and then turned and started to the back of the barn once more. Calliope smiled at the sight of his darling little swallowtail suit coat as he went.

"Why, Calliope Ipswich," Rowdy whispered to her, "what have you done to the boys in this town, girl?"

Calliope playfully jabbed his ribs with her elbow before turning and giving her sister Amoretta a hug.

"This is wonderful, Calliope," Amoretta exclaimed in a whisper. "So very wonderful!"

"I'm so glad you're here," Calliope whispered in return. "It wouldn't be nearly so wonderful without you and Brake."

Calliope's brother-in-law, Brake, winked at her over Amoretta's head. He leaned closer and teased, "You and Rowdy Gates, huh, Calliope? You little minx, you."

"You hush, Brake McClendon," she scolded him with a soft giggle.

"Here comes Evangeline," Rowdy said, nudging Calliope with his arm.

Calliope looked back to see Albert Chesterfield escorting Evangeline to her seat, with her escort, Mr. Longfellow, following them. Evangeline smiled at Calliope with excitement as she took her seat across the aisle.

"Beautiful!" Evangeline mouthed as Mr. Longfellow took his seat beside her.

Calliope sighed as she listened to Eva's beautiful playing. She watched as Mr. and Mrs. Ackerman were ushered in, followed by Kizzy.

Once everyone was seated, Eva looked to Calliope, and she nodded. Natalie Chesterfield appeared then and stood next to her sister Eva. As everyone's attention was drawn now to Natalie, Calliope's heart soared as she heard Natalie sing the first line of "Oh, Promise Me." Natalie's singing voice was beautiful! And although Calliope had heard Natalie and Eva practice many times, tears sprung to her eyes as she realized that now all of Meadowlark Lake knew how truly talented a vocalist the girl was.

Once Natalie and Eva had finished, leaving every woman in the barn teary-eyed with admiration and emotion, Eva again looked to Calliope. Calliope could hardly breathe as she nodded, and Eva began to play Richard Wagner's "Bridal Chorus."

"Settle down, darlin'," Rowdy whispered into her ear. "You're gonna bust your corset strings."

Calliope smiled at him and said, "I am not. And anyway, isn't it all so beautiful, Rowdy?"

"I don't know, honey," Rowdy said, however. "All I can see is how beautiful you are…and in that fancy blue dress. I can hardly think of anything else but you."

Calliope looked at him—gazed at him—wished she could kiss him! The past three weeks of being officially courted by Rowdy had been pure heaven to Calliope. His kisses were now so familiar, as was his touch—his very essence.

In a manner, she'd begun to wish that the Tom Thumb wedding were already passed and gone so that she could spend every free moment she had in the company of Rowdy, instead of pulling the play together. But now as they sat next to one another—he in his best dress suit and she in the blue gown she'd sewn just for the occasion—she was a bit melancholy at the fact that soon Shay would be wed to Warren Ackerman and all the fuss and fun would be over.

Still, as Rowdy winked at her, smiled, and drew her hand to his lips to place a kiss to the back of it, she felt soothed. The Tom

Thumb play had been her conceived delight before winning Rowdy's heart. And now that she had somehow managed to capture his feelings and affections, she wasn't so sad that the play would soon be over.

Nigel Gardener appeared first, walking down the aisle and toward the stage as stiff and as solemn as any clergyman ever was. His long, white, flowing robe reached to the floor, and the small yoke at his neck and shoulders was gathered to quite a fullness. His sleeves were large and billowy, and a broad band of black fabric fit about his neck and extended all the way down his front to the floor.

Nigel stepped up onto the stage and took his place center back, turned, and faced the crowd.

The ushers-turned-groomsmen, Willis and Albert Chesterfield, marched to the stage next, taking their place to the audience right on stage.

Lena Chesterfield slowly marched up the aisle and onto the stage. Her butter-yellow dress was lovely, and the way her mother had affixed lilac sprigs in her coifed hair became her perfectly. Calliope noticed the way her pretty bouquet of Dora Montrose's yellow roses and Kizzy's lilac sprigs quivered as she held it. Thus, she offered an encouraging nod to the maid of honor.

Mamie and Effie Longfellow walked slowly down the aisle then, their sweet little yellow dresses making them look like fairies scattering yellow rose petals along their way.

Next came Warren Ackerman.

"Ah, the groom himself," Rowdy whispered.

Calliope bit her lip to keep from giggling as Warren marched straight and tall, down the aisle to the stage. He looked so serious and yet just like a Tom Thumb groom. He was perfect.

As everyone in the audience turned then, quiet exclamations of delight were heard escaping everyone as Shay appeared on the arm of her father, Judge Lawson Ipswich.

"Oh, Kizzy! It's perfect," Calliope heard Amoretta tell their stepmother. "She's a living doll!"

And indeed she was. As Shay gracefully glided down the aisle with her father, even Calliope was amazed at her beauty—of how perfectly the albeit miniature but very elaborate wedding gown and veil fit her. She was the most perfect Tom Thumb wedding bride ever bedecked! Calliope was certain of it.

Once everyone was in position, Lawson took his seat next to Kizzy, Eva finished playing the "Bridal Chorus," and Meadowlark Lake's first Tom Thumb wedding began.

"Dearly beloved," Nigel the clergyman began, "we are gathered here today in the company of this assemblage of lovely ladies and courageous men, to witness the joining together of Junie Bee Junebride and Tom Thumb in the bonds of pretended matrimony."

Calliope again bit her lip with delight. "Isn't this just too adorable, Rowdy?" she asked the handsome man at her side.

"It's entertainin' all right," Rowdy agreed, smiling at her.

"If there be any among you who can show just cause that this man and this woman should not be joined, let him speak now, or forever hold his peace," Nigel continued. He put one hand to one side of his mouth, adding, "And if anyone *does* object, my mama will swat 'em hard with a willow switch out behind the barn later on this afternoon."

Everyone laughed, and Calliope wondered how many folks thought it was Nigel speaking his own thoughts, unaware that he had been directed to say it.

Turning to Warren, Nigel asked, "Tom Thumb, wilt thou take this woman to be thy pretendedly beloved wife? Wilt though pretendedly love her, protect her, and carry her across stream beds and wet bridges so that she will never soak her slippers clean through? Wilt though assist her in carving out pumpkins to serve as jack-o'-lanterns on All Hallow's Eve, and willingly tromp deep into the woods to cut a pine each December 15 to serve as a Christmas tree in her parlor?"

"I will," Warren strongly affirmed.

Turning to Shay then, Nigel the clergyman asked, "And Junie Bee Junebride, wilt thou take this man to be thy pretendedly beloved husband? Wilt though pretendedly love him, soothe him, and bake him a cake each Saturday night? Wilt thou always prepare bacon for his breakfast and never admit he has lost a hair from his head even though he may grow to be as bald as a goose egg?"

"I will," Shay agreed with a giggle.

Looking to Calliope's father then, Nigel called out, "Who gives this tiny bride to this man-one-day?"

"Her mother and I do," Judge Ipswich said, somehow managing not to break into amused laughter.

"Well then, Tom Thumb and Junie Bee Junebride, please join hands and gaze pretendedly lovingly into each other's eyes," Nigel continued. "Tom, repeat after me: I, Tom Thumb, take thee, Junie Bee, to be my pretendedly wedded wife. I promise to pretendedly love thee and protect thee from this day forward, for better or for worse, for richer or for most likely poorer, as long as your mama doesn't come to visit more than once a year, and when she does stays less than two nights."

Everyone laughed wholeheartedly. And when the laughter had subsided enough, Warren repeated.

Nigel turned to Shay then and said, "Junie Bee, repeat after me. I, Junie Bee, take thee, Tom Thumb, to be my pretendedly wedded husband. I promise to pretendedly love thee and swoon over thee from this day forward, for better or for worse, for richer of for most likely poorer, as long as you keep your toenails tidily trimmed and your handkerchief folded neatly."

Again the guests of the wedding laughed with merriment. And when they had once again settled down, Shay repeated her carefully rehearsed lines, concentrating so as not to giggle.

Taking one of Shay's hands and one of Warren's, Nigel tied them together at the wrist with a lovely yellow ribbon and said, "I now pronounce you the cutest little couple this side of the Mississippi...*and* pretendedly man and wife! You may kiss the bride, Tom Thumb!"

Calliope held her breath, quickly exchanging worried glances with Amoretta and Evangeline. All the weeks before, Warren Ackerman had been more than happy to chase Shay hither and yon, catch her, and plant a quick kiss to her lips. But all three of Shay's older sisters feared that Warren might not be so keen on kissing a girl in front of the whole town.

Yet when Calliope looked back to the tiny bride and groom on the stage, her mouth fell agape when Warren Ackerman unexpectedly wrapped his arms around Shay and smashed his mouth to hers in one big, smacking kiss!

"Thata boy, Warren!" Rowdy shouted as all the guests applauded with approval.

As Eva Chesterfield began to play Mendelssohn's "Wedding March" as the recessional piece, everyone stood and applauded, calling out their approval of the play the children had just performed. As Shay and Warren and all the other children on the stage bowed with appreciation, the joy in the Ackermans' barn was a tangible matter.

Calliope wiped tears of happiness from her cheeks as she applauded the children's incredible performance. Naturally there were refreshments to be had, cake to be served, and just plain camaraderie to be enjoyed. Yet Calliope's favorite part of the event had just ended. And so she sighed with a bit of the disappointment one feels when something they've anticipated for so long and enjoyed so much is at an end.

"So it's over," she mumbled.

Rowdy looked to her, and she could see the compassion in his eyes.

"You're sad it's over, aren't you?" he asked.

"A bit," she admitted.

Rowdy took her hands in his then, raised them, and kissed each one on the back. "It doesn't have to be over quite yet, Calliope," he said.

"Oh, I know," she told him. "There's still the food, the cake, and of course the photographer we asked to come and take the wedding party's photograph."

"No, I mean…there can be a bit more weddin' to all this, today," he said.

The look on Rowdy's face was so sincere, so filled with an expression of love, desire, and promise, that Calliope didn't even notice that the applauding had stopped and that everyone in the Ackermans' barn was now watching her and Rowdy and smiling from ear to ear.

"What do you mean?" she asked him. And then, as Rowdy Gates kept hold of her hands, as he dropped to one knee before her there in the Ackermans' barn, realization washed over her like an epiphany.

"Calliope Ipswich," Rowdy began, "will you be my wife? Will you marry me right here, right now, today?"

"R-Rowdy," Calliope began as tears streamed over her cheeks. "Really? Do you really want me for your wife?"

Rowdy nodded. "I've only ever wanted you, Calliope…from the minute I first saw you." He paused a moment, kissed the back of one of her hands, and then said, "Will you marry me? After all, you went to all this work and got everyone in town under the same roof. It'd be a shame not to give them a bit more to be happy about."

"Of course I'll marry you, Rowdy Gates," Calliope wept. "And I'll marry you here and now!"

"Good thing I brought the county judge along with me, ain't it?" Rowdy said as he rose to his feet and gathered Calliope into his arms.

Everyone in the Ackermans' barn created the most joyous uproar Calliope had ever heard—applauding and well-wishing so profusely radiant, heaven itself couldn't miss it.

"I-I'm not wearing a wedding dress though," she told Rowdy.

"That's all right," he said. "I like this blue one. But if you'd rather, Amoretta brought hers along."

"Amoretta?" Calliope exclaimed as she turned to look back at her sister. "How did you…I mean…how…?"

"Rowdy wrote to me and asked me to bring it…just in case you really did agree to marry him today," Amoretta explained as she hugged her sister.

Evangeline was there too—and Shay—and her father and Kizzy—all of them hugging her and telling her how happy they were for her and Rowdy.

🍎

A mere twenty minutes later, the citizens of Meadowlark Lake were once again sitting in their mismatched chairs in the Ackermans' barn. Judge Lawson Ipswich had taken the place of Nigel Gardener in the center of the stage. Evangeline, Amoretta, Blanche Gardener, Winnie Montrose, and Sallie Ackerman had joined Lena Chesterfield as bridesmaids. Brake McClendon, Fox Montrose, and Dex Longfellow stood near to the groom as groomsmen.

As Calliope and Rowdy exchanged much different vows than Shay and Warren had, Calliope found that her heart was so full of love and happiness she could hardly contain expressing it by shouting to the stars of it. Rowdy Gates had made so many of her dreams of him come true—and this was indeed his finest hour in that. Somehow Rowdy had known she would love nothing more than to marry him as part of the event everyone had worked so hard to present to the town. Somehow he'd known that she'd secretly daydreamed about it on more than one occasion.

And as she heard her own father's voice speak the words—"I now pronounce you man and wife. You may kiss the bride"—Rowdy completed the dream come true by taking her in his arms and kissing her the way she most liked to be kissed, careless of the fact the entire town was witness to it.

"I love you, my beautiful blue-eyed Calliope," Rowdy mumbled against her mouth as the audience cheered for them.

"And I love you, my handsome Rowdy Gates," she said.

🍎

"Well, the play's over, I guess. What now?" Warren asked Shay as they watched Rowdy and Calliope accepting the congratulations of everyone who had witnessed their marriage.

"Seems like life will go back to just plain ol' life, I guess."

"I'm so glad Calliope wore her blue dress for her weddin," Shay said, smiling. Taking Warren's hand in her own, she pulled him along to walking with her as she began to sing the song she so loved to hear her father sing.

There were three little girls dressed in blue.
Then one married and left only two.
Then one fell in love with a boy,
Who loved her and gave her much joy.
Then the last little girl had a dream,
And she dreamed she was saying, "I do."
And when she awoke it was true!
Happy three little girls dressed in blue.

"Well, that's a sappy song," Warren said as he continued to walk with Shay—continued to hold her hand.

Shay shrugged. "Maybe, but I like it."

"Hey," Warren began then. "You know how you say you've got some gypsy ways, Shay Ipswich?"

"Yes," Shay admitted.

"Well, prove it to me. Tell me somethin' about the future usin' your gypsy ways."

Shay giggled, stopped, and looked directly into Warren's eyes. "All right, Warren Ackerman. I'll tell you this. It will be years and years from now, but someday, you're gonna kiss me the way Rowdy Gates just kissed my sister back there in the barn."

Warren's brows crinkled in a disbelieving frown. "All long and sloppy like that? Heck no!"

"Well, let's just wait and see, shall we?" Shay said.

Warren frowned a moment longer and then exhaled a sigh of resignation. "You wanna walk around a bit longer or somethin'?"

Shay smiled. "How about we go down to the stream, and I'll show you how to sail frogs?"

Warren Ackerman smiled and nodded. "Now that sounds like fun!"

Stripping off his swallowtail suit coat and bow tie, he smiled as Shay tossed her bridal veil aside and kicked off her shoes. Hand in hand they ran away from the Ackermans' barn and toward the sparkling stream that ran by the summer meadow.

AUTHOR'S NOTE

The truth is, I'm not really a trilogy-type person, you know? Especially the middle, the second part of a trilogy. I'm sure a lot of it goes back to Star Wars (and so many things do, of course) and watching Han be encased in Carbonite and then having to wait, like, three years to see him released. Ahhhh! It was torture. *Back to the Future II* is another example. I *love* the first installment and the third, but that second one is not my favorite (though I do love the references to Clint Eastwood and his movie *A Fistful of Dollars*). The same goes with me for the Twilight books and movies. I'm just not a fan of the middle installment, you know? I like closure—a happy ending right away and to be able to sleep at night. Seriously, you have no idea how a cliffhanger affects me. And that's why I trend toward writing what would be known as stand-alone books. I actually wish I enjoyed continuations of stories, but they stress me out so much it's embarrassing!

However, when the idea knocked me upside the head for the Three Little Girls Dressed in Blue trilogy, I knew I had to persevere. And that would mean writing a middle book. And I'm not going to lie to you, Calliope's story was a challenge for me.

For one thing, Calliope is such a spirited, happy-go-lucky, positive young woman that I didn't want her to have a ton of terrible drama in her life. I mean, losing her mother and baby brother was bad enough. It's amazing she made it through to be as joyful as she was. In fact, I knew from the beginning—the very conception of this trilogy—that she would be the healer. Do you know what I mean? Calliope knows who she is and what she wants. She's good and kindhearted and very concerned for the happiness of others. Therefore, I didn't want to drag her through another heart-wrenching drama. And besides, she was in love with Rowdy, and he obviously endured enough in his life previous to meeting Calliope that he was absolutely meant to find her and to love her.

Therefore, Calliope's story isn't the most dramatic cliffhanger in the history of the world the way most second installments in a trilogy usually are. Rather it reflects Calliope's heart, soul, and very nature. Calliope is a bright and beautiful young woman—warm and sunshiny—like summer, you know? She loves lilacs and roses and all things summery because that is her character, and she is an effigy of radiance and warmth. It's why she has blonde hair and eyes as blue as the spring and summer skies. Which, by the way, was more challenging for me to write—being that I would linger in perpetual autumn if it were possible. Although I love summer—sunshine, heat, green, flowers, kids running through sprinklers in the backyard, summer thunderstorms—it's not where I nestle in and feel happiest and most content.

In fact, I have a friend that gives me the hardest time about liking autumn and the holiday season more than summer. She loves summer! But everyone has his or her own preferences. For instance, my hunk of burnin' love husband, Kevin? His favorite time of the year is May through October. In other words, warmest weather and football! (He's so cute sometimes—like the time he told me that he finally understood why I get so excited so early about Christmas. He said, "It's the way I start feeling in June—knowing football season is only three more months away." Exactly!) My favorite time of year is August through December—for obvious reasons—and thus, believe it or not, it's more difficult for me to write books set in summer. Summer just isn't where my heart lingers.

Having said that, however, I love Calliope Ipswich for the very reasons some people love summer. So I'm hoping that you felt that while reading her story.

Another aspect of this book that I hope you enjoyed (because it was one of my very favorite things) was the whole Tom Thumb wedding thread. I know that if you weren't familiar with Tom Thumb weddings before, you certainly are now, right? But just for fun, let me give you a little more history on how the Tom Thumb wedding originated, okay? I'll try to be brief (which is hard for me when referencing things I'm really intrigued by).

A boy named Charles Sherwood Stratton was born on January 4, 1838. Within five years of his birth, Charles Stratton (a little person) was touring the world with his distant relative, P.T. Barnum. Mr. Barnum gave Charles Stratton's his stage name—General Tom Thumb.

Tom Thumb was somewhat the Shirley Temple of the mid- to late 1800s, in that he began performing at the age of four. By 1843, General Tom Thumb was a *world*-renowned performer. But it was in 1863 when General Tom Thumb really made headlines! On February 10 of that year, Charles "General Tom Thumb" Stratton married the woman he had "at first sight" fallen in love with. Her name—Lavinia Warren. Lavinia was also a little person in the employ of P.T. Barnum. She and Tom Thumb were married in an extravagant affair held at Grace Episcopal Church. Fellow little person performer George Washington Morrison Nutt (stage named Commodore Nutt) stood as General Tom Thumb's best man. Lavinia's sister (who was even smaller than Lavinia) was Lavinia's maid of honor.

Following the wedding ceremony, Tom Thumb and Lavinia stood atop a grand piano in New York City's Metropolitan Hotel to receive reception guests. The beautifully bedecked couple greeted some ten thousand well-wishers! In fact, a sentence in the *New York Illustrated News* read, "The History of General Tom Thumb and Lavinia Warren reads so much like some fanciful fairy legend that it is nearly impossible to regard the affair in any other light."

During their honeymoon trip, Charles and Lavinia were invited to the White House for a visit with President Abraham Lincoln! I mean, wow, right?

(The above photo is of "The Fairy Wedding Group"—including Commodore Nutt, General Tom Thumb, Lavinia Warren, and Minnie Warren. At the time of their marriage, General Tom Thumb stood 2 feet 11 inches, and Lavinia stood 2 feet 8 inches.)

The Tom Thumb and Lavinia Warren wedding became known as "The Greatest Little Wedding" and was so adored by all that people began performing plays—miniature weddings with children as actors. These plays were dubbed Tom Thumb weddings. The popularity of these Tom Thumb wedding plays was so enduring that thirty-five years after the actual event itself, a publisher in Boston published *The Tom Thumb Wedding* in 1898. Many schools and churches performed Tom Thumb weddings merely for entertainment, while others performed them as fundraisers.

Performances of Tom Thumb weddings strongly endured through the Edwardian period, and once in a while, you'll still hear of one being performed today. If I were to ever jot down a real "dreams to do" list, putting on a Tom Thumb wedding would definitely be near the top! I've always been intrigued by the idea and would love to produce one. Naturally, I'd want to do everything in Victorian or

Edwardian style—swallowtail suit coats for the boys, fancy, fancy dresses for the girls. Ridiculous excess would be the result of a Tom Thumb wedding I would do!

And seriously, didn't you just love the Tom Thumb wedding Calliope and everyone else in Meadowlark Lake pulled off? How fun! I would have loved to attend.

And now my thanks to you for taking the journey through Rowdy and Calliope's story. I hope you enjoyed it as much as I enjoyed writing it for you!

Yours,
Marcia Lynn McClure

Snippet #1—Wanna know what the most difficult part of writing *The Secret Bliss of Calliope Ipswich* was? The fact that Evangeline's story was so, so, so strong and forefront in my mind that I found it hard to focus on Calliope's! It took me so long to push Evangeline's story aside so that I could write Calliope's.

Snippet #2—I don't know what it was about this book, but whenever I mentioned biscuits and butter, my mouth would just start watering so badly that I would have to stop writing and go whip together a batch of biscuits. I'm not kidding! In fact, one evening I went down to make some biscuits (so that I could take them right out of the oven, slather them with butter, and then eat them as the melting butter dripped all over my fingers), and my oven wouldn't heat up! Can you imagine the panic I felt at that moment? Fortunately, I have an angel for a daughter. I quickly called my Sandy and asked her if she would take pity on her mother and make some biscuits for me. Now, keeping in mind that this was at about eight p.m. and that she's the young, sleep-deprived mother of two energetic little boys, the fact that she instantly agreed and showed up on my doorstep twenty minutes later with piping hot biscuits for me to slather butter on is proof that she's an angel! And since Kizzy's biscuits are made from my own recipe, I thought I'd share it with you here in the author's note snippets. You'll love them! But there are a couple of little things that will help them turn out extra yummy that aren't in the recipe. First of all, make sure the dough is sticky. Not too wet and gooey but sticky. Also, when you cut your biscuits, make sure the dough slightly swells up in those two little holes at the top of the biscuit cutter. We don't want our biscuits thin and wimpy, right? Lastly, be sure and dab a little bit of milk over the surface of each biscuit before you pop the *glass* pan in the oven. I always bake mine in a glass baking dish, and I never grease the dish before putting the biscuits in. Yummy!

Kizzy Ipswich's Biscuits
(Makes 6–8 biscuits in an 8×8 pan. Double recipe and bake in a 9×13 for more!)

Ingredients:
¼ cup butter
1 ¾ cup flour
3 teaspoons baking powder
¾ teaspoon salt
¾ cup + 2 tablespoons milk

Preheat oven to 450°F.

Combine all dry ingredients, and mix well. Cut in butter until butter chunks are about the size of peas. Mix in milk. Dough should be kind of sticky.

Dump dough onto floured surface, and press out or roll to same thickness as a biscuit cutter (approximately 7/8 of an inch). Cut into biscuits and place in glass baking dish. Smooth a little milk over the tops of each biscuit to help with browning. Bake at 450°F for 10–14 minutes.

Note: I've been using this biscuit recipe since nearly the day I got married. I had to fiddle with it a little bit, but this one works just right! However, you may or may not want to increase the salt, per your personal preferences.

Snippet #3—Why yes, Rowdy Gates is named in honor of Clint Eastwood's character Rowdy Yates in the old TV western *Rawhide*! In truth, I've never seen one episode of *Rawhide*, although you know what a big fan I am of Clint Eastwood's old spaghetti westerns like *A Fistful of Dollars*. However, for as far back as I can remember, my mom would tell me how handsome she thought Rowdy Yates was on *Rawhide*. And since the Three Little Girls Dressed in Blue trilogy was inspired by and dedicated to my mom, I thought a hero whose name *she* would associate with a handsome cowboy would be just perfect!

Snippet #4—Mr. Longfellow and Evangeline are examples of my subconscious working without my knowing. I've always loved the name Evangeline. The meaning of Evangeline is very sweet: bearer of good news, or messenger of God. But I just think it's a very pretty name. I will confess that I derive my knowledge of the existence of the name from the most famous source—the poem *Evangeline: A Tale of Acadie* by Henry Wadsworth Longfellow. Evangeline was Longfellow's first epic poem and was published in 1847. It's a story of profound devotion and faithfulness—but with a very bittersweet ending. Thus, I've never read it all the way through. However, being that I do love the name so very much, one of Judge Lawson Ipswich's daughters was named Evangeline. It wasn't until I was almost finished writing this second book in Three Little Girls Dressed in Blue that I realized I'd included the character "Dex Longfellow" in the first and second books (whose name I derived from glancing over at a Longfellow poetry book when I was writing Amoretta's story)—and that I had Mr. Longfellow being somewhat smitten by Evangeline. Ha ha! Mr. Longfellow and Evangeline Ipswich—proof that my subconscious sometimes pops things into my stories without my realizing it!

Snippet #4—You know what I think is so sad? That nowadays elementary school kids can't play kiss-and-chase! Some of my best elementary school memories involve being chased by boys at recess and chasing them back in return. Those were the days! Kids can get expelled for doing that now. It's ridiculous. (Heavy sigh!) What is this world coming to when little boys and girls can't even play kiss-and-chase at recess? Simple pleasures are being taken from us left and right. I'm just so glad that Warren Ackerman and Shay were able to play kiss-and-chase—just for the nostalgia it brings to those of us who loved it so much when we were kids. (That Warren…what a little dickens, eh?)

Snippet #5—Photographs of vintage Tom Thumb wedding plays are very rare. And when you do come across one, it is very expensive! In fact, in my vast collection of vintage wedding photos, I only have one Tom Thumb wedding play photo (shown below), and I came by it purely as a stroke of luck! It's also not as old as others I've seen, but I cherish and adore it. I count it as one of my greatest photographic treasures! Do you just adore the pastor to the left? What a cutie pie!

The little bride and groom in the photo below look to be more Warren and Shay's age. Too adorable! :)

And now that you have a wee bit of history on Tom Thumb wedding plays, I'm sure you can see exactly why the idea so thoroughly appealed to the Ipswich sisters—*especially* Calliope!

And now, just in case you missed the first book in the ***Three Little Girls Dressed in Blue Trilogy***, enjoy the first chapter of ***The Bewitching of Amoretta Ipswich*** by Marcia Lynn McClure.

CHAPTER ONE

"But it is what it is, Amoretta," Evangeline reiterated. "We're here now. We're not going back to Boston. And Daddy is *so* happy here…happier than he's been since Mama died."

Evangeline paused, and Amoretta mumbled, "I know."

"Calliope and I are finding things to like about the West," Evangeline continued. She wasn't nagging—only offering encouragement. Therefore, Amoretta wasn't at all perturbed with her older sister; she just wished she owned a bit of Evangeline's endurance and ability to make anything seem positive.

"Of course it's very different here, but linger on the beauty of the vistas, if nothing else, Retta," Evangeline buoyed with exuberance. "Just three steps out of town and the entire world seems to roll out before you!"

"And people are so kind and friendly," Calliope interjected. "Everyone has been so welcoming and helpful. I know you miss Boston, Amoretta, but out here…" Calliope paused to inhale a breath of fresh western air. Smiling, she continued, "Out here things seem so adventurous and new. And after all, you've got a more adventurous spirit than either Evangeline or I. Quite frankly, I'm surprised it's you who seems so unhappy with our move."

Amoretta shrugged, still disheartened and nursing an inescapable feeling of lonesomeness—even for the sweet, loving company of her beloved sisters.

"I don't know what's wrong with me," she admitted. "So many things flit around in my brain, things that worry me to near nausea. And yet they're all things I know shouldn't bother me at all."

"Such as?" Evangeline prodded.

But Amoretta shook her head. "You both will think I'm silly, petty, and just a plain old pouty baby."

"No, we won't," Calliope assured her. "We all have our secret strangenesses, Amoretta. All three of us."

"Exactly," Evangeline agreed. "Everyone in the whole world owns little idiosyncrasies. It's what individualizes us. So tells us, Amoretta…what kinds of things are bothering you so? What's keeping you from being happy here in Meadowlark Lake?"

Amoretta Ipswich looked from one of her sisters to the other. She wondered in that moment how miserable life may have been if she hadn't been blessed with such loving siblings. She wondered how she would've endured her mother's and baby brother's deaths when she was just ten years old. She wondered whom she would've played with, confided in, and loved if not for Evangeline and Calliope.

She felt a smile curl the corners of her mouth as she studied her older sister. Two years Amoretta's senior, Evangeline Ipswich owned the strongest, most persevering character of the three of Judge Lawson Ipswich's daughters—at least that's how Amoretta felt. Evangeline had been just twelve when their mother had died, and yet she had comforted and cared for Amoretta and Calliope nearly as perfectly as their mother had. Amoretta had always admired Evangeline's classic beauty as well—her raven hair and dark green eyes. She'd always thought that, other than their mother, there was no more beautiful woman ever born than Evangeline Ipswich.

Amoretta looked to her younger sister Calliope next. Instantly a giggle bubbled in Amoretta's throat, for there wasn't a person on earth that could keep from smiling once they'd gazed at Calliope Ipswich. There was something in her countenance—a sweetness and implication of constant mirth—that bred amusement in whomever looked at her. Her sunshine-colored hair flounced when she walked, and her bright blue eyes seemed to hold the same twinkle of starlight. Calliope was exactly two years younger than Amoretta—to the day—and in that moment Amoretta grew anxious at the realization that she and her sisters were quite grown up. Calliope was already seventeen, officially a young woman, and somehow it caused a great melancholy to settle in Amoretta's bosom.

Looking from Evangeline to Calliope and back once more, Amoretta sighed, for there she sat—Amoretta Ipswich, with her plain brown hair and her plain green eyes. There she sat (plain old Amoretta Ipswich) right between the raven-haired beauty of Evangeline Ipswich and the golden-haired loveliness of Calliope Ipswich. She always mused how simply kaleidoscopic the three of them seemed, especially for sisters. Raven hair and emerald eyes—plain brown hair and plain green eyes—hair like spun sunshine and eyes as blue as the sky. Yes, it was how Amoretta perceived the physical appearances of herself and her sisters, like the varying patterns that appeared in the kaleidoscope her father had gifted their mother one Christmas.

Oh, Amoretta wasn't envious on any level. She just felt plain and simple in comparison with her sisters. She pondered a moment how different their personalities were as well, nearly as different as their physical appearances. Evangeline—strong, enduring, loving, and nurturing. Calliope—lighthearted and a bit silly-minded at times. Amoretta—adventurous, superstitious, and curious as a cat. She thought that if all three of Judge Ipswich's daughters were combined into one, they might well make the perfect woman.

Amoretta giggled at the thought, and Calliope urged, "What? What's so amusing? And you're supposed to be telling us your concerns."

"Yes," Evangeline confirmed. "What's bothering you? These things that are worrying you and keeping you from blooming where you're planted?"

Amoretta rolled her eyes with exasperation. "Evie...you *know* I hate that phrase," she sighed. "I've been hearing it from the moment we arrived here, and I'm tired of it."

But Evangeline was neither vexed nor impatient. As always she smiled with understanding.

"Just tell us your concerns, darling," she said. "Calliope and I will help you sort things out."

Exhaling a heavy sigh of resolve, Amoretta began. "Well, things like...like...and I know it's silly, for I know good and well Mama and baby Gilbert are in heaven and not here."

"But?" Calliope urged.

"But we just left them there!" Amoretta exclaimed. "We just left them there in their lonely grave, all alone, with no one to visit and no one to talk to! It haunts me...haunts my thoughts in the middle of the night." Amoretta wiped a sudden tear from her cheek. "I just think of them there all alone, cold when winter comes, no one to visit or talk to...no one to leave pretty flowers on their grave."

"But that's why Father had them buried together, Rettie," Calliope offered, "so that they wouldn't be alone there...even though they're truly in heaven and not even in the grave."

Amoretta nodded, brushing another insipid tear from her cheek. "I know that. But it haunts me all the same."

"And what else is haunting you, Rettie?" Evangeline asked.

"I'm not telling you the other things," Amoretta announced. "You'll think I belong in the lunatic asylum."

Evangeline giggled as Calliope said, "Oh, we already know you belong there, Rettie. That's not anything new."

Amoretta smiled, though she rolled her eyes with feigned disgust all the same.

"Come on now," Evangeline said. "Out with it. What else is keeping you from—"

"Blooming where I'm planted...I know, I know!" Amoretta interrupted.

"Besides Mama and baby Gilbert being left behind, what else is it?" Evangeline asked.

Amoretta shrugged. She knew she might as well confess—for she knew neither Evangeline nor Calliope would let her escape their interrogation and efforts to help until she did.

"It's the...well...it's the S in the peelings, if you must know," Amoretta purged.

"The Halloween apple peelings S?" Calliope exclaimed.

"Oh, heaven help us!" Evangeline sighed with exasperation.

"Four Halloweens running, Evangeline!" Amoretta reminded. "Four! You cannot deny the facts, Evie. Four Halloweens in a row, my apple peels laid out an S. Four!"

"I know, Rettie," Evangeline said. "Oh, believe me...Calliope and I both know. But it's only a Halloween game. You know that." Evangeline smiled, rolled her eyes with amusement, and recited, *"Pare an apple, miss or mister, and fling the peel behind you. The letter it shapes begins the name of your lover meant to find you."*

"Oh, wait!" Calliope giggled. "I like this one better. *Thrice around the apple go, with knife in paring whirl. Take the peel, and toss it back, whether you be boy or girl. Upon the ground the peel will shape the letter that begins your one true lover's given name, spelled out in apple skins."*

"I know it's just superstition," Amoretta interrupted, sighing with exasperation. "But some of us...some of us believe there may be a certain credibility to some superstitions."

"But even if that old superstition is true, which it's not," Calliope began, "your apple peelings shaping S does not mean you were meant to marry Sylvanus Tenney! There are hundreds of men in the world whose names begin with S. Sylvanus is only one."

Evangeline and Amoretta exchanged amused glances.

"I'm sure there are more than hundreds of men in the world with names that begin with S, Calliope," Evangeline teased.

Calliope rolled her eyes, shook her head, and corrected herself, "Thousands then...if you're going to pick nits, Evie." Sighing, she continued, "Regardless, Amoretta, your S apple peels do not mean you were meant to marry Sylvanus."

"And how can you be certain?" Amoretta asked rather daringly.

Calliope shrugged. "Well, it would make sense to me that if one superstition were true, then the others would follow with proof. And I don't remember you ever bobbing for an apple and retrieving one with an S carved into it...nor do I remember you ever confessing to us having seen Sylvanus appear behind you in a mirror on Halloween at midnight. Therefore, you can't convince me that the S your peelings have spelled out for four years running...you won't convince me it was Sylvanus Tenney's S, and there you have it." Calliope gestured with one hand that she'd proved her point. "You never, ever once saw Sylvanus Tenney's image appear behind you in a mirror held by candlelight at midnight on *any* Halloween past. Therefore, you cannot be sure it is Sylvanus's S that the apple peelings carved out."

"But I've always *felt* it was Sylvanus's S," Amoretta confessed.

"Of course you did," Calliope agreed. "Because Sylvanus Tenney was and still is the handsomest young man in all of Boston! Every one of us mooned about after him like a litter of hungry puppies. Add to that that none of us knew another young man of our family's acquaintance with a name that began with S, and of course you felt it was Sylvanus's S in your apple peelings."

Amoretta shook her head. "You've failed to convince me that the S of my apple peels—four Halloweens in a row, I might add—was not Sylvanus Tenney's S. And therefore, I worry that in leaving Boston and moving to this godforsaken West, my happiness has been obliterated before it had the chance to begin."

Evangeline puffed a sigh of frustration. "Amoretta...for pity's sake!" she exclaimed. Then, straightening her posture and seeming to find renewed resolve, she added, "Think of it this way, Rettie. If Sylvanus Tenney is meant to be your one true love and husband—if your Halloween apple peelings truly have been spelling out S for Sylvanus—then all will be well. Your paths will cross again when it is time. Don't you agree? After all, aren't you the one forever telling Calliope and me that true love always finds a way?"

Amoretta shrugged. "Well...well, yes, I suppose. But—"

"But nothing," Calliope interrupted. "You *are* always telling us that, and if you really believe it, then take heart and know that if you were meant to love Sylvanus and belong to him…then life will bring you together once more."

Amoretta shook her head, brushed one last tear from her cheek, and smiled. How could she linger in her dismal mood of loneliness with such wonderful companions as Evangeline and Calliope ever at hand?

"Fine," she sighed. "I'll make a better effort to bloom where I'm planted." Wagging an index finger at her elder sister and then her younger one, however, she added, "But please quit saying that! It makes me want to scream every time I hear it. 'Bloom where you're planted.' I'm not a tulip or daffodil. I'm a girl, a woman, and I was born in Boston, and it makes perfect sense I should feel…well, transplanted and underwatered if nothing else."

Evangeline and Calliope both laughed, and Calliope said, "All right! We won't think of you as a tulip…but rather as a snobbish, Bostonian woman who—"

"I'm not a snobbish Bostonian," Amoretta interrupted, giggling. "I'm a normal, Meadowlark Lake tulip, blooming where I'm planted."

"Or at least you will be one day," Evangeline offered.

"And besides, Rettie," Calliope began, "I've already seen several young men right here in Meadowlark Lake who are far better looking than Sylvanus Tenney."

"Well, I'll believe that when I see one for myself," Amoretta said, winking at her sister.

"You've got to meander around town a bit…actually get out of the house for a change, if you expect to see one for yourself, darling," Calliope added. "Maybe one will appear as we walk to Mrs. Montrose's house this afternoon for the sewing circle."

Amoretta forced a smile. In truth, Amoretta Ipswich felt no better about being dug up from her comfortable bed in Boston and plopped into the dusty, dry ground in Meadowlark Lake than she had before her sisters had endeavored to cheer her. But she would not allow Evangeline and Calliope to sense that all their efforts were once again in vain.

Thus, rising from the chair she'd been sitting in in the parlor, she said, "You're right, Calliope! It's time I got out and about…found some of these good-looking young men you're always telling me about. Perhaps even before we start for Mrs. Montrose's sewing circle this afternoon."

"Do you mean it?" Evangeline asked. "You're really going out? You haven't been out since we arrived last week. Well…for anything other than a visit to the outhouse anyway."

"Exactly," Amoretta said. "And it's time I changed my attitude, right?"

"Do you want us to go with you?" Calliope asked.

"Not at all," Amoretta answered. "I'm off on my very first, way-out-west, Meadowlark Lake adventure. After all, you two are always telling me I'm the adventurous Ipswich girl, right?"

"Right!" Calliope giggled.

The relief and joy were so plainly obvious on the faces of her sisters that Amoretta was glad she'd chosen to fib to them about having changed her perception of their move. She wanted them to be happy. They were both enjoying Meadowlark Lake, and it would only be selfish to continue to dampen their spirits the way Amoretta realized in those moments she had been doing—however unwittingly.

"And so, my darlings, I'm off for a stroll…off to linger in admiration of those beautiful vistas Evangeline loves so and those handsome young men Calliope admires." With a curtsy, and a secret satisfaction in the smiles on her sisters' faces, Amoretta hurried through the parlor, into the kitchen, and out the back door of the house.

Determined to be out of sight of her sisters before her true feelings erupted, Amoretta hastened past the old outhouse, through the line of fruit trees that backed her father's new property, and toward the wooded area she could see on the horizon. But being that the woods were more than a mile off, Amoretta knew her tears could not be withheld so long as it would take to reach the woods.

Suddenly, and without further warning, Amoretta burst into the bitter sobbing of disappointment, heartache, and unfamiliar loneliness. Oh, how she missed Boston! How she missed the plush, green grasses and flowering, fragrant shrubberies! Oh, how she longed to wander familiar byways. Meadowlark Lake only owned one major thoroughfare—a street that entered the small town at one end and exited at the other. All other streets and paths roundabout were simply wagon-rutted dirt roads or grassy trails that were more often than not hard to follow. Of course, her father saw things differently. Amoretta's father had told her the dirt roads and overgrown paths of Meadowlark Lake were wonderfully rural, picturesque, and simple adventures in themselves. But Amoretta's mind had known her father had seen what he wanted to see in Meadowlark Lake—a fresh start.

And it wasn't that she wasn't happy for her father. She was! It's why she had sworn Evangeline and Calliope to secrecy where their father's middle daughter's unhappiness was concerned. Judge Lawson Ipswich seemed so hopefully changed since the family had abandoned Boston for places west, and Amoretta truly wished her father happiness. She only quietly wished her own happiness could've accompanied his.

Brushing rivulets of tears from her cheeks and trying to catch something other than a ragged breath, Amoretta began to run. She didn't know whether her feet followed one of the rural, picturesque, and adventurous paths toward the woods; she didn't care. All she could think of was reaching the woods, hiding among the trees, and sobbing out her retched soul in peace.

Over and over the phrase she'd grown to despise echoed through her mind: *Bloom where you're planted. Bloom where you're planted.*

Oh, how she loathed that phrase! In those moments, Amoretta wished whoever had coined it in the first place had left well enough alone. She wondered who it was that spent his time making up such irritating metaphors. *Bloom where you're planted.* It made her want to scream!

She tripped then on a large root protruding from the ground. And when she found herself sprawled on the soft, fragrant grass, Amoretta Ipswich felt pure defeat. Not bothering to sit or stand—careless of whether she ever reached the woods and the privacy it offered—Amoretta folded her arms on the ground beneath her, placed her forehead on the protection they provided, and cried.

He'd seen the girl running—seen her trip and go tumbling forward into the grass. His powerful protective instinct caused him to rein his horse toward her. Yet when he heard her sobbing, heard her cry out, "Bloom where I'm planted? Never!" and realized no one was pursing her, he paused in offering assistance.

He figured she'd come from the new judge's house—figured she must be one of three daughters he'd heard tell the new judge had brought with him from Boston. And if there was one thing he didn't need, it was to attract the attention of a judge. Still, the girl seemed overwrought, and from the very marrow of his bones he wanted to make certain she was unharmed.

Still, his intuition whispered that this was one of those moments when a female just needed space and privacy in order to cry her heart out to the breeze—to purge her spirit of whatever was ailing it. Therefore, instead of descending on her unexpectedly and perhaps scaring the very life out of her in doing so, he simply lingered a moment and listened to the girl pouring her heart out to the grass (something about tulips). And when he was sure she was not in any sort of danger or experiencing truly life-threatening duress, he reined his horse to the left. He'd take the longer way to the woods. He'd have less chance of being seen that way anyhow.

As he rode toward the privacy of the tree line, he shook his head, realizing he'd best plan on taking the longer route to the woods from now on. Being that the new judge's house had a clear view of the woods and all those who might come and go into and out of them, it made better sense to take a little more time than to raise the suspicions of the new lawman.

Raising a curious brow, the man mumbled to his horse, "Looks like that new judge has his hands full if that's how all his daughters carry on." The horse whinnied as if agreeing with its rider.

The man chuckled. "Let's just get where we're goin', Gambler…before that girl sits up and sees us."

He urged Gambler into a trot, hoping the girl was still crying too hard to hear the rhythm of horse hooves.

Amoretta had no idea how long she'd been gone from the house—and part of her didn't care. Alone in the vast open field of grass between her father's house and the tree line of the woods, she'd somehow managed to cry herself to sleep. She'd awakened when she'd heard something—the unfamiliar, and yet beautifully serene, call of a songbird nearby. Her eyes opened slowly, and she was surprised by the sensation of delight that washed over her as the vision of the soft blue sky and white billowy clouds was what met her in those first waking moments.

She'd obviously rolled over during her out-of-doors nap, and there above her was pure wonderment in blue and white. She'd never seen clouds like these before—like giant kernels of the whitest of white popcorn, lazily drifting on a hue of bright blue she could have never imagined. The thought occurred to her that in Boston she would never have known such privacy—such quiet. Save the sound of the light breeze through the grass and the sweet song of the birds, there was not another sound—and she fancied her ears adored that fact.

The day was warm, and the air was light—not heavy and sticky the way it always was in Boston. And there were no unpleasant odors, it seemed. Amoretta inhaled several deep breaths, concentrating as she did so on discerning the scents in the air. There was no scent of rancid meat that often lingered in the marketplaces in Boston. There was only the fragrance of grass. There was no choking coal smell, only a freshness her vocabulary could not define.

An enormous yellow and black butterfly fluttered into her line of vision, and Amoretta smiled as it floated just above her. It seemed almost curious somehow, and when it did eventually land on the back of her hand for a moment, she smiled at the tickling sensation of its legs on her skin. She was astonished at how very long the butterfly lingered—several minutes actually—and she inwardly admitted that the pretty thing could not have done so in the bustling city of Boston.

Eventually the butterfly took flight once more. Amoretta sat up as she watched it meander on its way. It looked just like a large yellow buttercup caught on the breeze, and she was disappointed when it disappeared into the grass somewhere, having found something else to be curious about.

"Where have you been, Amoretta Ipswich?" Calliope chirped as she rather romped through the grass toward Amoretta. "Evangeline and I are ready to walk down to Mrs. Montrose's house for the sewing circle gathering. You are coming, aren't you?"

Amoretta giggled, delighted by the sight of her sister skipping toward her. The manner in which bright sunshine glinted on the gold of Calliope's hair gave her the look of wearing a halo—just like an angel—and Amoretta did indeed feel better. Boston suddenly seemed very far away. And though she knew her anxieties would return—the strange loneliness she felt at the thought of never setting eyes on Sylvanus Tenney again—in that moment Amoretta wondered if perhaps she really could find a measure of happiness out west in the small town of Meadowlark Lake.

"Of course I'm coming," Amoretta chirped. Calliope offered her sister a hand, and Amoretta accepted, allowing her younger sister to help her to her feet. "I mean, after all…what's more exciting than a sewing circle?"

Calliope giggled, adding, "And we wouldn't want to miss it and make the sheriff's wife feel slighted, now would we?"

"No indeed!" Amoretta agreed.

"Then come on," Calliope said, linking her arm with Amoretta's. "Let's be off to our very first Meadowlark Lake sewing circle! There's bound to be gossip and thereby much to learn about the people of our new town." Calliope paused, winking at Amoretta. "Perhaps there'll even be a mother or two with a handsome son to marry off."

"A son more handsome than Sylvanus Tenney?" Amoretta teased.

"Oh, much more handsome, Rettie! Much more handsome!"

Amoretta's smile did not fade, and her heart remained lightened. She wondered if perhaps her wretched sobbing had purged some of her misery after all. Perhaps there was another man in the world whose name began with S—the S the apple peels had been spelling out for her every autumn for the past four years. Perhaps she could learn to *bloom where she was planted*. Though she still despised the phrase and determined that she always would, Amoretta looked up into the bright blue sky with its white popcorned clouds and smiled. Evangeline was right after all. Her mother and baby brother were in heaven, not in the cold Massachusetts ground. And if her apple peelings had spelled out S for Sylvanus, then true love would ensure that Sylvanus found his way back to her—somehow.

To the man of my dreams…
My husband, Kevin!

ABOUT THE AUTHOR

Marcia Lynn McClure's intoxicating succession of novels, novellas, and e-books—including *Dusty Britches*, *The Whispered Kiss*, *The Haunting of Autumn Lake*, and *The Bewitching of Amoretta Ipswich*—has established her as one of the most favored and engaging authors of true romance. Her unprecedented forte in weaving captivating stories of western, medieval, regency, and contemporary amour void of brusque intimacy has earned her the title "The Queen of Kissing."

Marcia, who was born in Albuquerque, New Mexico, has spent her life intrigued with people, history, love, and romance. A wife, mother, grandmother, family historian, poet, and author, Marcia Lynn McClure spins her tales of splendor for the sake of offering respite through the beauty, mirth, and delight of a worthwhile and wonderful story.

BIBLIOGRAPHY

A Bargained-For Bride
Beneath the Honeysuckle Vine
A Better Reason to Fall in Love
The Bewitching of Amoretta Ipswich
Born for Thorton's Sake
The Chimney Sweep Charm
Christmas Kisses
A Crimson Frost
Daydreams
Desert Fire
Divine Deception
Dusty Britches
The Fragrance of her Name
A Good-Lookin' Man
The Haunting of Autumn Lake
The Heavenly Surrender
The Highwayman of Tanglewood
Kiss in the Dark
Kissing Cousins
The Light of the Lovers' Moon
Love Me
The Man of Her Dreams
The McCall Trilogy
Midnight Masquerade
An Old-Fashioned Romance
One Classic Latin Lover, Please
The Pirate Ruse
The Prairie Prince
The Rogue Knight
Romantic Vignettes
Saphyre Snow
Shackles of Honor
The Secret Bliss of Calliope Ipswich

Sudden Storms
Sweet Cherry Ray
Take a Walk With Me
The Tide of the Mermaid Tears
The Time of Aspen Falls
To Echo the Past
The Touch of Sage
The Trove of the Passion Room
Untethered
The Visions of Ransom Lake
Weathered Too Young
The Whispered Kiss
The Windswept Flame

CPSIA information can be obtained at www.ICGtesting.com
Printed in the USA
LVOW04s1917050914

402640LV00003B/3/P